The Hunting Wives

THE HUNTING WIVES

MAY COBB

THORNDIKE PRESS
A part of Gale, a Cengage Company

Thorndike Press, a part of Gale, a Cengage Company.

Thorndike Press® Large Print Core.
The text of this Large Print edition is unabridged.
Other aspects of the book may vary from the original edition.
Set in 16 pt. Plantin.

LIBRARY OF CONGRESS CIP DATA ON FILE.
CATALOGUING IN PUBLICATION FOR THIS BOOK
IS AVAILABLE FROM THE LIBRARY OF CONGRESS.

ISBN-13: 978-1-4328-8746-9 (hardcover alk. paper)

Published in 2021 by arrangement with Berkley, an imprint of Penguin Publishing Group, a division of Penguin Random House, LLC.

Printed in Mexico
Print Number: 01 Print Year: 2021

To my extraordinary mother, Liz,
who told me the story that inspired this
novel; you continue to inspire me
each and every day.

And to my fabulous husband, Chuck,
who guided me out of the depths
of writer's block by saying:
"Well, you better write something.*"*
This one's for you.

Prologue

I keep seeing her face, upturned in the pool. Her long hair darkened by the water, stringy and tangled and noodling around her neck. Her eyes are closed, her body floating. Her lips are parted just slightly, and it looks as if she's resting, tranquil and at peace.

Of course, it wasn't like that at all. Her body was found facedown in a puddle of mud-soaked leaves. A shotgun blast had shredded her back. She was slumped down next to the edge of the lake, and near the silty shoreline, the lake water is the color of rust, not a sparkling turquoise. But the pool was the first place I saw her.

A week later, she was dead.

1

Tuesday, March 13, 2018

Things are different tonight. Electric and humming. There's a charge building in the air, crackling and buzzing through me, and I can pinpoint the moment this morning when everything shifted.

When my flat, dull routine of walking from room to room, collecting wads of wilted laundry, became something more luminous, something pulsing with an energy of anticipation so that even then, as I stuffed the washer with clothes and shook a thin layer of soap flakes over the top, I knew my day would follow a different course than the one usually mapped out by me, a stay-at-home mom.

I'm at the local wine bar now, waiting for Erin. We're meeting for happy hour and I'm outside at one of the bistro tables, the light from the sun dancing in my glass of chardonnay, the taste buttery and sharp on the back of my tongue.

It was a frigid thirty-eight degrees here this morning, but by late afternoon, it had climbed to eighty, our first warm snap this spring, and I'm taking full advantage, sitting out here like this.

I'm tapping on my iPhone, scrolling through my Facebook feed, but finding nothing interesting. Just more back-to-school posts even though we're well into March. It's endless. Day #63 of second grade! Or Time please slow down! They grow up too fast! — the kinds of updates I wince at and can't bring myself to post. I place my phone down on the table and stretch my bare legs, letting the sun warm them.

It feels so good to be in a dress; I can't remember the last time I wore one, and I've piled my hair in a neat but relaxed bun. Hoping for chic, but effortlessly so. Silver earrings in the shape of feathers tickle my neck as I turn to scan the crowd, hoping to spot them as soon as they arrive.

This morning, when everything tilted, so that my day would end here instead of at the dinner table with Graham and Jack, watching Jack mop up spaghetti sauce with an elbow of crusty bread, adorable streaks of orange painting his cherub cheeks, I had just finished my morning jog on the trail that runs through the woods near our house. I had stepped inside the back door and peeled off my yoga pants, which were drenched with sweat and sucking and clinging to my thighs, and slid back into my comfy flannel pj's. It's cold here. Not Chicago cold, of course, but the humidity makes it a vicious, different kind of cold that grabs its icy paws around your bones and doesn't let go.

Still shivering, I padded to the kitchen and steamed some milk for a second latte and rubbed my hands together, trying to warm up.

I powered up my laptop in the home office — just a small nook, really, in the back parlor — and was just beginning to type in my password for Facebook when I heard a loud banging at the front door.

I figured it was the FedEx man with yet another of my online purchases. Maybe a case of Illy espresso — our favorite — which I used to buy at the flagship store in the city, or, perhaps, the set of lime-green throw pillows I'd been waiting for. It's hard to find cute textiles in this town, and lately I've fixated on making the inside of my house look like a dreamy spread from Pinterest, or, more specifically, how I imagine the inside of Margot's home looks.

I've only seen glimpses of the outside, of course, from our mutual friends' photos on Facebook, but all of that changed this morning when I was invited into her world.

The loud knocking was followed by the chime of the doorbell, then a quick, staccato rapping, so I jumped up and rushed to the front door. Where I found Mrs. Murphy from down the street. Yet again. She's persistent. Ever since we moved in, she's found an excuse to pop by at least once a week.

"Hello, dear," she said, aggressively thrusting a crate of blushing grapefruits toward me.

"Thanks so much for these, Mrs. Murphy. They're gorgeous."

She craned her head around my shoulder, clearly fishing for an invite inside. But I just stood there shivering as cold shards of wind blasted us, a plastic smile frozen on my face.

"Well, then," I said quickly, before she had a chance to fill the void, "I'd better get these beauties inside!" I leaned down and took them, gave her a quick peck on the cheek. "So nice of you to think of us. Jack and I will drop by soon, I promise."

"Oh, I would love that! And Erin's *so* happy you're back. She's been filling me in on everything." I flashed another smile and turned around, then walked inside and shut the door.

I plopped back down again in front of my laptop and finished logging on. My eye immediately caught the three new notifications glaring at me in red, which always give me a frisson of excitement. Sadly, not much else going on these days.

Janis White reacted to a photo you shared.

A heart, in "reaction" to a pic I posted of Jack, his hair wild with sweat, yesterday on a swing set.

Angela Cline commented on your post.

Same post. Love this little man.

But it was the third notification that drew heat to my face, made my heart flutter.

You are now friends with Margot Banks.

Margot Banks. She of the famed Banks family in East Texas. Oil money dripping out of their ears and pouring back for generations.

Last week, I finally caved and sent Margot a friend request after a few months of trolling her pics on Facebook. Her profile is set to private, but I would click through photos of her — pics she was tagged in by our mutual friends, like Erin, for instance — and find myself entranced.

I took a sip of my latte and felt the warmth spread through my chest; now that we were friends, I began scrolling through her photos.

There was Margot at an upscale restaurant, raven hair perfectly coiffed. Cut just above the chin line. She's leaning back in the booth, slender legs toned and scissor-crossed. Her candy-apple-red lips are slightly parted, as if in invitation. Heavy-lidded, smoky-gray eyes with a hint of smirk in them. Bedroom eyes, as Graham would call them.

I clicked on another photo: Margot draped in a glittering red evening gown. At a charity ball or some such event for the Junior League, no doubt. She's backlit. Her chiseled shoulders are bare, her olive skin flawless. She wears the same smirk, as if mocking the camera.

Next, I hopped over to her updates, scrolled through her posts. Landed on one dated from last Tuesday, from the local wine bar. The post read: Tuesday happy hour at Chino's — SO fun. I scrolled farther back and saw a similar post from the previous Tuesday, took out my phone, and texted Erin:

Up for happy hour tonight?

A second hadn't even passed and she was already typing back. Erin, always there, solid and dependable and as eager as a teenage boy on prom night.

Woo-hoo! YESSSS.

Her response was followed by a champagne glasses emoji. I typed back the thumbs-up, which usually wraps up her text-a-thons.

I swiped back to Margot's photos, clicked on yet another one. Margot on her front lawn wearing a black wrap dress, her arms draped around two children who look as if they've stepped from a Renoir painting.

My eyes were drawn to her plunging neckline with a pinch of cleavage. A single diamond dangled from a chain and rested just above her breasts. I zoomed in and, to my absolute horror, Facebook asked me, Who do you want to tag?

I panicked and closed out. I felt like I'd been caught watching a dirty movie. The latte screamed in my bladder, and I stood and went to the bathroom and checked the time. I realized an hour had passed.

I'm well into my second glass by the time Erin arrives, dressed in frumpy browns and blacks, harried and disheveled, a bead of sweat licking her hairline.

"Sorry I'm late!" She sinks into a chair and swings her mom-bag down next to her. She's wearing clunky sandals, and suddenly I'm a bit embarrassed to be seen with her. But it's better than being alone. Plus, I like Erin. Truly. She's reliably cheery with a toothy grin and childlike energy. And I hate myself for thinking like this, for judging Erin this way, but a decade spent in the lifestyle magazine business has me hardwired toward shallowness. It's something I'm keen to shake off, to leave behind me.

The waiter saunters over to take our order.

"Split a bottle?" I ask.

"Yes, ma'am!" Erin beams.

We order chardonnay, the brand they have on special for happy hour, and Erin launches into a ragged monologue.

"I SO needed this! Mattie was a complete tyrant today," she says, tucking a lock of cowlicked hair behind an ear. Mattie — short for Matilda — is Erin's five-year-old daughter, and she's a spitfire, an adorable brunette with ringlets of hair framing her face. I love her.

"She started in on me this morning with wanting to wear a miniskirt — and you know that's not gonna happen — and she was so keyed up by the time we hit school that I wanted to stab my eye out with a butter knife!"

Erin serves on the board for a bunch of civic stuff — the children's museum, the local library — and her husband, a teddy-bear type, works from home building websites. Erin's able to stay at home, too, doing volunteer work and raising Mattie.

The waiter stops by and refreshes our glasses. Erin is becoming more animated with each glass of wine and drones on and on. I nod in the correct places, but find myself unable to listen. I keep eyeing the street for Margot, slyly checking my Facebook feed on my phone.

Before I know it, though, more than an hour has passed and the night sky is turning to ink all around us. There's no sign of Margot and I'm more disappointed than I should be.

One Week Later

2

Tuesday, March 20, 2018

I'm in the car with Graham. He's driving us over to the party at the Banks estate. His hand rests on my bare knee; he looks handsome in his simple gray sports jacket and crisp white tee.

After tearing through my closet this morning, discarding old dresses and skirts to a heap on the floor, I finally settled on a spring-green eyelet dress with cream-colored espadrilles. I looked fairly casual, so I threw on a pair of ruby drop earrings with a matching necklace for safe measure.

I feel exhilarated, like the old days, like we're on our way to a gallery opening in Chicago. I place my hand on top of Graham's and squeeze it.

The Banks estate is in Castle Hill, the oldest section of Mapleton. The streets are dotted with 1920s mansions, all left over from the oil boom. And Margot's in-laws' is by and far the largest, and as we slip through the black iron gates, a long, winding drive leads us down a grassy slope toward a massive, two-story colonial that sprawls like a plantation home.

Ancient, twisted oaks shelter the plush green lawn, and white lights twinkle from their branches. Our wheels chomp the gravel lane until we arrive at the paved, circular drive that rims the entrance to the house.

A tall valet in a white tux opens my door.

"Evenin', ma'am," he says and guides me from the car to the lawn. The sultry night air bathes my skin like a balm after the chill of the car's AC, and I can almost feel my hair frizz. Graham circles the car, takes my arm, and leads me around to the back of the house, where the party is already well under way.

The backyard is even vaster, and like the front, it's studded with giant oaks, glittering with lights. A hundred or so people are gathered in gossipy clumps — mostly older ladies in all their finery — and for a second, I feel a bit self-conscious in my modest dress. But then I spot Erin holding court at the open bar. She's wearing a white skirt with a plain, blue knit top and chatting with her husband, Ryan, and a group of guys who are all in khakis and short-sleeved button-ups.

A string quartet is parked on the back steps of the mansion, the cellist sawing away sonorously. Dozens of waitstaff in white tuxes hover over the crowd, brandishing silver trays of hors d'oeuvres. One of the tux-clad men, tall and broad-chested, is parked under a magnolia tree in the corner of the patio and shucking oysters.

"You guys made it!" Erin says, her voice already slurry with drink. She's clutching a pewter mug stuffed with mint leaves and ice. She shakes it in front of her like a Yahtzee cup. "Gimme a refill, Ryan. And a few for our friends!"

Ryan waves at us and then turns toward the bar.

"Total freak show. Am I right?" Erin cackles, swinging her mug at the garishly made-up older women. Her breath smells of bourbon and mint. "But the food. Damn good!"

I decide I like her tipsy; she's funnier this way.

"Care for a lobster roll?" a waiter asks, and I pluck two from the tray and pop one in my mouth, passing the other one to Graham. We skipped a proper dinner, splitting, instead, a hastily made sandwich in the breakfast nook while Jack wove between our legs as we chatted with the babysitter, giving her instructions. My stomach rumbles but then Ryan passes me a mint julep, drops of condensation beading the mug.

I sip. The sugary, minty flavor coats my mouth and is so sweet the bourbon doesn't even burn as it slides down my throat. I drain the mug greedily and order another.

"Graham, if you see the crab cake tray floating by, swipe 'em all!" Erin says. "They're insane."

Graham raises his mug to Erin's, clinks it with a toast. "To insane crab cakes!"

"Hear, hear!" Ryan chimes in, and we all toast together.

As if on command, a waiter appears brandishing a wide tray covered in said crab cakes. Graham lifts several, passing them around. I stuff one in my mouth (they *are* insane) and nab another from Graham, hoping the food will sop up some of the alcohol that's already fuming through my bloodstream.

The sun is fading behind the treetops, smearing the sky with peach and orange streaks, and as the night darkens, the party becomes both more intimate and animated.

The string quartet has stopped playing and Katy Perry's voice sings blandly from the speakers at the DJ booth. A chorus of crickets has begun to trill, and everyone's chattering reaches such a loud pitch that you have to practically yell to be heard.

I peer across the crowd, trying to spy Margot, but I can't find her.

"Where's the ladies' room?" I shout to Erin.

"It's over by the bathhouse. A friggin' bathhouse!" She cackles and motions to a low-slung structure by the pool, which is the size of a small pond.

Before I turn to go, Graham palms me a flute of champagne, the bubbles fizzing from the glass, pinging the top of my hand. I weave through the crowd, feeling light-headed and buzzed, my legs unsure in my tall wedges.

The pool is a slate-blue oasis flanked by gray flagstone pavers. I circle it and steer myself toward the bathhouse, which has a line of overly perfumed ladies spilling from its mouth. I take my place in the queue and nurse my glass while the line creeps forward. I'm just about to enter the well-lit room when I hear a throaty laugh from around the corner.

I step out of line and snake around the building.

There's Margot, leaning against the shiplap wall, a glass of champagne dangling from her hand. My heart flutters in my chest. She's in a taupe chiffon dress, short and sheer, and her legs glisten in the glow of the bathhouse lights. I inch forward but there are three women circling her, whom I recognize from Facebook.

I shift on my feet, vying to be noticed, but the women seem to sway, too, forming an impenetrable wall around her. My palms are glazed with sweat and I feel foolish standing outside their circle, so I twist around to leave, when I hear Margot.

"Don't mind us, I'm just hiding from Mother," she purrs.

The other three pivot around and give me the once-over, their eyes veering from my shoes up to my throat. I guess they approve because they unlatch their ring and stand aside. A busty, attractive brunette flashes me a wide smile. Next to her: a broad-shouldered pillar of a woman in a simple black dress. Callie Jenkins. Margot's best friend, according to Facebook. Shoulder-length ash-blond hair molded in a sorority cut and eyes unsmiling as she takes me in.

The third is a diminutive-looking woman in a strappy white dress, arms crossed over her stomach, clutching a simple black handbag. She's pretty, in an understated sort of way, with jet-black hair and stark blue eyes framed in a sleek pair of cat-eye glasses. Prim but with an undertow of sexuality, like a librarian from a porn film.

"Need a refill?" Margot fishes a bottle from an ice bucket at her feet.

"Absolutely," I say, though my head swims. She fills my glass.

"I'm Tina!" the friendly brunette offers, shaking my hand vigorously.

"Sophie. Sophie O'Neill," I say. "Nice to meet you."

"And I'm Jill. Jill Simmons." The small-framed, black-haired one steps forward, planting her delicate hand in mine.

Callie just stands there, parked in place like a suburban until Margot elbows her and whispers, "Manners."

"Callie," she says, extending a buff arm toward me, palm sweaty, limp handshake.

"And I'm Margot, by the way," Margot says, her smoky eyes level with mine, her voice velvet-smooth. I search them for a hint of recognition, wondering if she recognizes me from Facebook, but she acts as though she's never laid eyes on me before. "This is my husband's parents' place. And this is our hideout," she snickers.

They all look at me expectantly, so I rush in to fill the void.

"I just moved here," I say, my voice creaking out of me, shaky and small.

"Me, too!" Tina says.

"You did *not,*" Margot snorts.

"Well, I guess it has been two years already," Tina says, her voice slinky. "But I'm from Fort Worth. I'm not native like the rest of these girls."

I glance around and notice they all seem as tipsy as I am. I bring the glass to my lips and sip. The champagne tickles my throat and scorches my still-empty stomach.

"So, where are you from?" Tina asks, diamond studs twinkling from her earlobes.

"Chicago. Or just outside of Chicago."

"What did you do up there?"

"I was the lifestyle editor at a magazine." As I say this, I notice that Margot is now leaning toward me, paying closer attention.

"You know, I was in charge of celebrity profiles, arts coverage, that sort of thing," I ramble on.

Margot locks her eyes onto mine. Her finger traces the rim of her wineglass.

"That's so cool! But how'd you wind up here?" Margot asks, crinkling her nose.

They all chuckle. Margot grasps the neck of the champagne bottle, refills my glass.

"I lived here for two years in high school. Junior and senior year. And I kind of liked it. It's nice here, no?" I ask, taking another huge mouthful. It's both flattering and unnerving to be under the sudden glare of her attention.

Even though the sun has set, the night is still warm, panting and heaving around us. I smooth my hair over one shoulder, hoping to cool my neck.

"It's okaaay," Margot drawls, "but it's no Chicago."

Callie strokes the pearls on her necklace, her eyes steady on me, her other hand parked on her hip.

"I wanted to slow down, get away from it all. I've got a kiddo now, and my husband's an architect, found good work here. We've been in Mapleton about seven months now."

I swivel around and look for Graham. He's leaning against the open bar, pinned in by Erin, who's no doubt telling him one of her endless stories. But his eyes are intent and warm, his head tilted to one side, listening. His hair is still pomade-perfect, and his smile is a shock of white, even from here.

"Is that *him*?" Margot asks, motioning toward Graham.

I nod.

"He's *so* good-lookin'," she says, hip cocked, still staring at him.

My stomach drops. The thought that she

thinks Graham is hot thrills me for some reason.

My eyes graze along the hem of her dress. Her thighs are flawless; I imagine the hours she must spend each day doing lunges.

From inside her purse, Jill's phone chimes loudly. She unzips it, spilling the contents on the grass.

"God, you're already drunk!" Margot howls.

"S'okay," Jill says, bent over and scrambling on the lawn. "I can stagger home from here."

She rises with her phone in hand. Turns to me. "I live two blocks that way." She waves her phone in the direction of the dark woods behind us. She swipes the screen of her phone.

"Well, who wants you now?" Margot teases.

Jill studies the screen, brows furrowed. "It's Alex. He wants to know if we can have a dinner date Friday night. Ugh! He knows Fridays are for you guys." Her shoulders slump as she types into her phone.

"I want to do something different this week," Margot says.

"I'm game," Tina says, her heart-shaped mouth curling into a devilish grin.

Callie shifts toward Margot, yanks on her

shoulder, mouths something in her ear.

"It's fine," Margot hisses to Callie, shrugging her off. She turns toward the group. "I actually think we should invite her."

Jill looks up from her phone, exhales, blowing her bangs skyward. I have no idea what they're talking about, but they're all studying my face.

"Don't you think we can tell her?" Margot asks Tina.

Tina shrugs, her radiant smile dancing all the way to her eyes. "I don't see why not. It's not like she knows anyone in town."

Callie narrows her eyes at me but Margot slides in between us. She leans in and lowers her voice. "We're in a secret club. A shooting club." Her breath feels electric against my neck.

"Every Friday night, without fail, we go out to my lake house and shoot skeet, sometimes target practice. Blow off some steam."

My neck smolders; my mouth goes dry.

"Care to join us?"

I nod robotically, willing to do anything she asks.

"See ya Friday, then," she says and pivots away from me. "Gotta go make an appearance," she says over her shoulder, and heads for the crowd, the other three trailing her.

■ ■ ■ ■

As we wait for the valet under a twinkling oak tree, its branches as chubby as a newborn's legs, Graham fishes out his wallet and fumbles with bills for a tip. Erin breaks away from Ryan and walks over to us, pulls me to the side.

"I noticed you were talking to Margot and her friends for a while tonight," she says, without a trace of jealousy in her voice. The silhouette of the oak tree is black against the bruised-purple night sky. "I was surprised," she says. Her buzz from earlier seems to have lifted, and her face is now edged with concern. "And I just need to tell you" — she leans in closer as if she doesn't want anyone to overhear — "be careful. Margot Banks is not a nice person."

One Week Earlier

3

Present
Wednesday, March 14, 2018

Lemon-yellow lights pills through the blinds. Too much of it; I've overslept. I check the clock — it's seven forty-five. I sit up in bed, my tongue thick and dry from all I drank with Erin last night at the wine bar, and a dull ache circles my head like a halo.

I peel myself out of bed and drift down the hall. Graham and Jack are in the sun-drenched kitchen, Jack at the breakfast table mopping up grape jam with his toast, and Graham leaning over the cutting board, slicing an apple for Jack's lunch. His hair is still slick from the shower, and a damp lock hangs over his forehead, making him look boyishly handsome.

My heart melts at the sight of them.

"Morning, sunshine!" he says, flashing me a teasing smile.

He was already asleep last night when I

slipped into bed and curled up next to him, snuggling into his warmth.

He's just made me a fresh latte and slides it across the counter toward me. My god, I love this man. I often wonder how I managed to land someone so solid, so endlessly good-natured. I grab his face and give him a quick kiss. Jack toddles over and wraps his sticky arms around my legs, and I bend down, tickling him until he squeals.

"I'll take him on my way in," Graham says.

"You sure?"

"Yep. We're already running a bit late. And your hair's definitely not church-ready." He grins and gives me a wink, scoops Jack up, and they head out the back door, their matching blond locks bouncing in time together.

I sip my latte, but what I really need is water, so I drag a tumbler down from the cabinet and fill it from the tap. That's one of the nice things about living here — the town's water is crisp and clean — and I drain it completely before heading out for my morning jog.

It's warmer here today; the sky is cloudless and sunny, so I slip off my hoodie and knot it around my waist. I head down our steep drive and walk toward the trail. The neighbor's fence is choking with honeysuckle vines, and today their blossoms are wide open and so fragrant that the air itself tastes like candy.

A few houses up I see the elderly lady who's always outside, tending to her flower beds. She must be ninety but there she is, stooped over a freshly tilled patch of dirt, planting a row of pink tulips. She raises a small, red-gloved hand at me and I wave back.

The neighborhood is old and established with 1960s ranch-style homes on sprawling lots. Grandma homes, I like to think of them.

Of course, when we bought ours (509 Sycamore Drive), Graham and I wanted to remodel it, so out came the aluminum windows, and in their place, we installed crank-out windows, the kind we saw in the South of France on our honeymoon.

We shaved off the popcorn ceiling, ripped up the pea-green carpet, and installed planks of gleaming oak. We painted the outside bricks slate gray (they were orange and tan originally) and trimmed the house in turquoise and black.

But I love these older homes, preserved in time, and also the quiet ticktock of the street, the way you can hear the birds singing. Or the tinkling of a watering can. Sounds that are all but lost in suburban Chicago.

It was one of the reasons we moved here. To slow down. To get away from it all. And on mornings like these, I think that it might actually work out here for us.

I remember the hot and languid day last summer when I finally snapped and decided we had to move from Evanston.

We were at a park near the center of town. Graham was scouting for a picnic table — they were all taken — and I was pushing Jack in a toddler swing, the cracked, rubber seat warm against my hand.

I looked up and realized we were stranded in a sea of skinny jeans, all worn by the men. Each of them also clad in Top-Siders or low-top Converse sneakers. Their hair graying, their hands frantic as they routinely checked their iPhones. The women all drenched in designer clothes. (And I love nice clothes myself, but on a Saturday morning? It felt forced.) And everyone keyed up on Starbucks and straining to be happy. Hovering over the children and looking downright exhausted.

Where was the wildness of my childhood? With packs of children running free through the neighborhoods, building forts in the woods? And if the parents were around — say, at a backyard birthday party — they would've all been congregated together, mixing cocktails and minding their own business, not swarming over the kids like bloodthirsty mosquitoes.

I cracked. I looked over at Jack and wanted something different for him.

I thought moving here would be the answer.

Mapleton, Texas. A town of fifty thousand. Small enough to feel quaint at times but big enough to have a Chipotle. A quick, ninety-minute drive due east from Dallas, but nestled deep in the piney woods so that it feels a world away. Also, a two-year stop on my mother's endless, whirlwind march through America.

My mother, Nikki Jones. A traveling ER nurse with a man in every port. Long blond hair and brash. Perpetually bronzed from the tanning salon. Currently stationed in San Diego, and she's made it clear that she wants to be a holiday-only, FaceTime-only grandma. And that's fine with me. Preferred, actually.

The last selfie she sent us a few weeks ago: Nikki in a string bikini with an American flag print. I passed the phone to Graham, rolled my eyes.

"Holy shit, did she get a new boob job?" he hooted.

I yanked the phone back. Studied her springy breasts. Why yes, she had. I tapped on the photo and hit delete.

My dad took off when I was five years old, and he's printed on my memory in smells and sounds — his broad, nicotine-stained hands that always smelled richly of oak and tobacco, his deep baritone voice making sugary promises he rarely kept. But mostly while growing up, I felt him by his absence, the void that my mother tried to constantly fill with new and different men.

Mapleton was the last landing place during my high school years. We arrived in time for my junior year, rented yet another bland house with equally bland rented furniture, and when Nikki (I'm not sure I ever called her Mom) got twitchy just before senior year, I begged her to at least stay and let me graduate. I had made some friends. Erin, for instance, whom I met in geometry class and who was one of the only girls who would talk to me.

You would think this would make me come unglued, but the fact is, it's made me crave stability all the more. So when Graham fell to one knee outside an Irish pub in Chicago just six months into our courtship and asked if I would marry him, I screamed, "Yes!" Squealed, actually, buzzed and giddy off my third pint of Guinness. I was happy to be absorbed into his corn-fed Kansas family, the very jovial and very Catholic O'Neill clan.

And I'm still happy. But maybe my mother's transient nature is in me, too. Maybe that's why I'm feeling so restless.

4

I'm at the entrance to the trail now. The trees are so tall and the path so narrow, it feels like you're stepping inside a cave. The temperature drops by ten degrees, and the feathery tops of the pines form a canopy, snuffing out the sunlight.

I unknot my hoodie from my waist, slip it on, and begin to jog. The trail is several miles long, and to the south, it borders spacious, sculpted backyards. To the north, a thick, tangled forest. This isn't the Texas of legend — all steers and dusty ranches — this is deep East Texas.

I jog down the hill. My calves and lungs start to burn, but I press on and run until I'm a good mile in. Until I reach my favorite bridge that crosses a clear, shallow stream. Stopping, I bend over and take in huge gulps of air, which is heavy and moist.

The stream gurgles and coos over moss-covered rocks, and ferns the size of small children drip with moisture. This place feels ancient, sacred even. And luxurious to me after the manufactured, concrete trails that ran behind our old subdivision in Evanston.

Of course, this trail is man-made, too, but the black tar path was poured so long ago, it feels like it's part of the earth now, the surface of it cracked and buckled like an old face.

I haven't seen a single soul on the trail this morning, which isn't at all unusual. I will sometimes pass the odd jogger or harried nanny pushing a chubby newborn in a stroller, but most mornings, I have the trail to myself.

"Are you sure it's safe, you being out there all by yourself?" Graham regularly asks me.

I remind him that I used to catch the L in Chicago late at night, to get home after an event.

"I'm perfectly safe," I always assure him. "Just me and the whip-poor-wills."

The trail is also a rich source for my Instagram feed, @sloweddownlife, except the feed's not so rich at all at the moment — I've barely fed it. But this morning, I find myself snapping pictures on my iPhone — of the wild blackberry bush strangling the little bridge, the woodpecker drilling holes into the auburn pine bark — and creating mental hashtags (#foresttherapy #nature-photography #lovewhereIlive), and today when I get home, I might even post a few.

Our thinking was that in moving back here, with the lower cost of living and the money we made off the sale of our house, I could ditch my day job and raise Jack in the slowed-down way I'd envisioned. Farmers' markets on the weekends, relaxed dinners that I'd actually have time to prepare, the three of us frolicking in a flower-studded field during lazy family picnics.

Also, I could pursue my dream of writing for myself with my blog and Insta feed that would hopefully blossom into a lifestyle picture book. I fancy myself a sort of "Pioneer Woman" without all the cast iron, a sort of everywoman's Gwyneth Paltrow, without all the eye-rolling nonsense.

Graham was up for partner at a boutique architect firm in Chicago, but he gamely agreed to the move, and with the oil boom in Texas, he was offered an even-higher-paying job here.

And I liked it, at first. But things that felt like a blast of fresh air when we first arrived — zero traffic, near-empty stores, bottomless hours in the day — have begun, instead, to feel oppressive.

Weekends are a snap. I have Jack and Graham with me all the time. It's the weekdays that can drag on. I can finish all my errands for the day in less than an hour, zipping around the open streets and rarely hitting a line at the market, but even with my blog and Instagram posting, there are all these endless hours to fill.

I snap one last shot of the trail — a wide angle of the swirling creek — before heading up the incline. I force myself into a sprint, until the hangover begins to loosen its grip, until the fog in my mind clears.

I'm near the top of the hill when I slow to a walk and notice the man standing in his backyard.

I tug my shades down and zip up my hoodie. He's harmless, I'm sure, but he's always out there in a pair of faded overalls, tending to something in the garden, a pair of binoculars slung across his bulging belly. His name's Harold; I think he mentioned that the first time we spoke.

"These are for birding," he had chortled, clapping the binoculars with his pudgy hands. "And my wife's just got me this iPhone for Christmas, so now I can take pictures of the little guys." He brandished the new phone from his front pocket, and passed it to me so I could examine it.

He was friendly enough, but something about him that day seemed a bit off. He's one of those types who never breaks eye contact while talking to you, and his eyes had lingered over my chest a beat too long. Since then, when I pass by, I instinctively throw my guard up and just give him the briefest of waves.

Today I don't even do that. I pull out my phone and fidget with it, pretending to be absorbed in a text message. But I feel the pull of his stare, and sure enough, when I've walked a good way down the hill, I glance over my shoulder and his binoculars are trained in my direction.

5

Thursday, March 15, 2018

It's morning. I'm sitting in my office, sipping a latte and gazing out the window while my laptop powers up. It rained last night and everything in our backyard is lush and green. I watch a red hummingbird dart in and out of the blossoms of our trumpet vine, their silky petals coral and tipped with golden yellow.

Today is maid's day. Not at our house, of course. At Margot's — 5 Kensington Drive. In the gilded and gated neighborhood Kensington Place.

I know this because two months ago on a frosty winter morning, I was parked outside the gates, and a weathered minivan, wheezing puffs of exhaust, had trundled to the entrance of the neighborhood. That's how bored I'd become in this small town. The driver, a middle-aged woman with frazzled hair, lowered her window and stabbed the keypad. The gates swung open and I trailed the minivan inside.

I had sat, idling, outside the gates a few times before, hoping to get a glimpse of Margot's house, but never had the courage to follow in, say, a gleaming Jaguar, or a Mercedes. But I somehow felt inconspicuous drifting behind the minivan in my five-year-old Toyota Highlander.

I already knew the address (another perk of small-town life: phone books still get dropped at your doorstep, and sure enough, all Margot's contact information was reliably listed under Banks), and I shadowed the van as it coasted through the parklike neighborhood. Immaculate, curving streets with bleach-white sidewalks.

Golf course–green lawns the size of small estates rolling out from enormous, newly built mansions with rooms fanning out like accordions. A glittering pond anchoring the center of the neighborhood, rimmed with willow trees combing the wind, and a fountain in the center of the pond shooting water orgasmically toward the sky.

The minivan parked at the lip of the curb just outside Margot's house, and I slowed my SUV and found a spot under a giant sycamore across the street a little ways up.

The woman lumbered out with cleaning supplies and scuttled toward the house. Margot opened the hulking wooden front door and they disappeared inside.

I had seen both an aerial and a street view on Google Earth, but somehow, the house was even more magnificent in person. A sprawling, Mediterranean-style villa. The stucco painted a creamy white and trimmed in reds and yellows. Climbing fig hugged the exterior, and a pair of black Mercedes as sleek as seals rested in the drive.

I sat with the heater roaring, the seat warmers toasting my ass for a few moments before I drove off.

Today, I don't have to do that. I hook up my phone to the computer, and while my photos are uploading, I head to Facebook, to Margot's profile.

I know I shouldn't. I should be working on my blog first thing in the morning but I'm having a hard time getting motivated with it lately. I don't have a ton of traffic yet, or followers on Instagram, so sometimes it feels like I'm slinging posts out into the abyss.

Unlike in the magazine world, there's no real gratification, say, from a published article or finished edition. Also, there are no deadlines to meet, no one to answer to.

Just five minutes, I tell myself. And then I'll get to work.

Margot's made it easy for me; she even has an album titled "Our Home" and I click through the photos and look through acres of rooms with gleaming floors and glittering chandeliers. Breathtaking, yet chilly. Even the children's bedrooms are too magazine-shoot perfect — not a toy on the floor nor a doll out of place. The boy's room looks ripped from a Ralph Lauren catalog, and I can see the trail of his future mapped out in the navy-blue-and-white-plaid color scheme: private school, Ivy League, Wall Street next, or perhaps law school.

Next up, the master bedroom. Creamy whites and taupes. Sensual. The king-size bed is dolled up with satiny throws and looks like a sumptuous gift waiting to be unwrapped.

I close out of her photos and go to my feed.

The first post that pops up is from Erin. A cute pic of Mattie playing in the creek. I click the heart button, leave a comment:

Adorable!

Another post from Erin:

Don't forget, tomorrow the food bank will be accepting canned goods.

I click "like" and scribble a note on a sticky pad to gather canned goods.

6

I first discovered Margot on Facebook shortly after moving back. Via Erin. Even though Erin is an earth mama through and through and doesn't care much for the socialite scene, because of her volunteer work, she sometimes runs in the same high-society circles as Margot.

A few days before Christmas, Erin was tagged in a splashy post with twenty or so other women. A post about a Christmas party — specifically a "Mommy and Kiddos Dance" — benefiting the local children's theater.

Almost instantly, my eyes found Margot in the lineup of all the women and kids in the group.

She was dressed in a black, one-shoulder evening gown with a slit up the leg so high it reached the top of her thigh. A diamond choker clasped her neck, and her dark hair was smoothed back, shiny as a new penny.

I found myself drawn to her, my eyes studying her sculpted thigh, her slender wrist. But more than anything, it was her expression that jolted me. Her fuck-me eyes, but also, while everyone else was flashing giddy grins, Margot's mouth was pressed into that same smirk she wears in nearly all the other photos I've seen of her. That smirk of irreverence that lets me know she is different from all the others in the photograph.

I took a sip of the chardonnay I'd been nursing all evening and swiped through the comments. The first was Erin's:

That was SO fun! Mattie had a blast!

Followed by a stream of others that echoed Erin's sentiment:

Yasssss!
We should do this every year!
SO fun!

Then one from Margot:

Ladies, paleez. There wasn't enough booze in the joint to make the night bearable.

I grinned. I noticed her comment had racked up the most likes — nearly forty —

and that people were still hitting the "like" button while I was looking at it.

I dragged the cursor and hovered over her name, which in and of itself sounded beguiling: Margot Banks.

I clicked on it. But her profile was set to private. A locked door. The standard Facebook message glared at me beneath her profile pic:

> To see what she shares with friends, send her a friend request.

But I wasn't ready to do that just yet.

All I could gather from her profile were scant biographical details:

Age: Thirty-eight. Three years older than me.

Birthday: August 20.

Friends: 3,121. *Jesus.*

Her profile pic: Margot in oversize shades with the tease of a smile curling on her lips. Her arms wrapped around a dashing man. I clicked on the photo. The caption simply read: "Me and the hubs." The person tagged in the photo was Jed Banks.

I knew of that name, not because I'd ever met Jed, but because the Bankses are Mapleton royalty. The local library, for one, bears their family name.

I clicked on it; his profile was public. But clearly untended, like those of most males his age. Just stale birthday wishes to him from last fall, none of which he ever replied to.

I scanned through a few of his photos. Dark, wavy hair, olive skin. Roman-god handsome. Every bit as much of a scorcher as Margot.

I headed back to Erin's page, dug around, and found a handful more of mutually tagged posts with Margot.

One from last Easter at the Piney Woods Country Club. A ladies' luncheon.

The sun-soaked dining room filled with women of all ages, sitting at long tables adorned with pink and yellow tulip bouquets. Margot sumptuously dressed in a white sundress dotted with red poppies, her expression exuding an air of boredom.

The comments section was ripe with the usual:

Fun, fun, fun!
Lovely day, Ladies!

And also sprinkled with some religious comments:

We serve an awesome God!

He is risen!

Then Margot's:

> Yes, fun. But if one more person in this godforsaken town tells me to have a blessed day, I'm going to commit ritual suicide.

I nearly spit my wine out reading that, I laughed so hard.

This very thing had actually become an in-joke between me and Graham. "And how many times were *you* blessed today?" he began to ask me shortly after we moved here.

"Was it this rabidly religious when you lived here before?" he asked me.

No, no it was not. It seemed that in the past twenty years, the town had gone full-tilt-boogie fanatical. Jesus signs in front yards. Perfect strangers inviting us to their Sunday church services under the guise of "being led by the Lord to ask" us.

So when I read Margot's comment, she felt simpatico.

I found myself looking forward to checking Facebook to try and catch posts she was tagged in. And thinking about her more and more, wondering about her life, which seemed so much bigger than my own. And yes, digging her name out of the phone book and locating her house. It wasn't envy, though; I didn't want to be her.

It was so much more than that. I wanted to be *near* her. For her to notice me, too. The idea of it took my breath away. It became powerful and even consuming.

7

Saturday, March 17, 2018

We're back home now and I'm carrying an almost-asleep Jack to his bedroom, his warm face lolling on my shoulder, his thumb plugged into his mouth.

We've been at Erin's all afternoon for a barbecue for Saint Paddy's Day. Just the six of us: Erin, Ryan, and Mattie; Jack, Graham, and me.

Mattie is two years older than Jack — but they get along great and Jack doesn't mind Mattie bossing him around, fussing over him. I think he craves the attention. They chased each other around the backyard while burgers sizzled on the grill. Graham and Ryan sipped craft beers while Erin and I shared a bottle of prosecco.

Their house is a funky 1960s ranch, all endless dark-paneled halls and a sunken living room, the windows lined with pots of houseplants in varying stages of germination.

I love it. Precisely because of its unhipness. It's refreshing, relaxing.

As the men talked sports and Jack and Mattie started a water gun fight, Erin and I stumbled into the house to refresh our wine. I was leaning against her linoleum counter in the kitchen, admiring the collage of photos on the wall, when I saw a flyer pinned to her fridge.

MINT JULEPS FOR THE MUSEUM

A Garden Party
Hosted by Mr. and Mrs. Roger Banks
Tuesday, March 20th, 6:30 p.m.
at their estate
710 Castle Hill

"What's this?" I asked, trying to sound nonchalant. There was no way, of course, I was going to tell her about my ridiculous online crush on Margot.

"Oh," Erin exhaled, swirling her prosecco around in her glass. "Yet another stupid fundraiser for the children's museum. And guess who's on the committee? So, I have to attend. Shoot me now."

I kept staring at it.

"Wait . . . do you and Graham want to go?"

"Actually, yeah," I said, a roar of excitement building in my chest. "It sounds like an excuse to dress up!" I had to bite down my smile, try and contain my open glee.

"God, you *are* bored," she said. "Hang on, I've got a wad of tickets to get rid of," she said, crossing the kitchen to wrench open an overstuffed drawer.

As she began digging for the tickets, I gazed out the window at Graham. His head was thrown back in a laugh, ever the affable houseguest.

We'd first met at a café on the ground floor of the high-rise where the magazine office and his firm were located. I had been behind him in line and he grabbed two trays and offered me one. I ordered everything he did — steak salad, dressing on the side, a fruit cup, and a Coke with no ice.

"Do you know you just ordered everything the same way as me?" he'd asked, the corners of his eyes winking in a smile.

"No, *you* ordered everything *I* did," I had replied.

"Well, are you going to pick the same table as me as well?" he asked, guiding me to a sun-filled two-top next to the window. By the end of lunch, I was smitten with him. His strong, caramel forearms against the white cuffs of his shirtsleeves; his wavy, golden hair that catches the light; but more than anything, his earthy kindness and wit. And by the end of our third date — a wine-soaked dinner at an Italian place where we lingered for hours — I was in love.

He was so starkly different from the boys I used to date in college and in my late twenties. And I'm using the term *dating* loosely here because my relationships never lasted more than a few dates and always ended abruptly. I was drawn to tortured, bad-boy types. The darkly handsome ones who'd never call but would magically re-appear just when you're moving on.

I had convinced myself that it was me, that I was damaged goods. I'd never even had a boyfriend growing up, but had attributed this to our moving around so much, to always being the new face at school. It wasn't my looks that I was unsure about — I mean, I'm no knockout and I'd always been self-conscious of my stringy hair and bony knees, but I'd gotten far too many men interested in me to think it was just about my appearance. It had to be something deeper, something inherently wrong with me that made men not return my calls after a few nights out. Was I too clingy? Too needy? Not needy enough?

But in walked Graham that day and everything just felt right for a change. Erin had told me, long ago, that when I finally met the right one, there wouldn't be any more games. And obviously, she knew what she was talking about.

Staring out the window at Graham just then and watching him chat with Ryan made my insides ache — at his dashing looks, yes, but also at the charming ease he always radiates.

Erin slapped two tickets on the countertop and refilled my glass. I guzzled it down in a few hard swallows and stashed the tickets in my back pocket.

I'm still stuffed from the giant burgers at Erin's, and Jack and I are curled up together on the rocker in his room, reading *Goodnight Moon.* His little doughy index finger points to the mouse in the story, finding it on each page. "Mouse, mouse," he says, his brows creased with concentration. His arm is slung around me; his hair tickles my cheek. Three is my favorite age so far, I decide. And as the last fingers of sunlight seep through the blinds, I could fall asleep right here with him, but before I doze off, his chin drops to his chest and he's out.

After a moment, I lift him up and nestle him into his bed, kiss his forehead, and tuck the covers around him.

I step across the hall to our bedroom, where Graham is sitting on the corner of the bed, remote in hand. The blue light from the TV flickers across his face. It's a baseball game; the sound is low.

"Already asleep?" he asks, shutting off the TV. I nod.

He reaches for me, pulls me onto his lap, and kisses my neck. "Good girl," he moans in my ear before slowly peeling off my shirt.

He's still wearing his white oxford shirt, but it's unbuttoned and it feels good to be pressed against his chest — which still smells like smoke from the grill — and to let his strong hands have their way with me.

Afterward, he's asleep on the bed, splayed out like an exhausted toddler. It took a bit longer with all the beer he'd had, but I enjoyed it, as I always do. I feel content lying here, but also, the contentment scares me: Is this what we are going to do every Saturday afternoon? Grill with our friends, as if our lives are already mapped out for us? I take a deep breath and try and push the thought aside, but as I pull the covers around me, my chest constricts and I feel as though the walls are closing in.

I climb out of bed and head to the kitchen to make myself a cup of tea. While I wait for the water to boil, I lean against the counter.

This was my idea, I remind myself. I used to sit in the noisy offices of the magazine's headquarters, parked in my tiny cubicle as cars whirred past the glass window, and daydream about this. Daydream about a life with less exhaust, more trees, more nature, more time. Slowed-down meals with Jack and Graham. Being there for Jack at every stage of his childhood. Making Shrinky Dinks together on Friday nights, burrowing into the sofa with a metal bowl of popcorn to watch movies. Having time for these things instead of being overworked, over-scheduled, our lives soldier-marched by a frenzied whip on our necks.

I look around the kitchen at Jack's finger-print paintings taped to the fridge, at the roots of the cilantro plants splayed on the cutting board, at the calendar hanging on the wall, blissfully tidy and not crammed with activity. I take a deep breath and remind myself that I wanted all of this.

So why isn't all of this enough?

8

Sunday, March 18, 2018

I've thrown the windows open, and fresh morning air, tinged with honeysuckle, floods the room. I'm in the kitchen whisking eggs in a wonky, oversize ceramic bowl I made years ago in college. I've got the jazz station from Chicago streaming on my iPhone; Nina Simone purrs through the room.

Jack sits at the table, swinging his legs in time to the music, slurping a bowl of Cheerios. Graham stumbles down the hall, all rumpled and worn-looking.

He tousles Jack's hair, says, "Morning, bud!" and comes over to me, his hands circling my waist. His breath smells like mint and he nibbles at my ear.

"Someone's in a good mood." He beams.

I smile back, and let him believe it was because of last night. But what I'm giddy about at the moment is something entirely different. Has nothing to do with him.

This morning I rose early, tiptoeing into the kitchen while Graham and Jack slept.

I logged on to Facebook.

Last night, before drifting off, I posted a picture of Jack and Mattie from Erin's barbecue, their arms wrapped tightly around each other, both of them flashing silly grins for the camera.

This morning, when I logged on, there were already forty likes and a dozen comments.

From Erin:

I didn't even know you snapped this! Too cute!

I tapped the "like" button and scrolled through the rest of the comments, clicking "like" on them all. But my heart seized in my chest when I saw a comment from Margot.

Too cute!!!

My finger hovered over the reply button. A bit shaky, I quickly typed:

Thank you!

But then backspaced over it and simply

hit "like" instead. I didn't want to seem too eager. And probably, she was directing that at Erin since they are longtime acquaintances, but it somehow made me feel a lot less nervous about going to the party at Margot's in-laws' Tuesday night.

So just now, when Graham sits down next to Jack and eats toast, I make them both look up at me, and snap another photo.

"Wait, is this for Facebook?" Graham asks, and when I nod, he sarcastically pulls a handsome, brooding face and says, "Okay, now we're ready."

I snap it and type, Sunday brunch with these guys! And quickly post it.

Three Days Later

9

Present
Wednesday, March 21, 2018

The garden party at the Banks estate was last night, and I still can't get over the decadence and sumptuousness of it all. And all that drinking on a near-empty stomach hit me hard. But I couldn't say no to Margot refilling my champagne glass. Margot. My neck flushes just thinking about her, remembering her breath on my neck.

I'm on the jogging trail. I got a late start this morning — it's nearly ten o'clock — and it's already boiling out. I'm running down the hill and it's so boggy, it feels like I'm wading through a swamp.

I don't see the man in his yard today, which I'm glad about. My T-shirt is soaked through with sweat and clings to my chest. I push harder, trying to outrun this drilling hangover. When my head hit the pillow last night, the room actually twirled and I had to screw my eyes shut and grab the side of the bed to make it stop.

I reach my house and am trudging up the drive when my cell dings. I shudder. And pray it's not Jack's preschool teacher. My plans for the rest of the day involve a cheeseburger and sinking into the couch. I'm not even gonna pretend to do any work. Stepping inside the back door, I slide the phone from my pocket.

It's a group text, with a string of numbers I don't recognize. But then I read the name of the group chat and understand:

THE HUNTING WIVES

903-555-8528: You know the drill. 6:30 pm, Friday night at my place. Jill — how did Alex take it?

903-555-0947 is typing. A few moments pass, then finally:

He's fine. Pouting but he'll get over it. Wouldn't lay a finger on me last night.

I'm piecing together who is who and creating new contacts as quickly as I can.

Margot: Oh poor baby. As if one night of no sex will kill ya.

Jill: ☹

354-555-8956: I'm in!

Must be Tina, Fort Worth area code. Then:

Callie: 👍

I couldn't believe Margot had actually invited me last night. I figured she was drunk, that she wouldn't follow through. But here she is, asking me. My head is spinning.

I start to type and then stop. Start to type and then stop. Then settle on: Sounds so fun! I'm in as well!

Margot: yay

Me: Just curious, how did you guys get my cell?

Margot: From Facebook. Where your life is laid bare.

I can't tell if she's talking about my life or everyone's in general.

Margot: and oops, here's my address: 714 Forest Lake Road . . . you'll drive forever, if GPS fails you, call one of us.

Tina: And boots! Wear some boots.

I type back: thanks!

I set my phone down next to me. My face is flushed, and my heart is pinging in my chest.

10

If Mapleton were a shape, it would be an oval. At the top of the oval is the tallest hill in town, the only real vista in Mapleton. Graham jokes that it feels like we're living inside a bowl. And he's right, of course. There are no sweeping views in town other than on top of the ridge, a sharp, jutting chunk of red clay that seems formed by a long-ago earthquake. The rest of Mapleton, the newer part — our neighborhood, the strip malls — dips down into the bowl where the sight line is obscured by a screen of towering pines.

The ridge is postcard Mapleton: the historical downtown district with its ancient churches and storefronts, the redbrick high school — ivy coated, with arched passageways — and the quaint library lined with stained glass windows. It's also where the money houses are, like Margot's. And also Margot's in-laws', the Banks estate, where the party was held last night.

It's midmorning and I'm driving past the outskirts of their neighborhood now, killing time while making my usual weekday stops. To the dry cleaner's to pick up Graham's lightly starched shirts, to the market for groceries and ingredients for strawberry cupcakes for a bake sale later this week at Jack's preschool.

The whole of Mapleton is encircled by a four-lane highway — appropriately known as "the Loop" — and as I cruise down it, past Castle Hill, then on past Margot's neighborhood, a flicker of excitement zips through me.

I know my fixation with Margot isn't normal. It's one step beyond normal, and I know what my old friend Rox, from the magazine, would say — that I'm once again chasing something unattainable, something unhealthy — and for a moment, I'm filled with a sharp longing to be back in Chicago, sitting across the table from her at the café we used to frequent, talking about our lives.

I hired Rox as the art director of the magazine just six months into my tenure as editor. She had short, spiky black hair with the tips dyed in bright greens or purples. Her blue eyes were so pale, they almost looked silver. She wore the same uniform most days — an army jacket or black leather motorcycle jacket over expensive jeans.

Before she came to the magazine, she had worked freelance as a graphic designer and photographer, and in addition to being knockout brilliant, there was something about her that I immediately liked the first time we met.

She had been a military brat — moving around abroad as a child and in the US as a teen — so we spoke the same language, and also, Rox was ten years older than me and streetwise.

We took to each other and I found myself wanting to hang out with her more than the twentysomethings at the magazine, the climbers.

Rox was there for some of my nastier breakups, and also for my courtship with Graham.

"Graham's the one," she'd said one day in her deep smoker's voice, gripping a cigarette and taking sharp, stinging drags from it. "And I'll never forgive you if you fuck this up."

We were sitting outside the café that afternoon on the patio. She was drumming the table with her long fingers that were adorned with silver skull-and-crossbones rings, inhaling her triple espresso. She'd noticed the flirty barista making eyes at me, and noticed me blushing at his attention and making eyes back.

"Look, we all have hormones," she said. "I get it. But you *do* want something stable; you *do* want happiness. And that schmo over there? Please."

"And what about you?" I asked, tilting my head, teasing her. Rox was always guarded about her past and even current relationships, but from what I gathered, she preferred quick flings over anything long-lasting.

"People like me don't get married. I can't be tied down. But you, it's what you truly want."

And I knew she was right.

Graham and I were six months away from our wedding, and for some perplexing reason, I'd developed cold feet. I had to find out why. So Rox and I took a long break from work that day and I spilled my guts to her. About how I was suddenly afraid of commitment, about how, even though I was head over heels for Graham, I'd become worried about whether he was the one. Marriage had started to seem like such a scary and final thing, and I was near panicked that day, but she coolly broke it all down for me.

"Look, what you're dealing with is a classic case of self-sabotage," she said, grinding her cigarette out in the metal ashtray. "I'm not trying to be an asshole here, but you have to trust me. It's *not* Graham. It's you."

Fear of intimacy. That's what she called it.

During our friendship, we'd sifted through the rubble of my childhood enough so that she knew about my father's abandonment and Nikki's tumbleweed-like nature.

"You don't feel worthy of love, or stability, because of the way you were raised. On some fundamental level, you're drawn to those who don't want you, because you didn't feel wanted by your mom or your dad," she said, lighting another cigarette with her dark purple lighter. "So when everything is going great, your instinct is to wreck it. But you *do* deserve happiness, Soph. You can be whole. This isn't just some psychobabble bullshit. I really mean it."

Before my friendship with Rox, I'd never given much thought to my childhood. I knew it hadn't been traditional, or even ideal, but it wasn't as though I'd been abused. But as Rox pointed out, my childhood hadn't been exactly stable, either.

▪ ▪ ▪ ▪

Nikki never kept us in one place for more than a year or two. The longest we'd ever stayed put was in our dark and dingy duplex in Prairie Garden, Kansas. We lived there from the time I was born until I was six. About a year after my father left.

So when I think of my childhood home, that's the place that's seared in my memory: orange shag carpet, peeling linoleum flooring in the kitchen that I used to pick at with my fingernails, the smell of Rice-A-Roni (one of Nikki's only forays into cooking) mixed with clouds of smoke from her perpetually needing-to-be-ashed Virginia Slims.

The biggest presence in the house, though, after my dad had hit the road, was Nikki's brittle moods. One day she'd be misty-eyed from a recent breakup — hands endlessly working a cigarette or her curling iron — and the next, she'd be giddy and humming while she squeezed herself into a pair of tight-fitting, acid-washed jeans for a date while leaving me in the care of our neighbor, Miss Denise, an ancient woman with hands the size of a trucker's.

I understood, very early on, that I was — for the most part — just a side note in

Nikki's life, so I often retreated to my twin bed and curled up to read one of my Nancy Drew books. But at least in Prairie Garden, we were in a proper neighborhood and I had friends up and down the street to entertain me.

After that we moved into more shiftless environments: a condo in Tallahassee, Florida (one of my favorite places, though — I loved the howl of the sea breeze and walking along the shore, collecting shells), followed by apartments in Ann Arbor and Tucson.

Nikki liked this unattached mode of living — never getting too close to others — so I was excited when we moved to Mapleton and she finally sprung for a rental house on a wide street lined with magnolia trees. Even though my only possessions were a bubblegum-pink dresser and wood-framed twin bed — the rest of the house Nikki filled out with furniture from Rent-a-Room — I could at least pretend to myself that our lives were veering toward normal.

Which isn't to say it was all bad growing up with Nikki. She did have her moments. As flighty as she could be with the rest of her life, she took her career very seriously, and by extension, took my studies very seriously, too.

We'd sit, knees touching, at the kitchen table, where she'd help me with my homework. Long division in the third grade, for instance, which I struggled with, but she made sure I finally got it. She was big on good grades and getting into college.

"You don't wanna have to rely on some no-good man," she'd say, time and again. "We take care of ourselves, you hear me?"

So obviously I didn't consult with Nikki about my decision to upend my career at the magazine and move to Mapleton. I knew she would never understand actually *wanting* to hang out with a kid as much as possible.

I didn't get the chance to consult with Rox, either. And now I wish I had. While I was on maternity leave, she took a job in Iceland — as a freelance photographer for an ad agency — and now she roves around Europe taking gigs. We stay in touch on Instagram (everyone in Mapleton is on Facebook, and it's as if Instagram and Twitter don't exist here yet), liking each other's posts, but I haven't actually spoken to her since a few months after Jack was born.

Rox got me over the hump that day in the café — over my fear of commitment and my college-years addiction to chasing bad boys — and I threw myself headlong into my marriage with Graham and headlong into my career. And I was content for a while, even ecstatic.

Soon after, I became pregnant with Jack.

And pregnancy — the surge of hormones, the urgent desire to nest — deeply bonded me to Graham. He would stand in the kitchen after working all day and make me elaborate dishes. Chicken piccata, mushroom risotto, cooking on a whim to satisfy my latest cravings, and as our evening drew to a close, we'd sink into our pillowy sofa and he'd cradle my feet in his strong hands, massaging them until I drifted off to sleep.

After Jack arrived, I loved them both with a fierceness I never thought possible. Jack was a colicky baby, his face beet red and screwed up into a wet ball most nights, but Graham would lift him from me and walk the floors until he was soothed while I rested in between feedings.

I felt like I wore new-mommy-hood well. I luxuriated in the whole attachment-parenting phenomenon — wearing Jack in a pumpkin-orange sling across my chest as often as I could, having him sleep tucked between me and Graham. And I stayed home from the magazine for a full six months before I managed to peel myself away from his tender, warm body that always smelled to me like peach cobbler.

I tried to put down roots in Evanston. Literally. I planted a showy rose garden in our backyard one Saturday morning while Jack snoozed in his stroller in a patch of sunlight.

I promised myself I'd be a better mom to Jack than Nikki was to me.

But after a year or so into Jack's life, my old bad-boy urges resurfaced when I profiled a painter for the magazine. He was an Austrian transplant named V, short for Victor, and the assignment almost led to a fling. After the piece ran, V — tall and tattooed — texted and begged me to go out for drinks in return for running such a glowing article.

I knew what he really wanted, of course, and I'm ashamed to admit that I wanted it, too. And fantasized about it. There were sparks between us, so one sunny afternoon, I left the office early and went to a pub across town to meet him for happy hour.

I strolled down the sidewalk in a yellow sundress, adrenaline shooting through me at the prospect of what was about to happen, but when I peered through the warbled glass door of the pub and saw the back of his head as he waited at the bar, I stopped in my tracks. He wasn't my Graham, and I knew what I'd be in danger of losing if I stepped through that door.

I turned and walked away.

Erin and I had been more in touch since having kids, and I was lured by the glimpses of Mapleton she'd show on Facebook: family picnics at a nearby berry farm with homemade pint jars of lemonade at their fingertips. The three of them — Erin, Ryan, and Mattie — at a Halloween carnival in downtown Mapleton, sipping mugs of apple cider in front of a giant pumpkin patch.

If I'm being honest with myself, yes, I wanted to move back here for Jack, for us, but also, it seemed like the kind of place where I could conform to the version of my very best self. In moving here, I thought I could become someone more wholesome, more grounded. Someone I could admire. Someone like Erin, for instance.

As it turns out, you can't outrun who you are. My darker urges simply followed me here and are even more amplified because it's so quiet, and sometimes so boring.

And though I'd do anything to be back in the café with Rox just now, talking through everything, I know exactly what she'd say.

She'd tell me that my feelings are normal. That I couldn't have predicted how isolating working from home alone could be, especially living in a small town. That it's understandable I was eager to ditch the hustle and bustle of the magazine world, but that there's a real part of me that misses the glamour of it all.

She'd tell me that I'm now getting my glamour fix from fantasizing about Margot, and that I need to find a healthier outlet. That I should find what I'm looking for within.

11

Friday, March 23, 2018

I'm driving out to Margot's lake house. The GPS says I still have twenty-three minutes to go and it's already six fifteen. I'm running late.

I told Graham about it last night during dinner. I made sure to top off his wine first, and between forkfuls of roasted chicken and potatoes (his favorite), I asked if he minded my going.

He swished the wine around in his glass and beamed at me. "Who are you, Annie Oakley now?"

I soft punched his shoulder.

"Who's going to break the news to Ryan and Erin?" he asked.

"What are you talking about?"

"I was going to surprise you, actually. I made dinner plans with them at the pub for Friday. And I booked a sitter." He raised his glass to his lips, took a sip. "And also, I think I'm developing a crush on Ryan."

"I think you're adorable. And I think you're just as bored as I am in this town," I said, and leaned over and kissed him on the cheek.

"Heeeey, Mommee!" Jack chirped. "I want iPad!"

His plate was licked clean, so I complied. "Sure thing, Jack-o-licious."

He scooted off his chair and ambled down the hall.

"But just one show before bed, remember, honey?" I called out after him.

"That was so sweet of you to want to surprise me, but can you cancel with them?" I asked. "But don't tell them why. I wasn't even supposed to tell you."

"Ooooh, a secret club," Graham said, his eyes flashing. "I like it!"

He slid the bottle across the table, refilled our glasses.

"But seriously," he added with a bemused smile, "why weren't you supposed to tell me?"

Shit. Maybe I shouldn't have. But I *had* to.

"Probably for no good reason," I said, hoping to dismiss it. "These women probably just like the *idea* of being a part of something exclusive, ya know?"

It seemed to work.

"Fair enough, Miss Oakley," he said, his eyes crinkling into a smile.

He took another sip of his wine and set his glass down. Laced his fingers through mine and pulled me into a kiss.

I'm turning off the main highway now onto a country road, the private road to Cedar Lake. The trees thicken and soar overhead, and the blacktop lane is so narrow, it feels as though I'm being squeezed through the forest. The road dips and curves like a roller coaster, hugging the lakeshore, which I catch glimpses of through the curtain of trees.

It's gorgeous out here, and a jolt of excitement sizzles over my skin as the robotic voice of the GPS announces my final turn.

Rounding a sharp corner, I see Margot's drive to the left; I turn in front of the barn-red mailbox with BANKS painted in black cursive on the side. I cruise down the crushed rock drive for what seems like a half mile until I finally reach the house.

It's the same ruddy, redwood shade as the mailbox, all wooden siding with endless windows trimmed in forest green. A 1940s California ranch, I would guess from first glance (I know this because of Graham's never-ending subscription to *Architectural Digest*), with three wings situated in a half circle. It sits atop a slight hill with a plush green lawn pouring down to the water's edge, and through the bank of windows I can see the lake.

I'm just ten minutes late, but the other four are all here already, churning on the wide front porch. Callie carries an armful of guns to one of three nearby four-wheelers, stacks them on the back.

Margot stashes wine in the saddlebag of a camo-colored four-wheeler while Jill and Tina chat on the porch. Everyone is dressed in knee-high leather boots, and I feel as if I've just stepped into a cover shoot for *Garden & Gun.*

The only boots I own are anklets, so I shoved some skinny jeans into them and threw on a red tank top. Driving over, I felt sassy, but as I step out of the car, I feel out of place and overmatched. Being this close to the lake, it's even more humid, and as I walk to the porch, my hair wilts. Tina and Jill smile and wave, but Callie ignores my arrival and focuses instead on strapping guns to the rack on the four-wheeler with canary-yellow bungee cords.

Margot pauses her packing, glances at me, and flashes a quick smile.

"You made it. Good." She sees me eyeing the house. "I'll give you the full tour later, but it's just thirty minutes till dusk."

She strides over to the wine-laden four-wheeler, jeans squeezing her curves. "Let's go, ladies," she calls out, and straddles it. Callie is already mounted on the four-wheeler that's loaded with guns, and Tina walks over and jumps onto the back of it.

"Guess you'll ride with me," Jill says, and I wrap my arms around her bone-thin body. She twists the key in the ignition, and the engine sputters to life.

We follow the others and head down a grassy lane that cuts through the forest. The surface of the path is engraved with deep tire tracks, and every so often, we sink into a dip and my chin pecks the back of Jill's tiny back.

We've driven about a quarter of a mile when we come to a clearing next to the lake. Jill slows and parks and I walk over to the water's edge before joining the rest. The lake is bigger than I had imagined it would be, so much so that I can see the opposite shore but can't make out any details other than the thick fringe of pines lining it.

"Our lake house is over there," Jill says, suddenly beside me. She's pointing to the far shore. "We really only use it in the summertime, but I love it out here." She stretches her arms above her head, yoga-style, and a satisfied smile spreads across her face.

The sun is still dangling above the tree line, and the reflection of it flickers off the surface of the lake like candlelight. The clouds glow nectarine orange, dripping from the sky like crème brûlée. Jill turns from the water, and I follow her to the center of the clearing where Callie is bent on one knee, loading bright orange discs into a small contraption.

Margot slides the guns off the back of the four-wheeler and hauls them over to Callie. Tina digs out safety glasses, earmuffs, and plastic wineglasses from a large black bag and places them on a small wooden table.

Margot uncorks a bottle of sauvignon blanc, icy from the cooler bag, and fills each glass.

"To Sophie," Margot says, eyes level with mine, raising her glass in a toast, "our latest member."

We all clink glasses and take sips.

Margot sets her glass down on the wooden table and pulls on a pair of earmuffs. I get the impression that she always shoots first. She opens the neck of a shotgun and stuffs it with ammo and snaps it back together. She slides on a pair of safety glasses and lifts the gun to her shoulder and yells, "Pull!"

Callie steps on the foot lever of the contraption, and an orange disc whizzes through the air. Margot fires, but misses.

"Pull!" she shouts, even louder this time.

"Callie always pulls for Margot," Tina snorts in my ear.

Margot's shot blasts the orange disc this time, shattering it. "Yeah!" she whoops, and spins toward us, sliding the earmuffs down around her neck and parking the safety glasses on top of her dark, glossy hair.

"Who's next?"

"Me," Jill says, already in safety gear. She strides toward Margot, who lays the gun in Jill's hands. Jill fidgets with her earmuffs and opens the throat of the shotgun to load it. She fumbles with the ammo before jamming it into place and closing the gun. She cradles the gun into her shoulder and stands slightly hunched over, her skinny legs slightly parted and planted in the yellow-green grass.

"Pull!" she shouts, but a breeze off the lake tosses her shout to the ground.

Tina, now at the helm of the contraption, stamps on the foot lever, releasing a disc. It zings through the sky and Jill fires but misses.

"Pull!" she shouts again. Another shot, another miss. She lowers the nose of the gun to the ground and turns toward us, chin down.

"You'll hit one eventually," Margot chides. "And I can tell you're not focusing like I told you to do. Here, more wine for you," she says, and swaps the gun for a full glass. Jill drains half of it in one long swallow.

"Sophie. You're up," Margot says.

"I really wanted to shoot tonight," Callie whines.

"Not enough time. The sun's almost set, and I want Sophie to have a shot."

I down the rest of my wine and put the safety glasses on. My hands are sweating, and when Margot hands me the gun, it's still warm from Jill's shots.

"Have you ever shot a gun before?" Margot asks.

I nod. "Just once, at a turkey shoot in kindergarten." I remember shivering in my autumn parka, the chill of the ground seeping through me, and feeling Saturday-morning tired. Glazed over from my breakfast of an Egg McMuffin and my father pulling me out of bed too early to go to the shoot. It's one of the few clear memories I have of us together doing father-daughter things. I actually won that day, and I remember after my shot struck the bull's-eye, my dad hoisted me on his shoulders and twirled me around, high above the ground that was covered in muted gold and red leaves.

"Well, that would've been with a rifle. This is a shotgun," Margot explains.

I'm surprised at how heavy the gun feels in my arms. "Let me help you," Margot says, and slides behind me, locking her arms onto mine. She smells of Chanel Allure, my favorite perfume, and the gold bangles lining her arm clank in my ear.

"Hold it close to your shoulder or it will kick," she says, her voice low and throaty in my ear. "And close one eye when you look through the viewfinder."

She releases me and I slide the earmuffs on. I take a deep breath and say, "Pull!"

The disc releases, and I track it and fire but miss it completely. My shoulder pulses from the kick of the gun.

"That hurt!"

"Hold it tighter."

And I do. I take a second and track through the scope at different targets. I used to play Nintendo until my elbows were shiny, and always prided myself on having good hand-eye coordination; I'm determined not to miss.

I can feel Callie sighing, but I take my time.

"Pull!" The sky is beginning to darken, but I track the disc this time and squeeze the gun to my shoulder and aim.

I fire and the disc explodes! I squeal and turn around.

"Damn, woman!" Margot sings.

Tina runs over and high-fives me, and Jill flashes a bright smile.

"It's not as hard as it seems," Callie snickers. "Shotgun blasts a wide area so it's not like a pistol or anything, requiring precision."

I pass the gun to Margot and rub my shoulder.

"Did it hurt that time, too?"

I nod.

"We'll have to toughen you up, sissy girl."

The last dregs of sunlight leak through the pines, so everyone starts packing the four-wheelers. A speedboat whines across the lake, sending waves crashing against the shore. I climb on the back of Jill's four-wheeler again, and even though we've been sweating for the past hour, her ribbon-smooth hair still smells cleanly of shampoo.

12

The kitchen is bright — all lustrous marble countertops and chalk-white cabinets with glass-front doors. Light ricochets off every surface as if everything had been freshly wiped down moments ago. Other than the sitting room at the entryway and the flock of bedrooms in the far wing, the lake house is basically one great room with a wall of windows running along the back overlooking the lake. A path of lights lines the pier to the boathouse, and the moon, nearly full, has floated above the water, smearing white light over the lake.

Callie, Jill, Tina, and I are gathered on a bank of sofas while Margot is in the kitchen shaking a martini shaker filled with vodka and ice. She lifts five chilled glasses from the freezer and drizzles the bottom of each with vermouth.

"Here, ladies! Filthy. Just like we like 'em."

We toast and sip. The glasses are cloudy

with olive juice, and tiny shards of ice float on the surface.

Margot then slides two trays out of the vast fridge and sets them on the bar. Cherry tomatoes speared with skewers and stacked against discs of mozzarella and fresh basil. The other tray has an assortment of meats — blackened chicken bits, pink curls of roast beef, smoked salmon — and cheeses with a spray of crackers.

We all descend on the food. I take a bite and a cherry tomato bursts in my mouth.

"This is delicious!" I say.

"Thanks, but I didn't make it," Margot says as she drags a cracker through a log of goat cheese. "Anita, my housekeeper, gets all the credit."

"Anita does *everything,*" Jill says between tiny bites of salmon.

"It's true, I'm guilty," Margot says. "I haven't touched a pot or pan in years. But she's getting older now, so we have a cleaning service. So, she doesn't do *everything.*"

"She raises your kids," Jill says, her blue eyes twinkling with mischief.

"Does not!"

"I'm kidding!"

"Jilly's just jealous because she doesn't have an Anita."

I'm puzzled because I've seen Jill's house

on Facebook — a gray stone mansion — and her husband is a heart surgeon. Surely, she can afford a housekeeper.

As if she can read my mind, Margot says, "She's too much of a control freak. Has to clean everything her way. Constantly down on her knees scrubbing the floors and walls. I honestly think she gets off on it."

A jangled laugh escapes from Callie. "I'm sorry, Jill, but it's true."

As I look at Callie now, her face flushed from the vodka, her blond streaks like frosting, she's more attractive than when I first saw her. There's something feral and rough about her that's hidden beneath her blank, cow-brown eyes.

"Well, I don't have a maid, either, but then again, I don't have kids. It's just me and Bill — what's there to clean?" Tina says, her voice already wavy with drink, her pink lipstick stamped on her glass.

"I don't have kids, either, but I damn sure have a maid," Callie says.

"You have a *staff,* dear," Margot says, giving her a sharp elbow.

The martinis are already drained when Margot says, "The wine! I forgot the wine! There's a whole bottle down there. Rock, paper, scissors for who gets to fetch it?"

"I'll go," I say, surprising myself. My head

is swimming from the alcohol and I could use a breather. Plus, I want to sober up before the drive home.

"The keys to the four-wheeler are in the ignition," Margot says.

"I'll just walk, thanks."

"You sure? Well, take a flashlight at least," Margot says and crosses the room, yanks open a drawer, and hands me a small Maglite.

I'm heading down the lane. The moon is high now and casts a silvery glow over everything, so I stash the Maglite in my pocket and walk along the trail in the bath of the moonlight. Russet-colored leaves, still damp from the recent rain, line the ground like a wet rug, muting my footfalls. All around me, though, the forest is alive and buzzing — a tense chorus of cicadas trills and hisses and seems to multiply with each crescendo. In the retreat of their swell, bullfrogs croak, and it occurs to me that I'd have to shout to be heard.

I shiver at the thought and fish my cell from my back pocket. I text Graham as I walk:

Going to call it a night soon, I think. How's J boy?

Perfect. Trying to get him down at the moment.

He texts me the kiss emoji and I text one back.

I'm at the clearing now and the lake is a white mirror with the moon perched above it. Water claps against the shore and a warm breeze skims over the lake, tousling my hair. I see the glint of the wine bottle in the center of the clearing and retrieve it. It's warm now, and the bottle swings from my hand as I head back toward the path.

The walk and fresh air have helped to clear my head of booze, and I'm about halfway down the trail when I can just begin to make out the orange glow of the porch lights. I start to feel as though I've stepped into a Robert Frost poem, when I hear a gunshot, loud and clattering, off the lake. A flock of doves explodes from a nearby tree and I drop to the ground, flatten myself against the damp leaves as the bottle of wine tumbles from my hand and rolls away. My heart bangs in my ears and I lie there for a moment, unsure of what to do next.

I'm slowly crouching on all fours, my breath ragged and shallow, when I hear a branch snap and footsteps approaching.

Squinting in the dark, I see a figure striding toward me. It's Margot, backlit from the lights of the house, with a shotgun propped on her shoulder.

"Whatever are you doing down there?" she asks, likely out of breath from the walk. "Oh, no! I scared you!"

I get to my feet and dust off the knees of my jeans. My neck is burning with embarrassment for being afraid, but the adrenaline has wrung me out so thoroughly that I feel limp.

"I just fired a shot because after you left, I remembered there've been feral hogs out here lately, so I wanted to fire a warning shot, keep you safe." Her breath is tinged with alcohol, and her perfume is even stronger now that she's sweating.

"Of course!" I say, trying for cheery.

"Wouldn't your husband kill me if you got speared by one?"

I try and laugh but it comes out strained.

"You're shaking," she says, putting an arm around me. "Awww, you really *are* a sissy girl." She says it in that way of hers where I can't tell if she's flirting with me or teasing me, or both.

The moon has fallen behind the trees and we walk together in lockstep, my stomach buzzing with excitement from being this close to her.

13

After the darkness of the trail, the inside of the lake house feels glaring. Margot sinks the wine into a silver ice bucket and twists the bottle around, chilling it. Callie fetches wineglasses from the cabinet, and fills each glass to the brim.

We toast and sip, but I only take the smallest of sips so I can safely drive home. Margot tosses back half her glass and sets it on the bar.

"So . . . who wants to go hunting?"

"Always," Callie says, winding a lock of coarse hair around her finger.

"I'm in!" Tina trills, rocking back and forth on her feet, her coal-black eyes squinting in a smile.

"Where?" Jill asks, demure, her face half-hidden behind her huge wineglass.

"I was thinking Rusty's," Margot says.

Jill sets her glass down, crosses her arms.

"Oh, please, Jilly! It's been forever. Don't

pout. I'll behave, I promise." Margot goes over to Jill, puts her arm around her. There's a perceptible shift in Jill's demeanor, a small succumbing to Margot's power.

I have no idea what they're talking about, but suddenly they're all looking at me. I take another small sip of wine, swish it around in my mouth.

"Who wants to tell her the rules?" Margot asks, her hip cocked against Jill's, her exquisitely shaped eyebrows hiked in a question mark.

"I will," Callie says. This is the first time she's addressed me directly, and there's a trace of a sneer in her expression.

"Rules about what?" I ask, nervously giggling, clasping my wineglass.

"Oh, please." Callie rolls her eyes. "Don't act like you're not bored in your marriage."

"Maybe she's not," Margot says, her voice playful. "Her husband's a hottie."

The flush of alcohol and Margot's hooded eyes on me make my face flame.

"I think *everyone* here is a little bored, except for Jill," Callie says.

"Yeah, Jilly, what did Amazon bring you this week? Do tell." Margot's unwrapped herself from Jill and crosses over to the bar to refresh her wine. "I want to hear all about your latest toy."

I catch myself gawking at Jill and quickly look away before she notices.

"Ooooh, a new toy," Callie says. "What role is Tom going to play? Will he be the police officer this time or the victim?" Callie snickers.

"You only *wish* you still had sex with your husband," Jill fires back.

For some reason, Callie answers to me, "He chases me around the house, but I'm over it."

She stretches her long legs across the length of the sofa, takes another mouthful of wine.

"So anyway, we're all a little bored and have to let it out somehow."

"Monogamy is so . . . monogamous," Margot chimes in.

The cold blast from the air-conditioning has fogged up the windows, so I can't see the lake anymore behind Callie, only the clouds of condensation frosting the glass.

My stomach registers a red-hot signal of danger; I don't know how I feel about all this. Graham and I have never been anything *but* monogamous, and I'm certainly not bored with him. Am I? I'm just bored, I think. But if that's the case, why am I so drawn to Margot and why can't I get her out of my head? If I'm honest, there's part of me that, despite the sense of alarm that looms in the air, likes listening to them. It excites me. Makes me feel alive. Maybe the most alive I've felt since moving back. No, not maybe. Definitely.

"So. The rules." Callie sits up now, rests her elbows on her knees. "There's only two, really. We only use our first names. And, we don't go all the way."

I nod dumbly, as if being read the instructions to a board game.

"So, you're in," Callie says matter-of-factly.

Again, that pinprick of danger at the back of my neck. And before I have a chance to respond, Margot fishes a set of keys off the wooden coffee table, stashes her Louis Vuitton clutch under her arm, and heads for the front door.

"I'm driving. Everyone load up," she says, and everyone rises and trails her to the entryway.

I take out my phone and check the time. Eight forty-five. I should go home; I know I should. I certainly don't want to get trapped all night by riding in Margot's car. But then, I don't want them to think I'm a scaredy-cat, either.

"I'll follow in my own car," I hear myself saying. My voice squeaks out, high-pitched and thin.

Margot freezes, turns around, and frowns at me.

"Early day tomorrow," I say, casting my eyes toward the floor.

She twists back around and steps out the open door. "Suit yourself." The others trickle out behind her. I follow.

Everyone is weaving toward Margot's Mercedes but Tina spins around.

"I'll ride with Sophie! In case she gets lost."

14

Before Tina climbs in the Highlander, I dust a constellation of Cheerios off her seat. How Jack manages to scatter them everywhere, I'll never understand. Tina's perfume, powdery and floral, fills the cabin, and she's so buoyant, she seems to spring into the seat next to me.

Her husband, Bill, she tells me with a lick of pride, lifting her voice, is a home builder. One of the biggest contractors in Mapleton. They live in a sparkling new development north of town. I've driven by and it's all castle-like homes with spires and arched windows.

As we wind through the lake roads, tracking the red eyes of Margot's tail-lights, I'm struck by how utterly dark it is out here and I notice, as we approach the country highway, that Margot is turning away from town, not toward it.

"So, what's Rusty's?" I ask.

"Oh, it's a little honky-tonk on the outskirts of town. Margot likes to pick out-of-the-way spots. For obvious reasons." She flicks down the mirror on the visor and applies a fresh coat of pink lipstick. "We don't go much, though."

"Hunting or to Rusty's?"

She scrunches her curls with her fingers, studies her hair in the mirror.

"I was talking about Rusty's specifically, but we don't go hunting that often, either. Maybe twice a month. But sometimes more. Depends on Margot's mood," she adds, snapping the mirror shut and darkening the interior of the car. "Margot's appetite for men is insatiable. You'll see."

I instantly like and feel comfortable with her but chew my bottom lip as I ask the next question. "So, do you, you know . . ." I'm fumbling, can't spit the words out.

"What? Cheat on my husband?" she asks, her voice bright and cavernous. "No. I mean, I kissed another guy once, the first time I went out with them, actually, but I hated myself for it. Bill and I are high school sweethearts. I can't imagine being with anyone else. So, no. I'm just here to watch the train wreck." She rubs her hands together in excitement.

The highway is empty but well lit. Giant

trees surf past us, cut by the strobe of fluorescent streetlights.

"Anyway, Margot's in some kind of constant war with her husband, a 'who can one-up each other' battle. You ever seen him?"

I shake my head no, though of course I've seen him on Facebook. Just never in person. Those scorching eyes, his bronzed complexion.

"Well, he's gorgeous. I mean, dead hot. But Jed cheated on her once in such a stupidly typical way, with his secretary. Got caught, too, in a stupidly typical way: sloppy texting. Margot paid the poor girl a visit to her apartment and ran her out of town. This was three years ago, but Margot does everything she can to punish him still," she snorts, shakes her head. "She keeps him under lock and key. I'm pretty sure he hasn't stepped out of line since, but Margot surely has."

Tina's fingers dance over the screen of my satellite radio. "Oooh, I *love* this song, mind if I turn it up?"

It's "Brass Monkey" by the Beastie Boys, and after she cranks the volume, she lowers her window and warm night air oozes through the car.

"Nights like these," she shouts over the

music, "I feel like I'm eighteen again!"

I roll my window down, too, and we both dance in our seats to the music.

As the song ends, I realize we've lost sight of Margot. I turn down the volume.

"Ummm, I don't see them anymore."

"No sweat, we're almost there, just one last turn."

I roll my window up, smooth my hair down, readjust my bra.

"So, what's Callie's story?"

Tina pauses for a second, seeming to consider as she fingers the silver hoop dangling from her ear. "She doesn't like anyone who Margot might like. If you're getting chilly vibes from her, that's why. I think it was a full six months before she even acknowledged me. Just ignore her."

We're approaching a light. Tina waves for me to turn left. We head down a two-lane road.

"She's all *Single White Female* with Margot. Lives on the opposite end of the street from her, drives the same make and model car. She wants to be her; she's a bit obsessed with her. Her husband Trip is just a big oaf with a lot of family money. Fishes all the time. Manages the family finances. Could pass for okay-looking, though, if he dropped some weight."

(I've seen him, too, on Facebook. Sort of a heavy, pasty Ben Affleck.)

I see the lights of the bar flickering in the distance. I slow the car and pull into the gravel parking lot.

"Callie and Margot went away together senior year of high school. Left Mapleton and went to that chichi boarding school in Dallas called Hockaday. Jill told me once that there were rumors that they were "together" while they were away. Not sure if there was ever a thing between them but Callie sure acts like it."

15

The air inside Rusty's is as cloudy as milk, thick with cigarette smoke. A row of clearly hard-living, hard-drinking patrons is parked at the bar, hunched over their beers. A jukebox in the corner floods the room with what Graham refers to as "hick hop," the annoying, twangy, country rap that we hear piped through the speakers on our rare trips to the local hardware store.

A weathered couple cling to each other on the dance floor — which has honest-to-goodness sawdust scattered over it — and a bank of pool tables lines the far wall.

This is hardly a place I'd imagine picking someone up, but there is a lone cowboy type, tall and darkly handsome, leaning against a wall with a beer dangling in his hand. He eyes Margot, who crosses the room carrying a metal bucket of beer on ice and hauls it over to a large wooden table where Callie and Tina are already sitting.

We each pull a beer from the ice, and Margot takes a long slug of hers, then thuds it down on the table. A waitress crosses the room. Her hair looks as if it's been singed from a box perm, and a ready-to-be-ashed cigarette hangs from her lips.

"Can I get you ladies somethin' else?"

"Shots! Five shots of tequila, please," Margot says, her gray eyes dancing. "And make 'em top shelf!"

Margot is practically vibrating in her chair. It's as if she can't sit still, so she doesn't. She pops up and soars over to the jukebox. Bends at the waist and folds her hands between her knees as she scans the display. The cowboy's eyes never leave her. She fishes a handful of quarters from a pocket, slides them into the slot, and punches in her selections.

"Where did you say you were from again?" Callie asks me. She's eyeing me suspiciously, as if I've been lying about something.

"Well, originally from a small town in Kansas. Prairie Garden. But I've lived all over. For my mom's work. She's an ER nurse and we moved a lot. That's how I wound up here, junior and senior year of high school." I take a swig of my beer, cast my eyes around the room. A neon wall clock reads ten p.m. I know I really need to be getting home.

Margot saunters back to the table and pulls another beer from the metal bucket.

"What year were you?" Jill asks in a friendly tone.

"Two thousand one," I say. "Same as Erin."

They all swivel and look at me. It's as if they haven't made the connection that Erin and I are friends, but, then again, why would they?

"Erin Murphy. Well, used to be Murphy, now she's Reed," I say, my cheeks blotting with embarrassment, though I don't know why I'm feeling the least twinge of shame.

"Yeah, we know her," Callie says, her blank eyes resting on mine and narrowing.

"Well, obviously she doesn't know anything about this," I stammer. "I mean, I know it's supposed to be a secret and all."

Callie's eyes are still trained on me, but Jill breaks the spell again.

"We're older than you, then. Class of '98. We would've been off to college by the time you hit town," she offers.

"I'm thirty-five. Turning thirty-six this December," I add lamely. So, they must all be thirty-eightish. And she's right, I don't remember any of them from high school.

The waitress comes over with the tray of shots.

We clink and slam them, chasing them with beer.

Patsy Cline's "Crazy" warbles from the jukebox.

"Good, my music is up!" Margot says, tilting back a beer.

Jill floats up from the table and drifts over to the jukebox. She leans her back against it, sways her hips. Closes her eyes and softly mouths the words. This is it, I think, the moment in the porno where the glasses come off and she's no longer a librarian.

Thc cowboy takes a long pull of his beer, his eyes trailing her swinging hips.

He walks over to her, leans down, and whispers something in her ear. Takes her by the hand and leads her to the dance floor.

She threads her fingers behind his neck, presses her hips into his.

"There she goes!" Margot whoops. She slinks down in her chair, throws a leg over Jill's empty seat, and watches Jill as if she's watching a movie, a sly grin creeping over her face.

The cowboy pulls Jill in closer, kisses her ear. She throws her head back and his mouth moves up and down her neck. Margot motions for the waitress; she orders another round of shots and a bucket of beer.

I grab my cell, text Graham.

Gonna be a little later than I thought. SORRY!

He doesn't text me back. Most likely, he's already long asleep. It's ten thirty.

"Who's up for a game of pool?" Callie rises and shuffles over to the pool tables without waiting for a reply. Tina shakes her head; she's too transfixed by Jill's unfolding situation on the dance floor to move, but Margot springs up and follows Callie.

My eyes are burning with smoke, and exhaustion is tugging at me. Jack wakes up early, usually by six a.m. I need to get going.

The door to Rusty's bursts open and a group of rangy, rowdy boys files in. They all look freshly showered and are wearing the same deep navy T-shirts with a golden tiger across the chest. On the back, their shirts read, TATUM TIGERS. Looks like the football team from the next town over.

Margot racks the pool balls and lifts her hips as she leans down to aim for the cue ball. Her throaty laugh blankets the air, and the stream of boys all turn toward her.

She acts like she doesn't notice them, but I see a satisfied line move across her mouth, as if she were expecting them. She cracks the cue, sinks a solid red ball. Leans her pool stick against the wall and watches Callie shoot.

One of the taller boys — with sandy blond hair and ice-blue eyes — walks over to Margot and sets a quarter down on the edge of the pool table.

She ignores him, grabs her pool stick, and lines up her next shot. Sinks another ball in the side pocket, dusts the chalk off on her jeans.

"I'd like to challenge the winner of this game," the boy says, tipping his cowboy hat to her. His friends snicker behind him. They can't be over eighteen, but the staff of Rusty's doesn't seem to mind.

"If you like having your ass handed to you, then be my guest," Margot says.

The boys laugh even louder at this. Blond Boy blushes, swigs his beer.

Tina elbows me. "See? She's a magnet."

Margot finishes clearing the table, Callie barely manages a point, and Margot turns to face Blond Boy.

"You rack," she says.

He does as he's told and Callie slumps onto a barstool near the pool table. The other boys stand along the wall, watching.

Jill is still dancing with the cowboy — Tammy Wynette is belting about standing by your man — but she notices Margot and Blond Boy.

Blond Boy shoots, sinks two balls in.

"Woo-hoo!"

"Don't get too cocky," Margot says.

She lines up her shot, misses. Blond Boy shoots again, sinks a corner ball.

Margot grabs her pool stick, rubs the end of it with chalk, and drapes the top half of her body across the table. Her pearl-snap shirt floats down and I can see her black lace bra. Blond Boy edges up behind her, puts his hands on her hips. She lets him. Margot shoots, sinks a ball, spins around, and throws her hands around his neck.

"On that note, buy me a drink," she orders. "A strong one."

His face is scarlet now and he heads to the bar, speechless.

Jill untangles herself from the cowboy, leaving him stranded on the dance floor, and strides over to our table. She yanks her yellow purse off the floor.

"I'm going outside," she says through clenched teeth. "I'll text Alex to pick me up." She clomps away. Margot watches her, cocking an eyebrow.

"What the hell?" I ask Tina.

"She hates it when Margot pulls this shit."

"What shit?"

"Messing with underage boys," Tina says. She licks her lips, drains the rest of her beer.

I nod as if she's just told me about the weather, as if any of this is normal.

Tina turns to face me, lowers her voice. "Okay, so last fall we were all out at Margot's land one Friday night for the Hunting Wives. And Margot and Jill had this idea that it might be fun to have a bonfire and invite the whole football team out."

I finish the remains of my lukewarm beer, then push the bottle away from me.

"Jill's son Brad is the quarterback," Tina continues, a grin tugging at the corners of her lips; she's clearly the type who loves to gossip. "Well, we were having a great time; the boys brought a keg out; it was all pretty innocent. But then Margot and Brad headed for the house, alone, to grab a bottle of whiskey. And when they came back, Margot's shirt was inside out." Tina's eyes flash conspiratorially. She twists her palms upward, as if in a shrug.

"I have no idea what happened between them, but damn," she says. "Jill was livid but didn't even say anything that night. She waited until we were all out to dinner the next week, with our husbands, and out of nowhere, she tossed a glass of wine in Margot's face."

I hadn't even realized I'd been doing it, but a shredded pile of napkins is building in front of me like a snowdrift; my hands have been tearing and twisting the paper into small wads.

"Margot wouldn't speak to her for three months. Jill tried to apologize but Margot is ruthless. And, of course, Margot should've been the one apologizing but she'd never admit anything had happened. She basically gaslighted Jill into thinking she was the one who'd done something wrong." Tina tilts her head back, snickers. "These women. They're my friends but they're also nuts. Jill doesn't talk about it, but I don't think she's ever forgiven Margot."

My head is fuzzy with cheap beer and this sordid gossip. I look up at Margot; Blond Boy has her pinned to the side of the pool table. Her legs are parted, and he's pressed against her, saying something urgently in her ear. Her croaky laugh pierces the air again, and every head in Rusty's is twisted in their direction, as if by force.

I rise and walk over to her.

"This has been so much fun but I gotta bolt," I say. "My Jack's an early riser."

Margot peels Blond Boy off her. "What? You're leaving already?" she asks, her voice climbing in pitch. "We're just getting started!"

She's pouting almost, and I realize that I'm part of her treasured audience. I'm about to add another apology when she hisses, "Whatever. Suit yourself." Darkness flickers across her eyes, then she turns from me and folds herself back into Blond Boy's arms. A curtain has fallen between us; she won't even meet my eyes and it's as though I don't exist anymore.

16

Saturday, March 24, 2018

My knees are damp from kneeling in the garden. I'm bent over, yanking clumps of grass out of the ground like fistfuls of hair, when my cell dings. Leaping up, I head over to the bench, swipe the screen. I was hoping it was Margot, texting me back, but it's only a notification to pay our wireless bill. My heart sinks and I set the phone back down on the bench, a little harder than I should; I'm irrationally mad at it for not coughing up a reply from Margot.

This morning, I had texted the group.

Fun times last night, ladies!

But only Tina responded, with the heart emoji.

It's Saturday afternoon and the sky is heavy

with dark clouds, as if on the verge of a shower. It's windless and muggy out, and I'd love the feel of a quick release of rain. Graham is sitting in an Adirondack chair on the back patio sipping a well-earned whiskey sour after my late night last night, and Jack is dashing through the sprinklers, belly-laughing each time the water sprays him.

I collapsed in bed after eleven thirty or so last night, and even though I was solidly sober by the time I steered myself home, my head felt leaden this morning when I first sat up in bed.

"Whoa, Annie. Get your gun," Graham quipped when he saw my shoulder, blackened with a bruise from the kick of the shotgun.

"It fucking hurt."

He rolled down the strap of my cami, rubbed the area around the bruise in small, light strokes. "But was it fun?"

I nodded. I didn't tell him about Rusty's. I wasn't sure how much I could or should tell, in case he ever crossed paths with Margot or the rest of them. "It was interesting. Sassy women. But I actually shot a skeet! You'd have been so proud."

"Well done." He grinned, tracing my lips with his thumb before kissing me.

■ ■ ■ ■

After a breakfast of spinach and mushroom omelets — one of Graham's specialties — we piled in the Highlander and headed to the farmers' market in the town square. I ordered us cappuccinos from the coffee trailer and Jack a donut, and we wove our way through the stalls — smelling handmade soaps and candles, trying free samples of baked goods, inspecting giant ribs of squash and zucchini.

"Wanna try a black bean brownie?" a twentysomething girl asked us, her voice coarse but friendly. "They're vegan." Her hair was dark and almost waist length. A trail of charcoal-colored tattoos trickled up her bare navel. She was dressed in denim cutoffs and Doc Martens. "They taste better than they sound," she coaxed, grinning and offering me one with her outstretched hand.

I popped it in my mouth. Grainy, but strangely delicious. "Mmmmm . . . they *are* good."

I handed her a ten and dropped two cellophane-wrapped packs in our cart before we headed toward the plants.

I loaded the cart with twenty basil plants,

their skunky smell filling the air when I pinched their leaves, while Graham picked out tomato and pepper plants.

"Pot-tee! Pot-tee!" Jack rocked back and forth on his heels. We are in the midst of potty training, but he only likes to use the toilet at home, so we stashed our goods in the back of the SUV and headed to the house.

I'm nestling the last basil plant into the warm, springy soil when the first drop of rain thuds on the back of my neck.

We escape into the chill of the house, wipe our muddy feet on the entryway mat. Rain is now lashing at the windows, and Graham steps into the kitchen to fix me a drink and refresh his own. I lean against the kitchen table, slip my cell from my pocket. No new notifications. Of course there aren't any; I just checked it moments ago before we came inside.

I know I shouldn't do this, but I can't stop myself. It's driving me crazy that I haven't heard back from her, so I text Margot directly.

Thanks again for having me out! Had such a blast!

I find the gun emoji and quickly tap send before changing my mind.

The sky outside the window darkens and grumbles, and I clasp the phone in my hand, willing it to chime a reply, but it stays mute.

One Month Later

The path to the clearing is narrow, the surface pocked with jagged tracks from the four-wheelers.

Even with the moon — which was half-full that evening — hanging in the clear sky, the trail would've been dark as soot, nearly impossible to see a foot in front of you.

I wonder if she was lured to the clearing that night, with the promise of something fun, something salacious. Or did she go against her will, fighting with adrenaline slinging through her veins?

And if she was lured, did she scream when she knew what was going to happen to her? But even if she did, the damp forest would've swallowed the sound whole, muffling her cries.

17

Present
Monday, March 26, 2018

We spent all of yesterday, Sunday, in the house, trapped indoors by the gushing rain. By noon, my hands were fraught with worry from endlessly checking my cell to see if Margot had responded (she hadn't), so I went into the mudroom and dragged down Jack's art bins.

Crafting with Jack always soothes me. Probably because as a child, it's the activity I most craved to do with Nikki but it was the kind of request she generally swatted away, preferring instead to lounge in her bedroom with a suitor, her too-loud laugh bouncing down the hall, her face only poking out of her room when she'd ask me to fetch her another peach wine cooler.

We worked on projects throughout the afternoon — gluing bits of pastel-colored construction paper onto poster board, cutting shapes out of felt with Jack's tiny plastic scissors, finger painting a mural to display in the hallway — and for a few hours, my mind drifted away from Margot and eased into the comfortable absorption of working side by side with Jack: his fingers sticky with glue and latching onto mine when he wanted help with something, his warm head slumping on my chest toward the end of our projects when he was ready for a nap.

Graham busied himself at the kitchen table, drafting plans for a new bid, and as dusk approached, I clicked on the gas stove and set a kettle of water to boil for our evening tea. As we sipped mugs of brisk Earl Grey, lightly creamed with milk, Graham resumed his sketching, and Jack, fresh up from his nap, abandoned me for the television and *Daniel Tiger's Neighborhood.*

My thoughts returned to Margot. Was she mad at me for some reason? Should I have stayed at the bar later? I swiped the screen of my cell, unlocked it. Checked Facebook. No updates or posts from her at all. I reread my text to her, inwardly scolding myself for not being wittier, punchier. And newly wired by the caffeine from the tea, I stepped out back as the rain continued to throb against the metal roof of the covered patio, and paced.

For some reason, a poem from college English lit came flooding back. Tennyson's "Mariana," about a woman waiting for her lover who never arrives. As I paced the pavers, it played over and over in my mind as if on a loop:

> Upon her bed, across her brow.
> She only said, "The night is dreary,
> He cometh not," she said;
> She said "I am aweary, aweary,
> I would that I were dead!"

18

Tuesday, March 27, 2018

It's morning. Graham has just taken Jack to school and I'm parked at the kitchen table, uploading photos of the garden to Instagram, hashtagging them: #amgardening #gardenlife #sloweddownlife #herbsforthesoul.

The rain broke in the middle of the night, and the morning sun twinkles in giant puddles on our back lawn.

Sipping my second latte, I'm trying to throw my concentration into something productive. Something other than incessant thoughts of Margot: my Instagram feed, my blog. I even circle the pages of a seed catalog, marking selections for the next row of vegetables I'll plant in the garden.

I get a flurry of likes on my Insta posts, some new followers and a few comments, and a smile steals across my face. I down the rest of the latte, stand up and stretch, and head outside to snap a few pics of the water-soaked backyard. The air is warm and close, the birds are belting out a frenzied song, and rainwater spurts and trickles from the gutters.

I step back inside, and despite my efforts to distract myself, Margot slides back into my brain. *Not now,* I say out loud, grabbing the keys and banging out the door.

I have to find something to do outside of the house today or else I'll go mad, so I head downtown to Gerald's, a quaint corner market, to stock up on wine and nibbles.

I'm drifting down the aisles, tossing items in my basket for a meat and cheese platter for tonight's dinner — I'm not in the mood to cook — when I hear the chime of the door and see Jill walk in with a tall young man who must be her son.

He's over six feet and hobbles on crutches as he and Jill approach me.

"Well, hey!" Jill says brightly. She leans in and gives me a quick peck on the cheek. "This is Brad. My teenager." She beams.

Brad is wearing a grass-stained, white-and-green football uniform. His thick, dark hair juts up at odd angles and is slick with sweat. He's gorgeous. His lips are full and his blue eyes are piercing like Jill's and fringed with long, dark lashes.

For a second, I imagine him with Margot in the lake house, Margot pinned to the wall as he kisses her neck. My face grows pink at the thought.

"Nice to meet you. I'm Sophie."

Jill is running her fingers over the assortment of olive oils, intently studying what she's going to select.

Brad dips his head in deference. "Pleased to meet you, ma'am," he says, his voice deep, his handshake strong.

Jill snaps out of her olive oil trance and looks at me as if she's forgotten I'm here. "Brad twisted an ankle today at practice. He says he's fine but they're making him walk with crutches just in case." Her eyes flutter up to her son. "He *is* the star quarterback, after all. And he has a full scholarship to Notre Dame next fall." She snakes a thin arm around his waist, leans into him. He blushes at the attention.

I try and read her face, scanning it for any evidence that I've been ousted by Margot or by the group, but it's a blank.

"See you soon?" I ask, with more pleading in my voice than I had intended.

"Sure, see you around," she says briskly, with a shallow smile.

19

Jack is sloshing water over the sides of the bathtub, slapping the surface of it and drenching Graham in the process.

I'm down the hall in my office nook, perched behind my laptop, but I can hear the clopping sounds of water and Jack and Graham's bright giggles.

I'm nursing a glass of merlot, taking small, peppery sips and watching the sunset flame behind the row of pines in our backyard. I tap the mouse, bring up Facebook.

I'm just starting to scroll through my news feed when Graham, towel in hand, ducks his head in the door.

"Want to help with bedtime? He's almost finished with his bath."

"Gimme a minute," I snap, a bite to my voice. "I'm paying bills," I lie.

He slinks down the hall. I feel guilty and should hop up and apologize, but I resume scrolling.

It's one of the first posts I see. From Margot.

Happy hour is the best hour!

And along with her status update is a photograph of the four of them: Margot in a flouncy blouse with short shorts; Tina right beside her, all grins and twinkling eyes, grasping her wineglass; Jill leaning against a barstool, her arms folded across her waist; and Callie with her hand parked on a hip, sneering at the camera. In triumph at me, I think.

A pit forms in my stomach, like an expanding pancake, and to my surprise, hot tears prick my eyes. I'm obviously out. I must be. Done and finished already as a member of the Hunting Wives. After only one week. I feel stung and a little betrayed by Tina, who seemed so genuinely nice. I grab my phone and hammer out a brief text to her.

Had so much fun the other night. Just curious (and I know this might sound a tad ridiculous) but I have to ask: did Margot seem peeved the other night because I left Rusty's early?

The Facebook post is from an hour ago.

Tina might still be with them but I can't help myself.

A moment passes and I'm mindlessly scrolling through the rest of my news feed when my phone chimes.

I wouldn't worry about it. If she was, she'll get over it eventually.

I guzzle the rest of my wine, twirling the stem of the glass between my thumb and middle finger. So, Margot *is* upset. Tina, the diplomat, dodged my question outright but in doing so, also answered it.

The room is now dark and I sit in the sickly glow of my laptop, my vision softening around the corners from the wine. I snap my laptop shut, pad down the hall, and slink into our bedroom. Graham is turned on his side, away from me. He's reading over his latest bid, his face crimped with focus, and I creak into bed and hug a pillow to my stomach.

I don't like feeling this way. This pinched state of agony waiting to hear back from Margot. I don't like what it's doing to me. When, for instance, did I become a shrew who snaps at her kind husband? I need Rox here to slap some sense into me.

I stare at the wall. My eyes follow the

groove of crown molding near the ceiling, and I hear Erin's voice in my head from the night of the garden party: *Be careful. Margot Banks is not a nice person.*

Erin. Sweet and uncomplicated Erin.

I slide my phone off the nightstand, text her.

Dinner Friday night? Our place or yours. Up to you if you're interested! I'll roast a lamb with rosemary from the garden and roll out the Slip 'N Slide for the kiddos.

I power my cell back off without waiting for a reply and curl myself around the pillow again. Tomorrow, I'll get the rest of the plants in the ground, including some transplants from Erin's garden. She's all into the food-as-medicine thing and has given me some dandelion greens (supposed to cleanse the liver) and some Chinese sweet potatoes (the leaves taste like spinach but don't leave that slimy film over your teeth).

I'll write a blog post, snap some more photos of the garden, make a chicken potpie for dinner with a crust made from scratch.

Slinging a foot over Graham's warm leg, I feel myself drifting off to sleep.

20

Wednesday, March 28, 2018

The morning is shiny and clear. A few low-slung clouds drift through the sky like barges on a river, but the sun is out and the sky is sapphire.

I'm on the trail, bright and early, and it feels as though a fever has broken. I feel like myself again. I'm running in inspired bursts and I even greet the man in his yard today.

"Morning, Harold!" I chirp as I jog by.

His binoculars thud against his chest as he lowers them, and his gaping smile reveals a mouthful of crooked teeth. "Beautiful day!" he answers, and tips his head.

Near the end of the trail, I slow to a walk and stroll down my street. The doves are cooing overhead, their soft, insistent murmurs sounding like a heartbeat, and I pause at a neighbor's yard to admire their cotton candy–colored tulip tree, just beginning to bloom.

I'm turning in to our driveway when my phone chimes. It's Erin, returning my text.

Erin: Sounds great! Our place. 7?

Me: Perfect.

Erin: See you guys then! I'll make the sides and dessert. ☺

Me: ☺

I heat the remains of a latte in the microwave, then float to the nook to my laptop, and pound out a punchy blog post about *Shinrin-Yoku,* the Japanese term for a "forest bath." I mention the health benefits — lowers your stress hormones, boosts your immunity — and select a few crisp pics of the woods and the trail, and click publish.

I feel motivated, possibly the most motivated I've felt since moving back, so I hop up before the feeling evaporates and cruise down the hall to the bedroom. I cast off my jogging gear and tug on an old pair of cutoffs. The denim is so worn and buttery soft that it feels supple against my skin, and I'm pleased to find I can comfortably button them without sucking in my gut — I haven't tried them on since shedding the baby weight. I pull on one of Graham's Chicago Bears tees and head outside to the garden.

I slip on my gloves, grab my till, and dig a fresh row for the rest of the tomato plants and Erin's transplants. Kneeling, I tuck them in the ground, tamping down the top layer of soil with the palms of my gloved hands.

I study the adjoining, empty raised garden and think about what to plant next. Probably heirloom tomatoes, from seed, from the earmarked catalog on the bench. I peel off my gloves, wipe the grit from my hands, and crouch down. When I'm nearly level with the ground, I snap a few pics of the freshly watered basil and compose an Instagram post: #basil #gardenlife #turningbasilintopesto.

I'm midway through hashtagging when a notification pops up on my screen.

A text.

My cheeks burn as I read the name of the sender.

Margot: Hey, there. Sorry it's taken me a while to get back to you. Things have been . . . kinda crazy. I'm about to head to the lake to lay out, if you wanna join. I have wine. ☺

My heart feels like it's drumming in my throat. I check the time. It's only eleven. I don't have to pick up Jack from preschool until two thirty. I take a second before I text back, trying to draw in a deep breath. But I can't. Adrenaline is surging through me and I quickly type:

Absolutely! Sounds fun. See you soon.

I'm smiling so wide my cheeks feel like they're going to burst. I must look like a madwoman out here in the yard, grinning and clutching my phone.

I leave the garden hose where it is, splayed next to the raised beds, and head inside. I'm practically shaking as I change into my swimsuit.

I stand over the sink, wash my face, and apply a fresh coat of lavender deodorant. (I hate the chemical, powdery stuff.) I toss on my cover-up, grab a beach towel, and race to the car.

21

When I pull up, Margot's on the wrap-around porch on the side of the house watering pots of tropical-looking plants. She waves and I walk over. She's wearing a straw sun visor and a stark white cover-up that's open in the front, revealing a red string bikini.

I'm grateful my eyes are shielded by oversize sunglasses so she can't see them roving over her chiseled stomach, her coppery legs, her pert breasts.

"See," she says, sprinkling the leaves of a hibiscus with water. "I'm not completely useless."

She twists the faucet off and bends over to grab a fabric cooler.

"Let's head down."

We walk down the grassy hill toward the pier, which extends over the water to a dock and boathouse. The sun is overhead now and I'm wishing I had thought to bring a beach hat.

I follow her to the edge of the pier and we step onto the floating dock. It's covered in a short layer of Astroturf, and Margot kicks off her flip-flops, so I do the same. It somehow feels plush underfoot like velvet, and there's a large wicker basket next to the pair of gray chaise longues filled with white beach towels, rolled to perfection. I feel silly with my faded, multicolored towel; I leave it tucked next to my beach bag as Margot lifts two towels from the basket and snaps them over our chairs.

She sheds her cover-up and we sink into the recliners. Unzipping the cooler, she slides out a bottle of sauvignon blanc and fills our glasses. We toast.

"Thanks for meeting me," she says as I shrug off my cover-up.

She eyes me. "That's super cute," she says of my green bikini. I'm self-conscious of my blinding white skin, still jiggly in places from pregnancy and approaching forty.

"Thanks," I manage.

She takes a long sip, leans back in her chaise longue. The lake is still and a lazy breeze bats at us, lulling me into a relaxed state.

"I'm usually out here on Wednesdays. But I don't normally invite the others. I get sick of them sometimes, honestly," she says, her voice hoarse and cracked. "Sometimes," she says, "I just wanna float away from it all."

A pontoon boat cruises past, sending waves that gently rock the dock from side to side. "I know what you mean," I say, because I don't know what else to say. I also wonder if this is her first nip of the day.

She sits up, pulls a bottle of suntan oil from her bag, and begins massaging it into her legs. Her skin is molten, not a freckle or wrinkle, and now she smells sweetly of coconut as she glistens with oil.

"Mind doing my back?" she asks.

I stand and lean over her as she rolls on her stomach and tucks her hair into her visor. Her bikini bottom is a thong; my breath stutters as I drizzle oil into my palm and work it into her shoulder blades. I wipe the remainder on the backs of my arms and then fish out my SPF-15 sunblock so I don't get seared.

She twists around and lies on her back again. Refreshes our glasses and traces the rim of her wineglass. "So, tell me about Graham."

I nearly choke on my wine. I'm not sure how to respond.

"He's, I dunno, nice."

"Mmmmm . . . seems to be," she says.

"Been married long?"

I know I'm just on my second glass, but I haven't eaten since breakfast, a slice of toast with butter, and that's long since vanished. The wine makes my head swim.

"Five years. I got pregnant during our second year of marriage," I say. "And you?" I ask, wanting to turn the conversation back to her.

"Fifteen long years. Two kids. Nina, my daughter, is eight. Harrison, my eldest, is ten. I would jump in front of a bus for them," she adds, slowly sipping her wine, "but marriage can be . . . tricky."

"Amen," I say, even though I don't mean it. Mine hasn't been. "What's your husband do?"

"Financial adviser. Boring stuff. Except it's not that boring lately. He's been super stressed out by work — I've never seen him under so much pressure. It's annoying." She sighs and stretches out a tanned leg.

"We knew each other growing up, hooked up in college. We were combustible then. Still are, I guess." She rolls over on one elbow to face me. Her breasts squeeze together, and the outer ring of a dark pink nipple peeks out of her suit. My stomach flutters, and for the second time today, I'm glad I'm wearing sunglasses. I know I'm fuzzy from the alcohol but there seems to be a charge building between us.

I down more wine and blink away the sunspots clouding my eyes, when my reverie is pierced by the sounds of voices, male and loud, floating from down the hill.

We both sit up and turn to look.

Margot springs to her feet like a cat.

I shield my eyes and recognize the taller one as Brad, Jill's son. He's wearing a pair of black swimming trunks with a white T-shirt pulled tautly across his chest. He's with a friend, a shorter, sunny-faced boy with hair the color of cantaloupe.

"Hey, boys," Margot says brightly as they amble down the pier. I can't tell by her tone whether she was expecting them or not.

Brad leans into her, and she gives him a quick peck on both cheeks.

"This is Jill's son, Brad," Margot says, turning to me.

"I know," I say. "We've met."

She looks at me askance but then Brad explains.

"Mom and I were at Gerald's this week and we bumped into her. Good to see you again, Sophie," he says, his full lips spreading into a smile. I'm shocked he remembers my name.

"Heeey, Jamie," Margot drawls, slinging

an arm around the other boy's shoulder.

He steps toward me, offers a hand. "Jamie. Jamie Smith." His burnished-copper hair is molded with product, and his eyes are a stunning, sea-glass green. Even though he's shorter than Brad, he's a good foot taller than me, and I gaze up at him and grin.

"Sophie," I say, shaking his hand.

Margot fills the glasses with more wine and passes them to the boys. They drink in eager gulps, then peel off their T-shirts. Jamie is lean yet ripped with small muscles, while Brad is all rock.

"I don't know about y'all, but I'm going for a swim." Brad dives into the lake and swims underwater for a few strokes before breaking the surface. "Oooh-heee!" he shouts. "Water's still cold."

"C'mon, Miss Banks!" he says, panting and treading the water. "I dare ya!"

Margot lowers herself down on the ladder, her face wincing, likely at the chill of the water.

"Race you to the cove?" Brad says, and they swim away from us, around the tree-lined bend where a long stand of cypress trees obscures the view.

I'm left standing on the dock with Jamie. He drains the rest of the wine into the glasses and we sit on the edge of the dock, our toes dipping into the icy water.

"Shouldn't you be in school or something?" I ask, already slipping into some kind of flirty voice.

He grins and scratches the back of his neck. "We're playing hooky. I was Brad's ride to the doctor — he sprained an ankle but it's all healed up — and he wanted to come out here."

I nod. I see him studying my legs, feel his eyes tracing over me.

"Not sure Abby would be too happy about it, though," he says, dragging a foot through the water in a circle.

"Abby?" I ask.

"Brad's girlfriend. Prettiest girl in school. Sweetest, too," he says, shaking his head.

I'm no longer tipsy, I realize; I'm plain drunk. I plant my hands next to my hips and heave myself up, walk over to my bag, and reach for my cell to check the time. It's one o'clock already. I need to leave soon. Fishing a bottle of water from my bag, I take a few slugs to try and sober up, and when I'm finished, Jamie is standing right behind me.

"You're getting all burned, you know?" he says. His voice is rich and deep.

I can tell; my skin is fever-hot, especially

in the places I couldn't reach with the sunblock.

"Your shoulders," he says.

I pass him the sunblock, lift my hair off my neck. His hands are warm, his touch firm. He continues massaging long after the lotion is set in, his breath hot and rapid on my neck. My pulse is racing and the wine is making me swoon.

I feel him tug on the tie to my bikini top. To my surprise, I let it fall. He grabs my shoulders, spins me around.

"My god," he says breathlessly. His bright green eyes roam all over me, and warmth spreads across my stomach as he steps closer, brushing his chest against mine.

He leans in to kiss me. A restrained, teasing kiss. My lips part but then I hear Margot's raspy laughter bounce off the water. Far enough away that it sounds like an echo, but close enough for me to snap out of it, pull back, and tie my top.

I peer at the lake and see Margot's face bobbing on top of the blue water as she swims toward us. She's smiling and I have no idea how much she's seen. Brad swims behind her, diving underwater and breaking the surface with loud gulps of air.

I stash my towel in my bag and turn to leave as they slither out of the lake.

"Gotta run get Jack, my son," I say. My voice is shaky from adrenaline.

"We're leaving, too," Brad says, toweling off. "Have to get back to school."

"Well, for the love of god, don't tell your mom about this," Margot says, her voice buttery and light. "You know she's not down with underage drinking."

She pecks him on the cheek again, and it doesn't seem sexual at all; it seems motherly, so I can't tell if there's anything between them.

22

The church is freezing after the blast of sun at the lake. I wrench my cover-up around me and pad down the hallway, my flip-flops slapping the linoleum floors as I make my way to Jack's classroom.

It's not a second past two thirty but he's the last one here, and Ms. Marcie, his sweet but overly zealous Christian teacher, is antsy. She's coating the surface of a little round table with a mist of Lysol and wiping it clean in agitated circles with a wad of paper towels.

Ugh. I'm becoming my mother. Something I promised myself I'd never do to Jack. Nikki arriving perpetually late to collect me from school, her waist-length hair shaggy and wild, excuses to the teacher spewing from her coral-lipsticked mouth. I can remember my face reddening when Nikki would interact with the other adults in my childhood sphere, and that peculiar, twisty feeling of being embarrassed for her.

I keep my distance. I don't want Ms. Marcie to smell the booze or sin on me.

Jack clocks me, drops a gnawed-on book to the floor, and toddles over, leaping into my arms. Hugging him tightly, I ask Ms. Marcie over his shoulder, "How was his day?"

"Fine! He got really into painting today. With a brush, not just finger painting. And he ate all of his lunch! No nap, though, just so you're warned." She smiles and returns to the can of Lysol.

I sling his backpack over my shoulder and we head for the car.

After I've buckled him in his seat, my phone dings.

Graham: I'm picking up Pizza King tonight! And also, a surprise!

My face slouches into a frown; my shoulders sag with guilt. I am a truly terrible person. I feel sunstroked and icky. How could I have done that to him? And, also, I completely abandoned making the chicken potpie, which makes me feel even worse about myself. If that's possible.

I text him back:

Sounds delicious!

I look in the rearview and Jack's eyes are sealed shut, his cherub mouth slung open with the tip of his tongue hanging out.

I drive around the wooded neighborhood near the church for a few minutes, cruising slowly through the wide streets, so Jack can have a full nap before heading home.

As I'm waiting for our garage door to trundle open, I check my cell. There is a text from Margot.

Margot: I swear I didn't know they were coming out! Please don't be mad!

I'm not sure I believe her. My hand is still slimed with sunblock and I clutch the phone, trying to figure out how to respond. I begin typing but see that she's working on a fresh text.

Margot: But it looks like you were having fun anyway. ☺

My neck burns with shame. She continues typing.

Margot: See you Friday? 🔫

Me: No worries!

I'm not admitting to anything.
I quickly add:

Me: And yeah, I'll be there!

Friday. Yikes. I'll have to cancel on Erin. Again. I hate to do it, but she's reasonable and understanding. She'll let me make it up to her, I hope.

I think about deleting the text. But Graham isn't the type who looks at my phone, so I leave it.

Anxiety pools in my stomach and chest. What have I done? I breathe. Remind myself that I didn't even really kiss him. But *still*. I can still feel his hot chest against mine; I can still picture myself standing there, half-naked in front of him. I wince at the image. I can't believe I did that.

I promise myself I'll never do it again. What bothers me, though, is the creeping sense that whenever I'm around Margot, I'm out of control.

23

We're in bed for the night — Jack is already zonked and Graham is rubbing small, careful circles of aloe vera into my sunburn.

"There's this new product that's out, you know," he says, a hint of a grin in his voice. "It's called sunblock. We could invest in some. You could use it next time you're gardening all day in Texas."

I nudge him with an elbow and he smooths my hair to one side so he can hit the back of my neck with it, too.

I didn't tell him I'd been at the lake. I couldn't.

He finishes, snaps the lid on the bottle, and blows on my shoulders to dry them. The chill of the gel is shocking, until it dries into a thin coat over my skin.

"Still in the mood to celebrate?" he asks.

His bid came through today; his bosses are thrilled. He picked up a bottle of nice champagne on the way home and we split it over pizza.

I turn and face him. Press him down against the mattress and straddle him. "I'm so proud of you," I say, nibbling on his ear. I feel filthy-dirty from my trip to the lake earlier, but also, so turned on. And even though my stomach is riddled with guilt, I can't resist Graham. I never could.

He slides a hand around the nape of my neck, kisses me, and with the other hand tugs my panties off.

Halfway through, I close my eyes, and out of nowhere, I imagine Margot in the doorway of our bedroom, watching us.

Later, we're lying on our backs. My pink skin is cooking the cool sheets; I'm spent.

"Ryan texted me, asked if he should pick up a bottle of scotch for Friday night. Thoughts?"

I roll to one side, drag a finger up and down his chest. "About that. We're going to have to cancel with them again. I'm going shooting. I didn't know if I'd be invited back, honestly, and I just found out today, I —" I'm grasping for words, fumbling for the best explanation when he stops me.

"I think it's safe to say this has been good for you," he says, his eyes grinning, his fingers tracing soothing circles on the top of my head.

■ ■ ■ ■

Oh, Graham, you have no idea.

24

Saturday, March 31, 2018

I come to in the back seat of Margot's Mercedes. My face is pressed against the glass, my mouth dry and parched. It's freezing inside the car. I grab my coat off the floor and wrap it around me.

Callie is driving, Jill and Tina are passed out next to me, slung over one another, and Margot leans back in the front passenger seat. Relaxed but alert. We're driving home from Dallas, winding through the lake roads. The frosty white display on the dash reads four a.m.

Four a.m.! Shit, shit, shit! I claw through my purse for my cell, dig it out. Six missed alerts. I swipe and read Graham's succession of texts.

9 p.m. Just got J down. Whew!

10 p.m. Hello, Ms. Oakley, do you copy?☺

10:45 p.m. Heading home anytime soon? Gonna go to bed and read.

11:30 p.m. Thought I'd wait up for you but looks like it's gonna be another late one. Be safe. Xx

2:30 a.m. Got up to pee and saw you weren't here — check in, ok?

3:30 a.m. Whatever.

Fuck. He's pissed.

Why wouldn't he be? I stare at my phone and try and think of something to text back, some excuse, but nothing comes to mind. I wonder if he's still awake. I wonder if I should wait to call him once I get in my car, but if he *is* still up, he's got to be worried. I let out a sigh and quickly type:

SO sorry! I'll explain everything when I get home. Which will be soon. Phone died!

I had promised I wouldn't stay out too late, that I'd get up and make Jack pancakes before we went to the farmers' market. I press the pads of my fingertips into my temples. My head feels like it's in a vise. My throat burns, as if I've vomited recently, and my stomach turns somersaults. This doesn't feel like a normal hangover. I fold my quaking hands together as the night comes back to me in flashes.

The beginning of the night I remember clearly; it's the end of the night that is stuttering: the loud, Cuban-themed nightclub in downtown Dallas, Margot's hand on my knee, pulsing strobe lights, and Jill straddling a man in a booth.

Before I left the house to head to the lake earlier this evening, Margot had group texted everyone.

Margot: Bring a change of clothes. We're going out tonight!

So I slipped a slinky top and a pair of black ballet flats in my bag and kissed Jack and Graham goodbye.

I rode with Jill again on the four-wheeler through the woods to the clearing. Margot shot first (she hit half of her targets), then Jill (she hit one; she squealed in victory), and finally, Callie shot. I declined to shoot; I didn't want to hurt my shoulder again and I didn't want to piss off Callie again, either.

Callie stood next to the skeet contraption, feet planted a foot apart in the grass as she raised the shotgun and fired. One after the other, she blasted all four of her skeets.

Margot shrieked, "That's my sharp-shooter!" and ran over, slapped Callie on the ass. The first real smile I'd ever seen crept over Callie's face, making her look like a small, delighted child.

After a robust round of martinis, Margot announced that it was time to change. Everyone else had garment bags with sleek dresses, so when I pulled out my top and flats, Margot briskly shook her head.

"Sophie. I don't mean to be a bitch but that won't do. Follow me."

I trailed her down the hall to the master bedroom and into the walk-in closet. She flipped a switch, and overhead bullet lights illuminated the closet, which was the size of my bedroom. Everything was organized by color, and strands of jewelry hung in glittering rows next to Margot's collection of handbags.

She stepped, barefoot, onto the plush white carpet and over to the corner where a row of little black dresses was dangling. She lifted one off the hanger and handed it to me.

"Try this," she said. She turned to select

her own outfit, so I slipped out of my clothes and tugged on the dress. It hugged my hips but otherwise fit perfectly.

"I'll zip you," Margot said, coming up behind me, lifting my hair out of the way. "You have beautiful hair, you know it?" Her hands were warm against my neck, and her breath felt like a kiss. My skin tingled; I hoped she didn't see the goose bumps rise over my arms. I swallowed the awkward lump in my throat and turned to face her.

"Gorgeous. I mean!" she said, her eyes zigzagging over me in approval.

She lifted off her own top, shimmied out of her jeans, and I turned to look away.

"Oh, please," she said, "don't be so old-fashioned."

She slid into a low-cut, emerald-green romper. The neckline plunged to the waist, and the shorts barely hit the tops of her thighs.

I blushed and stammered, "Looks fabulous."

She eyed herself in the mirror and slid her bone-thin wrist into what looked like a Van Cleef & Arpels pink gold bracelet.

"Want to borrow a necklace?"

I nodded. She looped her finger around one and pulled it down from a black velvet rack. A silver pendant with a simple diamond. She fastened it around my neck.

"You sure?"

"Yep. It's just costume. So, if you lose it, no biggie."

We all piled into Margot's Mercedes with Callie behind the wheel.

"She could make this drive in her sleep," Jill chirped from the back seat. "She has a condo in Turtle Creek. We sometimes make a weekend of it, shop, go out, and crash there. But we're coming back tonight, right, Margot?" she asked, leaning into the front seat. "You know I have to take Brad to practice in the morning. He's still not cleared to drive. Oh, and Abby — that's Brad's girlfriend," she said, turning to me, "asked me to take her prom dress shopping tomorrow afternoon! Isn't that adorable? Her parents are religious nuts and she doesn't want her mom to pick something out so she asked me! Just *love* her."

Margot gave her the thumbs-up and passed her an empty wineglass. "Refill, please." No one else would have noticed it, but when Jill mentioned Brad and Abby, I saw Margot's jaw tighten.

Jill pulled an icy bottle of chardonnay from the cooler and topped everyone off.

Callie wove through downtown Dallas, her eyes locked straight ahead onto the snaking traffic until we arrived in front of Club Havana. We left the car with the valet and hurried inside.

Inside, the club was a dark cave with multiple levels of dance floors and VIP areas roped off with red velvet cables. Loud, pulsing music. Latin music on steroids.

Margot nodded to the maître d' and we were shown to a private booth with a bottle already resting in a bucket of ice on the wide, circular table. We all slid around it, and Margot nudged in next to me. After we toasted our first glass of champagne, she slung her arm around me.

Callie fumed watching her, and after a few minutes, stormed off to the dance floor with Tina and Jill in her wake.

Margot refilled my glass, pushed it toward me.

"Fun place, right?"

"Very cool."

Margot slipped a lock of raven hair — polished by the loud lights — behind an ear, and I felt her leg graze mine. My pulse jittered and my breath grew shallow. I wanted to turn to her, stare into her eyes, and try to read her, but Callie returned with a well-dressed group of men.

Margot slinked out of the booth and introduced herself. They were all Russian, they explained, in town for business. They crowded themselves into the booth while flagging down the waiter.

They ordered the most expensive bottle of vodka available, and for the next hour, we all did shots. I was surprised at how little like alcohol the vodka tasted, but my eyes were beginning to swim, so I switched to water.

Margot was sandwiched between me and one of the men — he said his name was Andre, and he was at least six foot two with jet-black hair and flecked hazel eyes. A strong chin and chiseled cheeks. Movie-star handsome.

At one point, Margot rested her hand on my knee and didn't move it.

I could feel the violence of Callie's stare, but when I looked up, she simply smirked at me as one of the Russians, blond and edgily handsome, nibbled at her ear.

Andre tilted the vodka bottle toward my shot glass, but I covered it with my hand, shook my head.

"I'm getting a little tired of the vodka, too," Callie snorted, and floated up from the booth. She disappeared toward the bar.

Margot's hand was still on my knee, and she leaned in and whispered, "Ooooh, Callie's doing something nice for you."

Heat flooded my body, and Andre watched us hungrily.

Callie returned with two slender tumblers stuffed with mint and sugarcane.

"Here, drink this," she said, placing one down in front of me. "It's a mojito."

She took a sip, licked her matte-red lips, and watched me.

I took a long pull through the black straw, and the sugary drink coated my mouth. It *was* a nice change from the vodka.

"It's yummy, thank you!" I said cheerily. But she was already slunk back into the armpit of the blond man, who was now groping her hair.

As I drained the dregs of the mojito, Margot leaned over to Andre and whispered something in his ear. They slid out of the booth together, but Andre turned to me and held out his hand. I took it, and Margot grabbed his other free hand and led us upstairs to a darkened dance floor.

The lights were throbbing around us, and halfway up the stairs, the room seemed to flip. The floor became the ceiling and the ceiling became the floor. I looked up, and Andre and Margot were standing over me, mouthing words back and forth that I couldn't hear over the crushing music. I was slumped against the railing and I clutched my stomach, felt like I was going to be sick.

Andre leaned down and tucked a shoulder under my arm and guided me up the stairs.

"You had a little spill," he said in his richly accented English.

I let him lead me onto the dance floor. A slower, thumping song trickled from the speakers, and Margot was already dancing, swaying back and forth with her arms raised above her head, stretched toward the ceiling.

Andre circled her waist with a lanky arm and then pulled me into them. I tried to dance but I knew if I moved too much, I would stumble, so I let myself lean into his chest.

Margot moved closer to me, put her hands on my hips. Her charcoal eyes were steady on mine, and Andre slipped behind me, roping his arms around my waist.

Sweat beaded on my upper lip, and the room spun around me.

That's when my memory of the night starts to falter.

I remember staggering away from Andre

and Margot. Leaning on a barstool against the wall. The lights flickering as if someone were flipping the on/off switch. The music getting louder, faster, more jittery.

I peered down the stairs at the booth and saw Jill sitting on top of one of the Russians. Moving up and down against him. Tina sitting next to them, drink in hand, arm slung over the back of the padded leather booth. Callie with the blond still at her ear, but gazing up at me, her eyes narrowed and dark.

Margot. Andre. Andre slipping a hand inside Margot's romper, rubbing circles on a nipple. Andre leading Margot to a wall, hoisting her up. Sweat beading on my arms, clammy and cold. My eyes tweaking, my vision shifting.

Margot, eyes locked onto mine from across the room, as Andre had her right there on the dance floor, in the dark corner against the wall, her legs wrapped around his waist. Margot seemingly breaking the second rule of the Hunting Wives. *We don't go all the way.* Margot staring at me through all of it.

After that, I remember nothing.

I wrap my coat tighter around me. My whole body is racked with shivers. I rub my hands together to warm them, press them to my face, try and sober up.

I've never been good with mixing alcohol, but this feels like something different. I wonder if one of the men slipped something in my drink, but then again, I was the only one affected. And why would they single *me* out?

Callie pulls into Margot's drive just as the sun is oozing over the horizon. She notices me staring at her in the rearview mirror; she gives me a tight smile and a look. An unsettling look that makes me think of the mojito, the very last thing I drank, and a chill passes over me.

25

I wake with a start. The sheets are drenched with sweat; I reek of the nightclub — stale smoke swirled with alcohol and Andre's cologne.

Graham's side of the bed is empty, and Margot's little black dress is pooled on the floor. I wrench myself from bed and cross the hall and see that Jack's room is empty, too.

I wander to the kitchen. There's coffee in the pot but the machine is switched off and it's grown cold. A half of a silver-dollar pancake is stuck to one of Jack's Thomas the Tank Engine plates, and there's a terse note resting on the counter written in Graham's handwriting:

At the farmers' market.

It's nine a.m. Guilt racks my stomach and I fly down the hall to get dressed. I yank on some sweats and a T-shirt, twist my hair up with a jaw clip. At the sink, I nearly vomit while trying to brush my teeth, and my hands shake. Black eyeliner is smudged underneath my eyes; I look like a street mime, but I leave it and race for the car.

The farmers' market is packed and it takes me a while to spot Graham and Jack, but when I do, my heart leaps. I squeeze my way through the crowded rows, muttering apologies to those I'm brushing past.

Graham is at the black bean brownie table again, chatting with the girl from the other day. His head is tilted to one side, and a smile is pasted across his face. He's flirting, I realize, and the girl juts her hip out, twirls a ribbon of long hair around her finger.

Jack is crouched beneath the table, batting at Graham's calf, pretending to be a monster (his favorite game), but Graham ignores him and nods his head as the girl barks out a coarse laugh.

Jealousy pinches my chest, and all of a sudden I'm breathless, but I sidle up to my husband, slide my arm around his waist.

He doesn't acknowledge me. In fact, he peels my hand off his hip and takes a tiny, imperceptible step away from me.

■ ■ ■ ■

"I haven't tried that since college, but maybe I should again," he's saying to Brownie Girl, who flashes me an apologetic smile.

"We're just talking about juicing," she says to me with forced cheer.

"Oh?" I say dumbly. My neck burns with shame and anger.

"I'm into celery juice at the moment," Brownie Girl offers. She's turned her focus solely to me now, backpedaling for flirting with Graham. "It's super good for your immune system —"

"Maaa!" Jack crawls out from beneath the table, tugs on my sweats, blissfully coming to my rescue. I smile at Brownie Girl and nod, bend down and scoop Jack up.

"Ready?" I say to Graham. "This little tiger needs a nap soon."

"I'll just see you back at the house," Graham says, his eyes not meeting mine.

I stand there for a second, my mouth hanging open, feeling as though I've been slapped. I try and think of something to say, but no words will form, so I turn and bounce Jack on my hip as we head toward the parking lot.

▪ ▪ ▪ ▪

Back at home, I lift a sleeping Jack from his car seat and cradle him to my chest, trying not to wake him as I step through the back door. I ease down the hall and settle him into bed, covering him with just a thin blanket so he won't stir. I hear the back door open and I sigh, steeling myself for a fight with Graham.

When I walk down the hall, he is in the kitchen, washing the dishes from this morning's breakfast. His sleeves are rolled up and suds bubble on his forearms. He won't make eye contact.

I come up beside him, place a hand on his back. He tenses at the touch.

"I'm so sorry about last night," I sputter. "I drank way too much. I passed out, actually," I say, casting around for sympathy. "And since it's out in the woods, I don't get great cell reception, so I'm on roaming a lot, which drains my battery," I lie. "I finally found a charger that would work, and that's when I saw all your texts."

He jerks open the dishwasher door and turns away from me, silently loading our everyday china into the machine.

Sweat stings my armpits, and my mouth

is a box of gravel. I need something to drink. I move away from him, grab a glass, and fill it with water. Take a gulp and set it down. He's still turned away from me.

"Well, say *something,*" I beg, my voice turning into a shriek.

He twists around, trains his eyes on the floor.

"What am I supposed to say?" he asks, flipping his palms up in exasperation. "I just feel like there's something you're not telling me. And if it's someone else, some other guy, I want to know —"

I grab his face, press my lips to his. I know it's the only way to defuse the situation. He resists for a second but then his lips go soft and he lets me kiss him long and slow. Eventually, he slides his arms around my waist.

I pull him closer, wind my fingers through his hair. "God, I'm such an idiot."

He exhales and I feel his whole body sigh against mine.

"I'm sorry, too," he pants in my ear. "It's just weird you staying out so late and I'm here alone with Jack. It's just . . . my mind ran away last night when I woke up and you weren't home."

"No, *I'm* sorry I made you feel that way." And I am. I hate myself for it. I want to come clean and tell him there is no other man. But I can't. Because there *is* someone else. Margot. And, of course, I won't tell him about her because I don't even understand myself what's going on.

"I promise never to do that again," I say instead. "I was out of control. These women are out of control."

I squeeze his hand and look into his eyes, which have begun to soften.

A grin flickers across his face. "I want you to have fun. You know I'm not uptight —"

"Of course, I know that! You're the most laid-back creature I've ever known and I don't deserve you," I say, pillowing my face into his shoulder. "It was a dick move on my part and I promise not to act like a teenager again and make you worry like that."

He laces his fingers through mine and leads me to the bedroom. Jack's snores purr down the hall and we close the door to our room, sinking into bed together.

I'm exhausted, so I'm relieved when Graham doesn't undress. He just pulls me into him on top of the fluffy down comforter, and my head rests on his chest as his fingers hunt around for the remote.

"Last week's *Downton Abbey* since we never got to watch it?" he asks.

"Sounds perfect," I say and snuggle into him even tighter.

I wake to the sound of something rapping at the window. It's afternoon; Graham snores beside me while *Downton Abbey* still plays quietly on the TV — the servants are in a tizzy about something, all lace collars and black uniforms and cockney accents — and I grab the remote and squeeze the off button. I like this show but Graham *loves* it, and after last night, I'm not in the mood for their grating, whining voices.

The soft thudding at the window continues. It's probably the thin branches of the pecan tree being whipped by the wind, but an unsettled feeling crawls over my skin, so I climb out of bed, creep toward the window.

I tug the cord to the blinds and peer out. A squirrel shimmies down the arm of a pecan branch, knocking a few pecans loose, but other than that, the backyard is empty. I exhale, and when the breath leaves my body, my lungs burn from the secondhand smoke I inhaled at the club last night.

My head is still clasped by a wrenching headache, so I head to the kitchen to get more water, and drain the tumbler in three greedy gulps. As I walk back down the hall,

I pass by the picture window in the living room and see a figure moving down the street.

I scramble over to the front door and creak it open, poke my head out, and see the back of a man in a black trench coasting up the hill, away from our house.

I can tell it's Harold, the man from the trail, by the bulk of his body and the way he shuffles up the street. I shudder and close the door. Surely, he wasn't just in our backyard at the window. Surely, my mind is just cartwheeling, playing tricks on me from my delirious debauchery last night.

I click the door shut and lock it. Wrapping my arms around my chest in a hug, I head back to bed.

26

Wednesday, April 4, 2018

I've been good all week. I've written two zingy blog posts — one about the perils and joys of homemade yogurt, the other about DIY Easter crafts. I've cooked a bubbly veggie lasagna with fresh herbs plucked from the garden and even marched a square of it up to Mrs. Murphy's. Yesterday morning, the seeds arrived from the catalog and I've already planted them all.

The garden is well looked after, weeded and maintained. And this morning, I'm chopping up a row of tomatillos, locally grown, to blend up into a salsa for a tray of chicken enchiladas for dinner. I toss the juicy green bits into the blender, cover it with homemade chicken broth and diced cilantro, pinch a hearty dash of cumin on top, and blend. Pouring the salsa over the rolled enchiladas, which glisten like cannoli, I tuck the tray into the oven.

It's a beautiful spring day and I've thrown the kitchen window open. Birdsong splashes through the room, and a breeze hits my face, lifting my hair in refreshing bursts. I untie my splattered apron, drop it in the washer, and cross the kitchen to make another latte.

As the espresso machine whines and gurgles, I lean against the counter. Even though my kitchen is practically humming with delight, I think of the boring, lonely day ahead of me — a day with no social contact until I collect Jack from preschool — and the same unsettled restlessness skulks over me, making my skin crawl, making me feel like I can't breathe.

What's wrong with me? Why can't I be content with normal, quiet, lovely things? I mean, I *am* happy; there's part of me that *is* fulfilled by all of this, but obviously, there's another part that is decidedly not. I feel terrible even having these feelings; Graham is golden. Maybe everyone secretly feels this way about their lives?

People who've never been abandoned don't know what a hole it leaves. When my dad left us, it made Nikki rootless, unable to stay in one place for very long. And it made me clingy, first to Nikki — which she couldn't really handle — and then with the bad boys I chased.

So even though I longed for this, longed for someone stable like Graham, stability feels foreign to me, and I have to fight my impulse to fidget at every turn.

I sometimes catch myself staring at Graham, at his open happiness and fulfillment with family life, and find myself envious of how uncomplicated, how simple his needs seem to be.

I'm tired of being the complicated one.

When the machine gives its final belch, I pour the ink-black espresso into the bottom of my white mug, top it with steamed milk, and sip. My thoughts slide back to Margot. Not that they're ever far from her, but at least these past few days, as I've thrown myself into domesticity, I've managed to have whole moments where she becomes more like background noise, ever present but a bit more muted than usual.

But as I stand in the kitchen just now, taking a break and drinking my latte, here she is again, front and center, spotlit in the forefront of my mind.

Margot in the nightclub with her slender hand pressed to my knee, the heat on my leg. Margot whispering in Andre's ear. The two of them leading me up the stairs. Margot's hands on my hips on the dance floor. Her eyes on mine as Andre fucked her.

A shiver runs over me. My mouth goes dry thinking about her and what might've happened if I hadn't been so wasted. How far would I have let things go?

I try and push the thoughts aside but I can't. Warmth is spreading through my chest, and before I know it, I'm walking down the hall to change clothes.

It's Wednesday, the day Margot's usually out at her lake house, so I slip on my bikini, pull on a T-shirt with a pair of cutoffs, and decide to head out there. Surprise her.

We haven't spoken since Saturday night, other than the group text Tina sent the next morning.

Tina: Sophie honey, you okay?

Margot: Yeah, seriously. Can someone say lightweight? ☺

Me: Totally fine. Just hung like the moon.

Nothing from Callie or Jill.

I climb into the Highlander and head for the highway. The air is thick and tangy, and I lower my windows and let the wind do with my hair what it may. As I turn down the country lane, I spy a lovely farm stand on the side of the road with buckets of brightly colored flowers. I slow down and park and think, Why the hell not? I could bring Margot a bunch as a thank-you for including me in the group, so on a whim, I fish a crumpled twenty from my wallet and give it to the old lady in the straw hat whose skin is puckered from the sun.

The bouquet fills the car with an earthy, sweet smell, and I roll the windows up, not wanting to sever the delicate tops of the flowers.

Easing into Margot's drive, I see her Mercedes tucked near the front of the house. A smile spreads across my face. I park and walk up the grassy lane, and a warm gust from the lake rushes toward me like a hug.

I step onto the cedar porch. My knuckles are about to rap on the door when I spot something out of the corner of my eye. I step in front of the window and see Brad sitting on the couch.

His head is tilted back, his eyes are closed, and Margot's on her knees below him with her back to me. His jeans are pooled around his ankles and he's stroking Margot's hair as she rhythmically rocks back and forth between his legs. I freeze in place and watch them for a moment, and then, to my horror, Brad slowly opens his eyes.

It takes him a second to take me in, but when he does, he unfolds his hands from behind his head and places them on Margot's tanned shoulders, leans down, and whispers something in her ear. And before I can turn to leave, she twists around and sees me. Her eyes aren't mad, though, and her lips rise up into a sly smile.

I turn and walk toward the car, feeling stupid with the flowers in my hand, so I aim them at the ground, dropping them.

My heart is drilling as I climb into the Highlander. I close the door and exhale; I'd been holding my breath and my head swims. I feel dizzy.

Driving away, my face sizzles with embarrassment. I feel foolish for going out there unannounced and am trying to figure out what to say to Margot, when my phone dings.

I pull over on the shoulder to read the text.

> Margot: So . . . now you know. I'm busted. And I know I don't have to tell you this, but don't tell the others, they

wouldn't understand. You'll keep my secret, won't you? ☺

My hands are glazed with sweat and hover over the screen as I try to think of a reply. A fist is clenching and unclenching in my stomach; I don't know what to think of this, but I let out a long, ragged breath and type:

Secret's safe with me. Xo

27

After dinner, as Graham tucks Jack into bed, I step into our master bathroom and run a bath. I fill the tub with scalding water and drop in a silk sachet filled with fresh rosemary from the garden. The last dregs of sunlight bleed through the blinds, and soon, the room smells like the sharp, clean scent of a forest.

I dip a hand in the water — it's still too hot — and quickly pull it out, my skin turning bright pink. I light a small, white candle in a glass votive, take a deep breath, and wait for the water to cool.

On the bathroom counter, my phone vibrates, zigzagging across the white quartz top. I dry my hand and snatch it — I had turned the ringer off earlier so it wouldn't wake up Jack. It's a group text.

Margot: Sorry ladies. No hunting this Friday night. Family stuff.

A few minutes later, Tina responds.

Tina: Understood! Bill wants to go to Shreveport to the casino that night anyway, maybe I'll join him.

Callie: We never miss. What the hell??

Jill: I was sooo looking forward to it. But honestly, I haven't recovered from Dallas yet so prolly for the best.

I wonder if Jed somehow found out about Brad. Or if Margot's going to meet up with Brad. I don't know how to respond, so I just type the thumbs-up emoji.

I set the phone back down and sink into the tub. Closing my eyes, I feel my muscles go slack in the warm water. Of course I'm disappointed that I won't be seeing Margot, but also, I'm relieved she's canceled; I need a break. I'm still shaky from Dallas, and from what I saw Brad and Margot doing. But more than that, Graham and I are back to normal and I don't want to rock things. I can't.

28

Friday, April 6, 2018

I'm tearing crisp ribs of romaine lettuce for a salad over a large weathered bowl. Erin stands next to me, whisking the ingredients for a Caesar dressing. The rhythmic thump of her spoon against the glass bowl is soothing. So is the open bottle of prosecco we're sharing as Graham and Ryan hunker over the grill in our backyard, searing the steaks.

Mattie has pulled Jack into her lap on the sofa and she's absentmindedly combing her fingers through his blond locks as they watch yet another episode of *Doc McStuffins.* Jack's baby quilt is balled up in his lap, and he sucks his thumb, eyes glazed over from the TV.

"So, Graham told us that you've been busy with freelance work," Erin says. Her voice is warm and bright and filled with so much sincerity; I feel a stab of guilt as I lie.

"Yep, sorry I've had to miss out on our

dinners lately. But yeah, it's been good for me. You know what they say about idle hands and all that."

I grab a chunk of Parmesan and grate shards of it over the salad.

"That does sound really good for you. I'm happy. I know this town can be awful and boring, believe me," she says.

Erin left, too, after high school. She went away to the University of Texas at Austin and majored in world history and planned to never return. But one summer night, at a friend's wedding in Mapleton, Ryan asked her to dance and they fell in love. Ryan was already established here — he owned the house they live in now; his business was just picking up steam — and he made it clear that he wasn't going anywhere. So, Erin finished out her senior year and packed up her tidy duplex and moved in with him.

We kept in near-constant touch during college. I fled north, to Northwestern University's School of Journalism, and all throughout my freshman year, as loneliness sat like a hippo parked on my chest, I looked forward to my phone dates with Erin.

I'd sit cross-legged in baggy sweats on the thin mattress in my dorm room and curl the beige phone cord around my finger until it turned red. We'd talk for hours, about our classes, about the new cities we found ourselves in, but mostly, we talked about boys.

Erin was a serial monogamist, dating one studious guy for a year and then moving on to someone equally as serious as the last. I, of course, was knee-deep in my flings with bad-boy jerks.

I would tell Erin every agonizing detail of these tortured relationships and welcome her grounded, nonjudgmental reactions. I told her everything but skipped the one-night stand I'd had with a woman named Lisa.

Lisa was a senior when I was a sophomore and I met her in philosophy class. Everyone idolized her, men and women alike, but she made it clear she wasn't into men. She had charcoal-black hair, cut short, high cheekbones, and dreamy lips. She was outspoken, always organizing rallies and protests, and I was drawn to her and nursed a crush for weeks before she ever even spoke to me.

When she did finally notice me, one day after class when a group of students were gathered in the leafy courtyard next to the philosophy department, she looked at me and said, "You and me, drinks tonight."

She took me to a dive bar, and we sipped

foamy pitchers of cheap beers and sat at the scarred wooden bar, tacky with spilled booze. When she leaned over and kissed me, a gang of frat boys burst out in whoops, so she took me by the hand and led me back to her chalk-white bungalow around the corner.

She pulled me into her room, which smelled richly of incense, and traced her fingers over my lips before kissing me again, this time even harder. She kissed better than any boy I had ever been with, and my stomach did somersaults as she slid her hand down my pants and touched me.

The next morning, over pancakes at a nearby diner, she had me jot my phone number down on a napkin and promised to call. All that day, alone in my dorm room, I shuddered with desire, remembering her touch, and imagining us a power couple, strolling through the tree-lined campus together, her fingers laced in mine, but she never called and then ignored me for the rest of the semester in class. I was crushed.

I never told anyone about Lisa, until I met Graham. One night during our early and heady days of dating, we split a bottle of velvety red wine over a steak dinner in Chicago. We traded ghosts-of-relationships-past stories (like Erin, Graham had been a serial monogamist), and I blurted out about my torrid night with Lisa.

His neck turned crimson and his eyebrow arched in curiosity.

"I'm straight, though," I quickly added. "I was just experimenting."

I didn't want him to be a guy who dreams of a ménage à trois or open relationships or any of that malarkey. After the string of bad boys and jilted loves, I craved something solid.

Erin empties the last of the prosecco into my glass as I'm pulling a homemade persimmon pie from the oven. The crust bubbles and oozes, and as I'm walking it over to the counter in my oven mitt–clad hands, my phone dings. Erin leans over as if to check it but then turns away.

I set the dish on a hand towel and tug off the mitts, scoop up my phone. It's a group text, from the Hunting Wives. I can't tell if Erin saw it or not. And I can't believe I'm hiding something this big from her. Not that she'd be interested in joining us, but I do feel bad that she's excluded.

Jill: Pool party at the lake on Sunday? My place? I'm missing my ladies. Margaritas and nibbles.

Tina: Sounds SO fun. I'm in!

Margot: Yasssss!

A thumbs-up from Callie; I can feel her haughtiness even through a simple emoji.

I'm about to type back when Erin sidles up next to me.

"Work?" she asks.

Good. It doesn't seem as though she read the text.

I chew my bottom lip, angle slightly away from her. "Yep, sorry."

I type:

Sounds delicious! See you guys Sunday!

I flick my phone to silent and flop it over on the table in case more texts pour through.

I uncork another bottle of wine, this time a smoky merlot.

"Ryan's driving tonight, so bottoms up!"

Erin leans against the kitchen counter and clinks her glass to mine. I drain half of it in one long gulp, and the wine washes warmth across my whole body. I think of Margot, tanned and toned in her red bikini, and the prospect of seeing her in it again, poolside, makes me shiver with excitement.

I feel like a college kid again, only wanting to talk about boys and escapades, so I blurt out, "So . . . Margot Banks. You told me she's not a nice person. What did you mean?"

I want to snatch back the question as soon as it's left my mouth, but it hangs there in the air between us.

"Why do you care?" Erin's face is pricked with curiosity.

"I just bumped into her at yoga one day. Just curious," I lie.

She seems to accept this at face value and swirls the wine around in her glass, a bemused smile tickling her lips. She's sinking into gossip mode.

"Well," she says, lowering her head to mine, "her husband Jed is a total pig. He's always been such a prick, coming from money and all. And Margot, too. She comes from even more money."

She slams her glass of wine, holds the empty glass out to me for a refill.

"But back to Jed, he's super sleazy. Word is he banged half his staff. But never got caught until Margot showed up in his office one day and walked in on his secretary blowing him under the desk."

Erin's face blooms red as she continues. "Anyway, Margot ran the poor girl off. I mean, she wasn't an *innocent* girl, but what Margot did, or at least what I *heard* that Margot did — and this is between us, I don't want to be on her shit list — involved a gun and a death threat." Erin rubs her arms vigorously as if trying to shake off a chill.

"I mean, who the hell knows if it's true or not," she says, suddenly backpedaling. It's as if she is also afraid of Margot. But I can picture it, knowing what I do about Margot and guns, but, of course, I can't say that to Erin.

"The rich bitches in this town are crazy. And I avoid them at all costs, except when I *have* to be nice to them. There's this one woman, Jessica Bates, for instance, who was up for a board vote, to be vice president of the planning committee for the children's museum. And Jessica's nice, too, and fairly normal. And she was a shoo-in. But the week before the vote," Erin says with a flourish, swinging her wineglass in front of her, "she *slightly* disagreed with something Margot had to say. So, guess what? Not only did she lose the election but she was closed out from just about everything else."

I suck in a slow breath, nod.

"You know, just Grade A typical rich bitch stuff," Erin snorts. "Cut me off after this glass, please, or I'll be fucked in the morning," she slurs.

I'm at the kitchen sink, filing away the last dish from dinner into the dishwasher, when the urge to sneak into my office hits me.

Graham is in Jack's room, tucking him in for the night, so I tiptoe down the hall and slink behind the laptop. I've banned myself from Facebook all week long, and I'm proud that I haven't even had a peek, but just now, the need to see Margot overtakes me.

The first story in my feed is a post from Tina, at the casino with Bill. He's red-faced, strongly built, with watery blue eyes, and he looks like the sort of person you'd wanna split a bottle of scotch with. Fun. Spirited. Tina has snapped a selfie of them at the bar in the casino and she looks drunk and happy.

I smile but don't click "like." Because of Erin, I've tried to be discreet on Facebook with the group.

I scroll through other posts, but nothing jumps out until I see the most recent post from Margot, which isn't recent at all, it's from nearly a week ago, the Sunday morning we got back from Dallas.

Margot is in front of the Mapleton Methodist Church, one of the older churches downtown, and she's standing on the lawn underneath a bare sycamore tree with her husband, son, and daughter.

She's wearing a pale pink Jackie O–style dress with matching jacket and her hair is perfectly sleek, face perfectly made up. She certainly doesn't have the look of someone who just dragged in from a bar only four hours earlier. I'm impressed.

Her children are picture-perfect, too, and Margot's hands rest on the tops of their shoulders. The only thing off about the photo is her husband, Jed.

Not his looks — he's wearing a shirt and tie, and his dark, coffee-colored hair is sumptuously molded and swept to one side. He looks like a print model.

It's his expression, grim-faced and cold, that chills me. Something tells me he knows what's going on with Margot. And that he doesn't like it.

29

Sunday, April 8, 2018

I'm the first to arrive at Jill's lake house. Even though her pearl-white Lexus is parked in the drive between a camo-colored Jeep and a red work truck, she's the only one inside as I trail behind her through the house.

If Margot's lake house is rustic, old-money chic, Jill's is opulent and modern — a white stone mansion with two-story windows lining the back wall that look over a teal infinity pool that seemingly flows into the lake.

The rooms are massive and airy — all polished granite and light gray surfaces, the floors covered in Italian tile. Sunlight drenches the living room and kitchen, which make up one giant room.

"It's perfect you're early. You can finish the guacamole while I mix the drinks," Jill says, cinching the waist of her gauzy cover-up around her white one-piece. She pushes her black-framed glasses up on her pert nose and hands me a lime squeezer.

While I work on slicing open the limes and draining the juice over a glass bowl, my eyes feast on the liquor banquet she's laid out for us. Honey-colored tequila, perfectly measured out in five crystal shot glasses that line the countertop. A sliver of lime rests on the salt-dusted rim of each glass.

Jill grasps an expensive-looking bottle of tequila by the throat and glugs it into her giant blender until she's satisfied with the amount. A few splashes slop over the side and she grabs a white kitchen towel and mops it up, her face strained with concentration.

"Now, for the OJ, I think," she says, as much to herself as to me, licking a finger and turning the page in a glossy cookbook. She feels me eyeing her. "And yes, I'm using a recipe; don't judge."

I'm not judging, I'm impressed with her fastidiousness and the colorful array of ingredients she already has at her fingertips. I want to photograph it all but I wouldn't want Erin to see it in a post and don't exactly feel comfy asking Jill for permission.

With a paring knife, I get to work slitting the dozen or so avocados open on a cutting board. Jill takes a glass pitcher of freshly squeezed orange juice from the fridge and empties it into the blender.

"It's the secret ingredient," she says, winking at me. I hadn't noticed before how long and dark her lashes are, but here, in the sun-splashed kitchen, her face is blindingly beautiful. Behind her on the fridge is a family portrait of Jill, Alex, and Brad; they all have the same piercing aquamarine-blue eyes. Alex is a blond with high cheekbones, and he towers over them in the photograph, making Jill and Brad almost look like brother and sister.

"That's a recent picture," Jill says. "I wanted to have one last professional photo done before Brad leaves for college. I'm happy with how it turned out," she adds. She walks to the freezer and pulls down a roll of frozen lime juice. "I like to mix frozen and fresh," she explains, tearing open the package and dunking the bright green tube of frozen lime into the blender.

I take the knife and make crosses on the faces of the avocados before squeezing their buttery flesh into the bowl. The rest of the ingredients — diced jalapeños and tomatoes, cumin, garlic, and cilantro — are all in tiny bowls at my fingertips ready to be tossed in.

When I finish mixing everything together and dousing the guacamole with lime juice, Jill snaps a piece of Saran wrap over the top and presses it down over the mixture. "Keeps it from browning," she says as she lifts the bowl away from me and parks it in the fridge.

A timer chimes, and Jill spins around and bends down to open the oven. I can't help but notice how exquisitely chiseled her calf muscles are and how her biceps flex as she hauls a tray from the oven.

"Voilà!" she says, a hint of excitement brightening her face. "Peach-glazed short ribs! I made the peach preserves last week and marinated the ribs in it overnight."

"They're gorgeous," I say, my mouth watering. Jill transfers the shellacked ribs to a cobalt-blue platter and nudges the oven door shut with a perfectly pedicured foot. She then pulls a bowl of salsa from the fridge — presumably homemade, too — and empties a fresh bag of tortilla chips into a large wooden bowl.

"Finished! Everything looks great! Thanks for your help," she says, placing her hand on top of mine. Her fingernails are painted in the palest of pinks and her skin is creamy white and baby-butt smooth.

"I love this stuff, are you kidding?" I say.

"It's what I do, actually, I'm working on a lifestyle blog and —" I'm about to say more and finish explaining, when the front door gushes open and Margot spills inside.

Her hair is spiked with product — perfectly beach-mussed — and her face is hidden behind oversize black sunglasses. She's wearing a neon-orange string bikini, even stringier than her red one, and the top of it strains against her breasts. A jolt of lust zaps through me. Her lacy, black cover-up barely hides anything, and my eyes trail down to her waist and to the delicate orange ties at her hips.

"Hey!" she says in a husky voice, setting her straw beach bag down on the floor. She crosses the room and gives Jill a quick hug, then walks over to me. She hugs me, and her lips graze my cheek. "Sophie! Lookin' good as always," she says, a cloud of coconut from her skin perfuming the air between us. I blush and look down at my red one-piece, which I fished off the rack at Target yesterday. It's a basic suit but the neckline plunges just so, and it was the only one that was even remotely flattering.

"Thanks," I say dumbly.

Margot lifts a shot of tequila to her lips, tosses it back.

"You were supposed to wait for the rest of

us!" Jill says, her voice high and nasally.

"Oh, shut it. You know I'm good for another one," Margot says, bumping her hip playfully against Jill's. I see Jill study Margot's bikini; I can't read the expression that flashes across her face. Envy or desire or something else, I can't tell.

Callie bursts through the door next, followed by Tina, and all of a sudden the room is buzzing with greetings and chatter, the voices clattering off all the polished surfaces.

Callie is wearing a black one-piece, and the neckline vees all the way down to her hips. A gold band circles her waist, and she's also wearing gold cuffs on each wrist. She looks like a sexed-up Wonder Woman. Tina is in a ruby-colored, prim two-piece that covers everything but her midriff. Fringe hangs over her tanned waist, and silver beads line the straps. Her chocolate-brown curls are satin-smooth and her feet are nestled in bright red peep-toes. She looks like a million bucks.

We all settle around the bar and shoot tequila. A dense cloud crosses in front of the sun, momentarily darkening the room, and I look around at each of these women, polished to a high sheen, and I feel downright dowdy. Margot tips more tequila into our shot glasses while Jill works the blender, blasting my ears.

"Callie, help me out with the food, will ya?" Jill asks as she pours slushy margaritas into oversize glasses. She places them neatly on a tray and follows Callie outside to the deck. Jill steps back inside and clasps her hands together. "Oh! I almost forgot the sangria! Callie, could you —" she says, but Callie is already back inside next to her, dragging a jug of crimson-colored wine from the fridge.

Margot leans over and whispers in my ear. "Callie may seem like a bull, but she does everything she's told. At least she does for me." The tequila is thick on her breath, so thick that I'm quite certain it's only a fraction of the booze she's already had today.

We wander outside to the deck. The sun is still snaking behind thick clouds, but the wood on the deck radiates heat like a sauna. After we graze on the dazzling buffet, I park myself on a lounge chair in the shade, underneath a white umbrella. Jill and Tina sink down into the chairs next to me, while Callie and Margot take the chairs on the adjoining side of the pool.

I realize I'm holding my drink close to my chest — I guess I'm afraid to let it out of my sight with Callie around.

Jill meanders over to the pool, sits on the side, and drags a foot through the water. "So, Margot, do tell. What's the family drama?"

Margot's eyes are still hidden behind her Jackie O glasses, and she lifts her margarita glass to her lips, takes a sip. Next to her, Callie stiffens as if she already knows the answer and is bracing for Margot's reply.

"I don't wanna talk about it," Margot says dismissively.

"Kiddo stuff or hubby stuff?" Jill prods.

"Hubby stuff, if you must know, but seriously, drop it."

Then Margot turns to me as if letting me in on a group secret. "Not everyone's in this perfect relationship where their husband thinks they're an angel." She dips a finger into her margarita, swirls it around, takes it out and licks it.

"I am *not,*" Jill says.

"No shit," Margot says, sitting up and adjusting her top.

I take a long sip of the margarita, and my mouth puckers at the tanginess of it.

"But Alex, excuse me, *Alexander,* fucking worships you. If only he knew —"

Jill cuts her off, her thin voice teetering. "And that's why we keep our stuff a secret." She looks like she's on the verge of tears, and she stares down into the pool water, her eyes trained on the tiny waves she's making with her legs.

"Of course," Margot says, her tone softer. "Sorry, Jilly. I'm just on edge. Jed is stressed out at work and he's taking it all out on me."

I think of his recent picture on Facebook, his almost menacing expression, and wonder if this is true. And I wonder, again, if Jed has found out about Brad.

"You should try fucking him sometimes. It does wonders," Jill says. An impish grin spreads across her face. She lowers herself into the pool but immediately scrambles back to the side and climbs out. Goose bumps line her flesh, and the tips of her dark hair are dripping with water.

"A little does go a long way," Tina pipes up.

Her glass is empty and she stands and saunters over to the giant pitcher for a refill.

"In Shreveport this past weekend, I had sex with Bill," she says conspiratorially. "I wasn't even in the mood, but we were in the hotel room and I knew he needed it. So, I did it! Quick and easy, like folding laundry," she says, licking the salt off the rim of her glass. "And I must say, I actually got into it once we started. I mean, when we first got together, I couldn't peel myself off of him, but after ten years of marriage, it does start to get a little predictable," she giggles.

No one is laughing with her or even really listening. I feel bad, so I smile and nod as if I understand everything she's saying.

Margot rises from her chair, slinks over to the pool. Dips a toe in the water. Her olive skin is slick with suntan oil and she absentmindedly rubs the tops of her thighs.

"How long *has* it been?" Jill asks Margot.

"God, would you ever fuck off with that?" Callie snaps from across the pool.

"And you *really* need to get some," Jill says, pointing at Callie. Callie shoots her the middle finger.

"How 'bout you, Sophie?" Jill asks. Her perfectly shaped eyebrows arch and there's a trace of a slur in her voice. The booze is catching up to her. My cheeks flame. All eyes are glued on me.

I stutter, and consider lying, but instead I tell the truth. "Last night."

"See? That's why she's glowing. It's okaaay to have sex with your spouse, even if you hate 'em," Jill says with too much glee oozing out of her small frame.

"Okay, hot shit," Callie says. She's standing now, hands parked on her hips. "Why don't you tell Sophie about the chest of drawers?"

I have no idea where this is going so I take another slug of my margarita, giving myself instant brain freeze.

"Absolutely not," Jill says.

A barking laugh erupts from Tina. "Sorry, Jill."

I'm too intrigued and starting to feel buzzed so I blurt out, "What is Callie talking about?"

Jill's face turns scarlet and she crosses her arms in front of her waist.

"Alex and Jill have a secret dresser. Dedicated to their sex toys! The bottom drawer is for the whips —"

"Stop!" Jill whines.

"The next one is for the restraints," Callie says. A smirk ripples across her lips. "And the next one —"

"I hardly know *her,*" Jill says, gesturing toward me. "She's gonna think I'm such a freak!"

"I'm okay with it," I offer, mainly because I *am* so intrigued and beguiled by Jill and how this demure, petite woman is apparently into bondage.

"They are into crazy, freaky shit," Callie continues. "Alex barking like a dog while Jill whips him, Alex wearing a cuff around his neck while his arms are in restraints."

This is the most I've ever heard come out of Callie.

"If only the hospital staff knew what a *very* bad boy Alex has been," Callie says, licking a line of margarita slush off her well-lipsticked lips.

Instead of looking angry, Jill seems to be actually blushing with pride, tipsy and swaying on the deck to Beyoncé, who's piped through the outdoor sound system. She looks to me to see if I'm rattled, so there's only one way to show her I'm not.

"Sounds fun," I say, lifting an eyebrow.

I feel Margot's eyes on me, alert and intrigued. "Do you guys do that kinky shit?"

There she is again, wondering about me and Graham. It's both terrifying and titillating. I don't want him in her sights, but I also like that she thinks of us in that way. I'm not sure how to answer. I wobble, then say, "I mean, no, nothing like that, but we like to have fun."

I'm grateful when Tina pipes up again, saving me from mindlessly blurting out any more. "Bill likes it when I suck on his toes," she says sheepishly.

"Ewww, that's just gross, honey," Margot says.

■ ■ ■ ■

The sound of a boat whining from across the lake cuts the conversation off. It's a blue-and-white-striped pontoon boat and it's heading for Jill's deck.

"Oh, great! They've made it back safe and sound!" Jill says, lifting her cover-up off the back of a chair and protectively wrapping it around her.

"You didn't tell us fucking kids were coming," Callie says.

"Well, it's not like they're going to wanna hang out with us, so chill," Jill says.

I see Margot sit up in her chair and shield her eyes, staring at the approaching boat. Brad is driving and Jamie sits in the back with his arm slung across the padded seat. A girl with long blond hair sits in the passenger seat next to Brad. She's wearing a ball cap the way young girls and celebrities do, with her hair completely covering her ears and the cap parked precariously on the top of her head as if it could blow off at any moment.

As the boat reaches the dock, Jamie steps to the front and loops a rope around a wooden pole that's attached to the pier. He's topless in red swim trunks, his lean chest glistens with sweat, and I blush, thinking of our moment together at Margot's.

"Hey!" Jill calls out to them. "So happy y'all are back! There's leftover food to snack on and, Abby, dear, would you like some sparkling water? Iced tea?"

The girl steps from the boat toward Jamie. He offers her his hand and guides her down to the dock. She's in an army-green string bikini, and her petite build is exquisite. Amber-colored skin and taut. She removes her aviator glasses to talk to Jill.

"No thanks, Mrs. Simmons," she says. "I have a bottle of water in my bag." She points behind her, and Brad trundles off the boat, beach bag in hand, hair whipped up by wind and sweat.

"Well, let me introduce you to the group!" Jill says. Her speech is sloppy from the drinks and she puts an arm around the girl's waist like she's holding on to her for support. "Ladies, this is Abby. Brad's girlfriend, the one I talk about *all* the time!"

Jill winks at Abby, rubs her hands briskly up and down Abby's back. "But only good things, of course! I'm always bragging on you. Abby's a junior and she just made varsity cheerleader! Also, she's on the honor roll. Beauty *and* brains. We are so pleased!" Jill beams.

"That's Tina." Jill points and Tina waves, flashing a warm smile. "And that's Callie over there, trying to decide if she's brave enough to get in the pool." Callie rolls her eyes at Jill but walks over to them and extends her hand toward Abby.

Margot is flat on her back, sunglasses on, seemingly oblivious to Jill's cheery round of intros.

"Margot," Jill calls to her. Margot raises up a few inches, supports herself with her elbows, and dons a fake smile. "Margot, meet Abby," Jill says.

"Hey," Margot says, and gives a little wave of her hand.

I swing my legs to the deck, climb out of the chaise longue, and walk over to them.

Up close, Abby is even more luminous. Her eyes are lettuce green and she has a spray of caramel freckles that spackle her nose. She's gorgeous, but still, she's no match for Margot.

"And this is Sophie. She's new to town," Jill says. I reach out my hand and shake Abby's.

Whereas most teenage girls would roll their eyes at being paraded around like this, Abby seems genuinely polite, even nervous.

"Pleased to meet you," Abby says, with a deferential dip of her head. I want to take her in my arms, lead her out of this dysfunctional mess, tell her she can do better than Brad, who is barely masking his greedy stares at Margot.

Brad's parked in the corner of the pool, his long, ropy arms supporting him while he kicks at the water. "Mom, the pool is still cold, what the hell?" I'm taken aback that he still calls Jill *Mom.* It jolts me to think about the fact that this hunky young man is still just a teenager.

He catches me staring, shoots me a sly smile as if to say I'm in on his dirty little secret with Margot, who's so far taken no notice of him.

Jill disappears inside the house, calling out over her shoulder that she's off to mix more margaritas.

Jamie leans against the wooden railing. The sun is just beginning to set behind him, turning his copper hair even more golden.

His eyes are locked on Abby, and as soon as Jill unlatches herself from her, Abby walks to the edge of the pool, dips a toe in the water.

"It's freezing!" she says, her voice high and girlish.

Jamie sneaks up behind her and grabs her around the waist, lifting her up before they both tumble into the pool together.

Abby breaks the surface, water beading on her face and eyelashes. "Jamie!" she squeals. He's facing her with a devilish grin, and she splashes water in his face.

"Admit it, you would've never gotten in otherwise," Jamie says, pleased with himself.

Brad eyes them. But outwardly, he doesn't seem bothered by their banter.

Abby bounces in the water, clearly trying to warm up. Jamie watches her and begins treading water, his shoulder muscles flexing with each stroke.

After a moment, Brad sinks into the pool and swims over to Abby. She wraps her arms around his neck and he moves her over to the wall of the pool, where there's an underwater ledge to sit on.

He pulls her into his lap, grabs the sides of her face with his hands, and starts kissing her, marking his territory.

Abby pulls back, blushing, clearly not wanting to make out in front of all of us.

Jamie swims to the edge of the pool and turns his back to them. He parks his elbows on the deck and rests his chin on top of his folded hands.

He's right in front of my chaise longue and he looks up at me, his eyes tracing my body. His liquid green eyes make my stomach drop, and I'm praying that no one notices him. I give him a quick smile but then lean back in the chair and stare up at the salmon-colored sky.

I turn my head to the side and watch Margot. She's now flipped on her stomach, probably so she doesn't have to see Brad and Abby together, leg-locked in the pool.

Another squeal escapes Abby and she swats at Brad, who's tickling her. I forgot just how noisy, and grating, teenage girls' voices can be.

Not to be outdone, Margot tugs on the bikini strap around her neck. She's still on her stomach, her legs slightly parted, but she raises herself up on her elbows, and when she does, her top slithers down. I'm sitting perpendicular to her, and I can see the outline of her perfect breasts and the dark pink circle of her nipple, which is hard.

I see Brad notice, too, and watch as he immediately looks to Jamie as if to see if Jamie is watching Margot.

He is.

Brad's face hardens. He watches Jamie for a second longer and then moves Abby off him. He climbs out of the pool and towels off, water dripping from his moppy hair. Abby clambers out after him, seemingly oblivious to what is happening.

And as if Margot can sense Brad behind her, she rolls over on her back. Her breasts are now fully exposed and she runs a hand nonchalantly through her hair, like being topless in front of everyone is the most natural thing in the world.

Jamie's eyes are locked onto her, as are Tina's and Brad's. Abby puts her hand over her mouth when she notices Margot, and tilts Brad's head away from the sight with her hands. From where she's sitting, Callie's milk-dud eyes betray nothing.

"C'mon, Jamie, we're leaving," Brad orders, and tugs on his faded jeans. "Abby's gotta get home."

Jamie breaks his gaze and pushes himself up out of the water.

"Bye, ladies," Jamie says, slinging a towel around his neck and following Brad and Abby into the house.

Jill passes them on their way inside. She's carrying a freshly made pitcher of margaritas, and her expression twists into confusion at the sight of them leaving.

"But you just got here," she calls out before setting the drinks down and noticing Margot.

"Margoooot?" she huffs, the second half of Margot's name rising up in a high-pitched reprimand. "What the hell?"

At this, Margot sits up. My eyes haven't left her chest since she flopped on her back, and electricity courses through me at the sight of her half-naked.

"What?" Margot asks, annoyed.

Little, whiny sounds snake out of Jill, whose face is beet red with obvious anger. She can't seem to form words, so instead, she fans her hands around her breasts. "This . . . this —"

"Oh, for god's sake, don't be such a prude," Margot says, exhaling upward into her bangs.

"Seriously, what did you think you were doing?" Jill seethes.

"What do you mean? And I can promise you, your precious Brad's seen a lot worse. I'm sure he's privy to Mommy and Daddy's sex games," Margot says with a snort.

"I don't prance around in front of him topless!" Jill shrieks.

"I wasn't prancing! I was on my stomach the whole time until a few seconds ago when I turned over to take a drink."

Jill falters, as if wavering between anger and something else. Regret, it looks like.

"But you know what?" Margot says, refastening her top around her neck. "I'm out!"

Margot rises from her chair, slides her feet

into her black flip-flops, and pads to the back door. She yanks it open and slams it so hard behind her that the glass shudders.

"Way to go, Jill," Callie says, pulling her sunglasses on and swiping her keys off a side table. "She *just* told us she's going through a lot and then you lay *this* shit on her." Callie shakes her head.

Jill stammers around for a comeback and, instead, settles on an apology. "I'm sorry, I didn't mean to ruin our ladies' day, I just, it was weird, it was . . . I guess I overreacted. Do you think I should follow her out?"

"I don't think that's a good idea," Callie says, an air of disdain on her face.

Callie wrenches open the back door, vanishes inside the house. I look over to Tina. Her expression is stunned, her mouth hanging open.

I, too, want to follow Margot out, even though I know she knew exactly what she was doing, so I stand and take a deep breath, exhale, and head inside.

The house is empty, so I walk to the front door and pull it open. Margot is sitting in her black Mercedes with the engine running. Her face is stone, her sunglasses shielding her eyes.

Callie is leaning into the driver's side window, talking softly to Margot.

They haven't noticed me, so I stand there and watch. Margot stares down into her lap. Callie leans in further, smooths a hand over Margot's hair. Margot seems to melt. She leans back in the driver's seat and her mouth forms an O, exhaling.

I want to go over to her, to be the one who's consoling her. But she's not mine to console; she's Callie's.

Callie bends further at the waist so she's now eye level with Margot. She presses her lips to Margot's cheek, runs a hand along Margot's face. But Margot removes Callie's hand and shakes her head.

Before they can see me, I dissolve back into the house and shut the door.

30

Friday, April 13, 2018

I'm driving out to Margot's lake house, heading there a little early. I want to arrive before everyone else; I want to see if she'll open up to me. I didn't hear from her all week after the scene at Jill's, so I sent a text, checking on her. But she never responded.

She only sent a group text just yesterday, short and clipped.

> We're back on for tomorrow night. I expect to see everyone there.

Jill was the first to respond with an overzealous:

> Great! Can't wait!

Then Tina:

> Woo-hoo!

Then Callie, with just a thumbs-up emoji. I texted that I was excited, followed by a rifle emoji.

Before I left the house tonight, I kissed Jack on the top of his shampoo-scented head and wrapped my hands around Graham's neck, promising to be home no later than midnight.

"Go get 'em, shooter," he drawled in his mock Southern accent before nibbling on my ear and pulling me into him.

We hugged for a long minute before he released me. "But seriously," he said, suddenly stone-faced and solemn, "don't pull an all-nighter."

"That's not happening, I promise. There's no way I'm doing that," I said, my eyes never leaving his face.

Even though it's still early, the sun is beginning to set, a wedge of mango sinking into the treetops. It's even warmer than it has been, and the balmy, late-afternoon air feels good against my neck. I'm wearing a yellow sundress and some vintage boots I found at the thrift store this week. My windows are down as I curve around the lake roads, filling the car with the forested scent of the woods. Delicate wildflowers sprinkle the sides of the road, and when I round a sharp bend, a meadow opens up and the lake shimmers beyond it, sparkling and rippling like a breathing thing, and again, I'm struck by the picturesque splendor of the area.

When I pull into the drive, Margot is standing on the porch, leaning against the house with a bottle of amber liquid in her hand. She's wearing a cherry-red tank top with painted-on, faded jeans tucked into cowgirl boots that look like they cost thousands. Her hair is sleek and perfect, and a pair of diamond studs twinkle from her earlobes.

Callie is already here. Of course she is. I let out a long sigh and my shoulders slump in disappointment.

She reaches for the bottle from Margot, takes a long pull, and then passes it back to her.

Callie then begins loading shotguns onto the back of a four-wheeler, but when she sees me inching closer to the house, she gives me a blank stare and a quick wave. She's wearing a tight black T-shirt, and her ropy, blond hair is pulled into a high ponytail.

I climb from the car, walk over to Margot.

"Heeey," she says, her voice relaxed with drink. "Want some?"

I eye the bottle. It's bourbon, which I like, so I take it from her and knock back a long sip. The buttery alcohol burns the back of my throat, and I choke and let out a sharp, jagged cough that makes Margot jump.

"Damn, girl," she says, a wicked grin slinking over her face, "take it easy."

I pass the bottle back to her, and when she grasps it, her fingers brush mine.

She lifts the bottle to her lips, tilts her head, and tosses back another long slug. I study her profile — the curve of her chest and the silver chain that dangles from her slender neck. I try to read her expression but her eyes are trained forward. She's gazing into the distance, seemingly lost in thought. Staring at the ground, I drag a paper-thin gold leaf off the porch with the scuffed toe of my boot.

While Callie is out of earshot, cramming equipment onto the four-wheelers, I want to ask Margot how everything is at home, if she's forgiven Jill, but even though I'm standing close to her, inhaling the seductive scent of her perfume, and even though she all but beckoned me into a three-way that night in Dallas, a lump aches in the back of my throat and I don't feel I have the right to ask her anything personal.

Without looking at me, she passes the

bottle of bourbon back over and I take a smaller swig this time. Jill's Lexus snakes into the drive, and as it gets closer to us, I see Tina in the passenger seat next to Jill, her face animated and her hands gesturing in front of her as if she's telling a dramatic story.

They pile out of the car and walk toward us. Jill looks diminutive, dressed simply in a white lace top with a blue jean jacket, and her eyes are filled with caution as she approaches Margot.

Tina lingers back, letting Jill and Margot have some space.

I instinctively step away and walk over to Tina, passing her the bourbon.

Out of the corner of my eye, I see Jill and Margot hugging, a tight embrace that's charged with emotion. They don't speak, but I see Margot smooth the top of Jill's hair down before breaking away from her.

"Ladies!" Tina says warmly. "I'm *so* ready to party tonight! Bill pissed me off so much — he sprang a last-minute trip on me. We have to get up at five a.m. to drive to Dallas for some work thing when he *knows* I like to stay out late with y'all."

Even though she's supposed to be angry, Tina is smiling and excitement sizzles in her liquid brown eyes.

She knocks back the bottle of bourbon and takes three healthy glugs before she pulls the bottle off her lips.

"Whew!" she says, wiping her mouth with the sleeve of her black leather jacket. "Stuff'll put hair on your tits!"

She tips the bottle toward Jill, who takes it and slings back a greedy gulp herself. "I needed that, thank you," she says, passing the bottle over to Margot.

"Let's roll," Callie says over her shoulder before revving up the engine to one of the four-wheelers.

As before, I climb on the back of the four-wheeler Jill is driving and we head down the grassy lane toward the clearing. Sunlight sifts through the trees, turning the forest bright green and golden, and I have to squint because the light is so vibrant.

At the clearing, we drink wine. White, crisp, and chilled on a bed of ice in a fabric cooler. Nobody mentions anything about the pool party; it's as if it never happened. But Margot has an air of distraction about her. She seems half-in, half-out of the shallow, almost nervous conversation that ensues.

As always, Margot shoots first. She blasts the first two rounds, her triceps flexing as she pulls the trigger, but misses the next two.

"Dammit," she says, whipping off the earmuffs, which now dangle from her neck. "I'm off tonight. Who's next?"

"I am," Callie announces, taking the shotgun from Margot. As Tina crouches at the skeet machine, getting ready to pull for Callie, I notice that Margot slinks away to the edge of the lake. She digs her cell out of her pocket and turns her back toward us, head aimed down, as if she's reading a text.

Callie raises the shotgun and takes aim. Tina releases the skeet and it skitters across the sky until it explodes with Callie's shot.

"Pull!" Callie hollers, her blond ponytail swinging behind her as she tracks the next one. She misses it, but hits the final two and swings around to us with a satisfied smirk pasted across her face.

Margot lumbers over from the water's edge and gives Callie a high five. "Nice work, woman!"

"Sophie, you're up," Callie says, handing me the shotgun. I don't want to shoot; I feel the kick of the gun in my shoulder again, but I also don't want to look like a wuss.

As if she can read my mind, Margot says, "We brought Daddy's gun; it doesn't kick as hard. Promise."

I slip on the earmuffs and goggles as Margot walks over to the four-wheeler strapped with guns, slides one off the back, and passes it over to me. It's heavy in my hands, and the butt has a weathered sheen to it. If I were to guess, I'd wager this gun kicks even harder than the newer ones, but I take it and cradle it into my shoulder.

"Pull!" I say, and a bright orange disc zings across the horizon. I'm not focused, so I fire and miss, but Margot is right, the gun barely kicks at all. I turn and give Margot a thumbs-up.

"Pull!" I track the skeet more carefully this time, squeeze the trigger, and watch the disc burst into tiny bits that scatter to the ground.

Even though I'm in the zone now, I still miss the next two rounds, but adrenaline courses through me — I can see why they're addicted to shooting; I could do this all night. But Callie walks over, lifts the gun from me, and handles it like it's diseased.

The sky is now jack-o'-lantern orange as the sun evaporates behind the trees, so Margot tips the remains of the wine into each of our glasses. We clink and toast as cicadas buzz all around us before we load up and head back to the lake house.

31

Inside, we gather on the sectionals in the great room, the lake twinkling behind us as the last slices of sunlight cut through the pines.

Margot is at the bar, pouring bourbon into shot glasses. It's frigid inside, and she's wrapped a knee-length black cardigan around her. She sets the glasses on a silver tray and takes the few steps down to the sofas.

"Cheers, ladies," she says, and we each down our shots. Mine tastes so strong that it makes me shake my head.

Now that the sun has vanished, it's dark inside the house. Only the bullet lights above the kitchen sink are on, little stabs of white light, so Margot switches on a table lamp and it fills the great room with a golden glow.

She leans into the corner of a sofa and pulls the cardigan around her even tighter.

Her lips are glossed in crimson red and she's staring out the window, the same mask of distraction as before covering her face.

Callie uncrosses her legs, refills everyone's shots.

"I don't know about you guys, but I could drink this whole bottle," Callie says, exhaling toward the ceiling and kicking off her boots.

"I'll drink to that!" Tina beams.

"Same!" Jill chimes in.

We all toast and shoot again, but the energy in the room is flat and lifeless. It's Margot. Or rather, it's the absence of Margot. The usual Margot who is charged, crackling with electricity, directing our every move.

I look at her, trying again to read her face. She's wrapped her arms around her legs and is resting her chin on the tops of her knees. She's rocking back and forth, fidgeting. She fishes her cell out of her back pocket, stabs the keypad.

Jill and Tina gossip in the corner of the opposite sectional, but I notice that Callie is studying Margot, too.

Margot tosses her cell on the cushion next to her, stands and yawns, stretching her arms over her head.

"You guys, I'm sorry. I just don't have it

in me tonight. Can we make it an early one?"

"We just got here," Callie says flatly.

"Absolutely!" Jill pipes in, clearly still eager to keep things smooth with Margot. "I have to get up early, take Brad —" But she stops here, catching herself. "We have a lot of stuff to do tomorrow."

Tina rises from the sofa and loops an arm around Margot's waist. "You okay, honey?" she asks, her voice as warm and saccharine as a school counselor's.

Margot quickly nods, then shakes her off. "Totally fine, just bushed for some reason."

"Well it's no big deal to me, like I said, Bill's dragging me to Dallas first thing in the morning. Maybe we can have lunch later this week?"

"Sure. Text me," Margot says.

My cell chimed a few minutes ago, so I root around in my bag until I find it. It's a text from Graham, I'm sure, and I'm secretly relieved that Margot's calling it an early one so I can get home when I promised.

But when I look at the screen, I see that it's not from Graham at all. It's from Margot.

Not you. I want you

She hadn't finished typing the first text, so there's another one tacked on.

to stay. If you're up for it.

I want you. Was that an accident that she didn't finish typing out the rest, or a message? My face flushes and my pulse quickens. When I look up at her, her eyes are locked onto mine. I slowly nod.

Jill and Tina are at the door, blowing air-kisses to the rest of us, but Callie stays moored on the couch as if she has no intention of going anywhere. She drags the bourbon across the coffee table, downs more straight from the bottle.

"Sorry, woman, I'm whooped," Margot says, sinking into Callie's lap and slinging an arm around her neck. "I'll make it up to you, I promise," she says, planting a kiss on Callie's cheek.

I don't know what to do with myself, so I mumble an excuse about having to use the bathroom and head down the hall to buy more time until Callie leaves.

When I walk back into the great room, Margot is slung across the couch, her legs stretched out in front of her. She gives a quick jerk of her neck toward the kitchen. I see a light coming from the mudroom, the small nook off the kitchen, and inside, I see Callie lining up the guns in the glass-front gun cabinet.

"I was going to clean them tonight," Callie calls out. "You know I like to clean them regularly."

Margot rolls her eyes at me, twists her neck in Callie's direction. "Thanks, but just leave 'em, sweetie. I'll call you tomorrow."

Callie stomps out of the mudroom, huffs at the sight of me still here. I stand frozen in the middle of the great room with my bag in my hand.

"Oops, left my cell in the bathroom," I lie, then head, once again, down the hallway. I'm just about to step inside the bathroom when I hear the front door slam. I turn around and creep back toward the great room.

"Coast is clear!" Margot says brightly. "Never thought I'd shake her off tonight."

She moves around the island in the kitchen, pulls down a pair of stemless wineglasses.

"Red or white?" she purrs.

"Red, please," I say, and walk the few steps up to the kitchen.

It's still dark in here, except for the trio of bullet lights, making everything feel candlelit and intimate. Through the windows lining the back of the great room, the half-full moon glistens over the lake, and orange-yellow lights from the neighboring boat-houses sparkle against the night.

"Mmmmmm," Margot says, after taking a sip of her wine. "This tastes so good."

My heart is racing from being all alone with her. I lift the glass, swirl the wine around, and take a gulp. It *is* delicious.

"Yum," I say, "*so* good."

Margot leans back on the counter and crosses an arm in front of her.

"I just wasn't in the mood for them tonight. Ya know? But I wasn't ready to head home just yet, either. So, thanks for sticking around," she says, but I still sense that air of distraction about her, like she's talking to me but also not really talking to me.

I want to set my glass of wine down, move toward her, lean in and kiss her, and see what happens. But every time I think of doing it, I stop myself. My palms are glazed with sweat, and my heartbeat drums in the back of my throat. I keep drinking instead, and the room grows softer with each sip I take.

I'm just working up the courage to ask her how her week went when she steps away from me and heads down the hall. "Nature's calling," she says over her shoulder.

I lean against the kitchen counter and stare out the window at the rippling lake. I take another slow sip of wine, swish it around in my mouth. It tastes like cherries and oak. Maybe I'll use that as a conversation starter when Margot gets back. God, I really am schoolgirl nervous.

I reach for the bottle to refill our glasses, and out of the corner of my eye, blue-white light flashes through the kitchen like miniature lightning strikes.

It's Margot's cell, vibrating on the kitchen counter. I peer down the hall. She's still in the bathroom, the light seeping from beneath the door, so I creep over to her phone and risk taking a peek.

There's a text notification from "B," which I assume means Brad. I quickly swipe the screen and a stream of their texts blooms into sight. The latest one reads: Where are you? So I scroll to the top to get the full conversation.

Margot: I'm not gonna wait around all night.

B: Sorry. Still at dinner with Abby's parents.

Margot: Figure it out.

B: I can't just leave. But I'll get out of here asap.

A few minutes later.

B: Ummm . . . Hello? Why aren't you texting me back? I tried to end it & she threatened to slit her wrists. So . . . give me time. I need to let her down easy.

B: You know you're the one I wanna be with.

A minute later.

Margot: Like I said, figure it out.

B: Trying

Margot: Get rid of her.

Ten minutes later.

B: Leaving now.

B: Where are you?

My mouth has gone dry snooping through her texts. I'm praying that Brad will text back so she won't be able to tell I've checked her phone. I slide it back toward the charging station, exactly where it had been before. I look up and Margot is heading down the hall, walking toward me. I glance back at the phone, willing it to spring to life, but it's just a blank screen.

I smile at her and she smiles back as she grabs the bottle of wine.

"Let's finish this, shall we?" she says, stepping closer to me. She's cast off her cardigan, and as she leans over the counter to refill our glasses, my eyes drift over her breasts, ample and almost bursting out of her low-cut tank top. Butterflies flurry in my stomach as I inch closer to her.

"Sounds like a fine plan," I manage to say.

As she pours, I risk a stare, looking straight at her. She brings her glass to her lips and, behind it, flashes me a seductive smirk that reaches her eyes.

I take another sip of the wine. Set my glass down. I'm ready to make my move. I stare into her smoky eyes, slide my hand across the counter, inch my hips even closer to her. She's still staring at me when the blue-white light from her cell flashes on the counter behind us.

She twists around and grabs her phone. Studies the texts. It doesn't seem like she's noticed I've read them.

A smile creeps across her face. She exhales, then bites her bottom lip, still grinning. She types a message into the cell, sets it down, and looks up at me.

"I hope you don't mind," she says, walking over to the sink and primping her hair in the reflection of the window. "I thought it was going to be just us. But Brad is on the way." She adjusts her bra and tugs down on her top, exposing even more cleavage.

"That's fine," I say, trying not to show how disappointed I am. "I should be getting home anyway."

I check the time on the microwave: nine forty-five.

Margot walks over to me, places a hand on my wrist. A shiver courses through me.

"Stay," she says, her mouth open, her lips supple. "It'll be fun. Promise." She winks at me and keeps her hand on my wrist.

"Okay," I say, staring down at the counter and hoping she won't notice my face blushing.

She slips her hand away and empties the rest of the wine into our glasses, takes a long sip, and then checks her cell again.

She steps into the entryway and gazes out the window, watching for Brad's headlights.

32

Nearly an hour later, Brad steps through the front door. His thick hair is slick with product, and the armpits of his shirt are ringed with sweat. It looks as though he's been jogging, and he gives off the spicy, pungent smell of a teenage boy's cologne.

While we were waiting for him to arrive, Margot returned to her earlier state of fidgeting and distraction: running her fingers through her hair, reglossing her lips with apple-red lipstick, and anxiously checking her cell.

I had parked myself on the sectional, hoping that she'd settle in next to me, but she live-wired through the great room and kitchen, uncorking another bottle of red and pacing between the two rooms.

"Sorry, it took me longer to get away than I thought," Brad says as he grabs Margot into a hug. She says something harsh to him that

I can't make out and bats him on both shoulders with balled-up fists. He lifts her up and spins her around until she relents and squeals with pleasure.

He glances my way and notices me, half-drunk and smeared into the sofa.

"Jamie should be here shortly. In fact, he should've already been here by now," he says to me as if this were a double date, an arrangement I'd previously agreed to.

My neck burns at the mention of Jamie, and the wine sours in my stomach. I should get up, leave now before he arrives. I check the time. It's nearly eleven o'clock. I set my glass down on the coffee table, unfold my legs from beneath me, and stand.

"I really do need to get going," I say to Margot, who's pressed her back into Brad's chest. Her fingers are laced behind his neck and she's the old Margot again, radiating fierceness and sexuality.

"Don't leave just yet!" she says, her face scrunched up, looking at me as if I'm insane for even considering going. "Seriously. Stay for at least one more drink."

The wine has made my legs feel syrupy, so I sink back into the sofa. "One more won't kill me, I guess." I dig in my bag for my cell, check for texts from Graham. Nothing. I let out a sigh and my shoulders relax.

But I type him a quick text.

> Leaving soon! Home before midnight so I don't turn into a pumpkin. xx

I press send and drop the cell back in my bag. I've texted him as much for his own sake as for mine — I want to be held accountable. I want to keep my promise to him.

Brad and Margot join me in the great room. They are all over each other — Margot sits in his lap while Brad twirls a lock of her glossy hair around his finger. Clearly, she's forgiven him for running behind.

"Miss Sophie," he drawls, cobalt-blue eyes trained on me, "lookin' good tonight."

Margot jabs him in the rib cage but nods in agreement. "She's a star," she says.

But she's not looking at me. She's tracing a finger over Brad's lips before leaning in to kiss him.

I look away from their tangled mess, swallow hard, stare at the polished oak floorboards. The room suddenly feels overheated and swampy, and I'm all but squirming in my seat as they make out. I should leave, I'm clearly just the third wheel here, but an irrational, stubborn part of me thinks that

I'll be next with Margot.

I rise and step into the kitchen. "Wine, anyone?" I call out, hoping to break their spell.

"Yes, ma'am," Brad says, moving Margot off his lap and striding into the kitchen. He grabs Margot's empty glass and holds it out for me to fill. I refill my own and we toast before draining our glasses.

"It's making me all swoony, the wine is," Margot says. "I'm switching back to bourbon."

"That's my girl," Brad says. He shoots me a quick wink. Something about the way he's paying attention to me makes my stomach twinge. It feels like he's checking me out, and I'm both flattered and mortified.

I glance at Margot but she's oblivious, busy filling three tumblers with the rest of the bourbon. The bottle is only about a fourth full, so she evenly distributes it between our glasses. She turns to the fridge and scoops a handful of ice from the freezer, wraps it in a rag, and sets it on the counter.

"Brad likes his whiskey on the rocks. And he likes the ice to be jagged," she says, taking a mallet from the drawer and hammering away at the folded bundle. She unrolls it and drops the slivers of ice into his glass, which pop against the heat of the bourbon.

"Hear, hear!" Brad says, raising his glass to ours.

I take a small, scorching sip and set the glass down. I need to take it slow or I'll be too drunk to drive.

Margot pulls up a playlist on her phone, and soon Willie Nelson is crooning in the background. She slugs her tumbler of bourbon, licks her lips, and moves her hips slowly back and forth to the music with half-closed eyes.

Brad and I watch her performance. His mouth hangs open and his full lips are shiny with whiskey. His eyes are following her hips, and soon, he goes over to her and pulls her into a two-step.

I take another slow sip and watch as his hands slither over her faded jeans, around her waist, and down to her ass.

I'm grateful when I hear Jamie's knock at the door. Margot breaks away from Brad and wrenches it open.

"Howdy, you!" she says, her voice loud and giddy. "Glad you could finally join us."

I flick my eyes toward the clock on the microwave. Eleven twenty. I will leave soon; I have to.

"Yeah, man, what the hell took so long?" Brad asks. "I thought you would've beaten me here."

Jamie lopes into the kitchen, glances around for a drink.

"We just polished off the bourbon, sorry about that." Margot says. "But . . . I've got vodka in the freezer. Martinis, everyone?"

Jamie nods and looks down at his hands, which seem to be shaking. He's jumpy and has barely made eye contact with me, but seems to settle once Margot pours him an icy shot of vodka.

"An appetizer," she says.

He slams back the vodka, then holds his shot glass out for another pour.

"Somebody's thirsty." She grins approvingly.

He downs his second shot. "Wooo! Aaah, much better." His neck flushes red with the alcohol and he turns to me, taking me in with those glittering green eyes.

Brad walks over to him, playfully punches him in the shoulder. "Seriously, where you been, dude?"

Jamie scoffs, his breath hissing out of his mouth. "What is this? An interrogation?" He looks at me with a bemused smile, rolls his eyes at Brad.

Margot strains the shaker of martinis into glasses and drops a pair of olives in each one.

"Enough chatter, boys, let's drink," she

says, lifting the glass to her lips. "And let's move to somewhere more comfortable."

We each grab the stems of our glasses and step into the great room. Margot kicks off her cowgirl boots and pushes the coffee table up against the wall. She struts over to the windows, throws them all open. A rush of warm air blankets the room, and I plant myself on the sofa beneath the picture window overlooking the water. A breeze tickles the back of my neck, and the honeyed globe of light from the table lamp encircles us, making it feel like we're nestled in a cocoon. I'm walking that razor-thin line between tipsy and drunk, so I take small nips of the giant martini, which is briny with the taste of olives.

Margot slinks from the sofa down to the floor, spreads her legs out in a V.

"I've got an idea!" she says, her voice pitched with naughtiness. "Brad, go and grab the bourbon, would ya —"

"But it's empty —"

"Shush it, I know," she says, slowly shaking her head. She sounds on the far side of the tipsy spectrum as well. "Just grab it, bring it here, will ya?" Her tone is snappy, her earlier anger at Brad resurfacing.

He stands and rakes a hand through his lush hair, which promptly falls back over his eyes as he skips up the few steps to the kitchen.

Jamie sits on the sofa opposite from me, his eyes glued to mine, the corners of his mouth turned up in a flirty grin.

Heat rises to my face and I smile back. "How've you been?" I dumbly ask.

Still grinning, he bites his bottom lip, nods his head. "Very well," he says, his voice silken and deep, his eyes still locked onto mine. I fight the urge to go over to him, sit on his lap, and kiss his neck, which is still blotchy with scarlet streaks.

Brad returns with the bottle, tosses it to Margot.

"Okay!" Margot says, placing it on its side in front of her. "Everyone, on the floor. We're playing spin the bottle."

My pulse races and I move directly across from Margot as the boys take the other spots, forming a circle.

"What — is this going to lead to an orgy or something?" Jamie asks, his eyes smoldering as he looks between Margot and me.

"I'd be down with that," Brad says, leaning back into the foot of the sectional, clasping his hands behind his head.

Margot gives him a playful kick with her sock-footed toe. "Hush. And just for that, you go first."

Brad leans forward and gives the bottle a sharp twist. It spins and wobbles before stopping right in front of Jamie.

"No way," Brad says. "I'm not kissing him."

"Oh yes you are," Margot says.

A surge of excitement moves over me as Brad kneels and knee-walks over to Jamie. He pecks him on the cheek.

"No cheating," Margot says, her voice firm and husky.

Jamie leans in and grazes Brad's lips with a quick kiss.

"Y'all are lame, but that will do, I guess," she says.

I don't know why, but quickly I blurt out, "I'm next."

"Ooooh, Sophie's ready," Margot says.

I grab the bottle and give it a good spin, hoping it lands on Margot. It whirls on the wooden floor before stopping at Jamie's knee.

His grin widens and he rubs his hands together. I move over to him. His breath, hot on my neck, smells like cinnamon. Our lips meet and he kisses me, his tongue playful and teasing like his kiss on the dock. Warmth spreads over me, and I want to continue kissing him but he pulls back, a satisfied smile spreading over his face.

Margot's mouth hangs open. "Well, that was hot."

She leans forward and puts her manicured hand on the bottle. Her nails are painted a deep purple, and they clack against the neck of the bottle as she gives it a weak spin. Just weak enough, in fact, to land right in front of me.

This is no accident, I'm sure of it, and electricity zaps through me as she cat-crawls her way over to me.

"Now we're talkin'," Brad hoots, but Margot ignores him, her eyes drilled onto mine, her cleavage spilling out of her top as she moves on all fours until she's right in front of me.

She's on her knees, so I get on mine as well and lean toward her. Her lashes are long and she bats them at me before clasping my face in her hands. My heart is palpitating.

She first plants a small kiss on my forehead, her breasts aimed at my eyes. Her skin smells like her customary Chanel Allure, and she drags a warm finger across my face until it reaches my mouth. She traces a circle on my lips and I feel a pinch of lust between my legs; I'm all but shuddering at her touch. I can't resist any longer, so I grab the back of her neck and kiss her. Tentatively at first, but she's kissing me back now, long and slow.

She pulls back for a second, breathless, her charcoal-gray eyes swimming with desire, before pulling me into another kiss, this one harder and faster. A warm breeze gusts through the window, coating the room with the marshy scent of the lake, and I can't help it; I slip a hand under her tank and rest it on her scorching stomach. I take my other hand and graze my fingers over her neck, down toward the top of her breasts. She moans in my ear. My own breath is rapid and shallow, and heat drenches my body.

Brad and Jamie erupt into whistles and cheers, and Margot leans back and sits on her legs. She stares down at the floor, an almost bashful smile creeping across her face. She exhales, tucks a lock of hair behind her ear.

I wonder if I've taken things too far by touching her. But I know by her kiss and her molten eyes, the way she looked at me, that that's not the case. And now she's beaming, clearly pleased to be the center of attention once again.

She leans forward and grabs her half-finished martini and slams the rest.

"Who's next?" she asks.

Jamie and Brad are motionless. It's as if the entire room is frozen in desire.

"It's Jamie's turn," Brad says, knocking the bottle toward Jamie.

Jamie leans down, bats at it. It zips around in a frenzied circle before settling in front of Brad.

"Jesus Christ," Brad says. "Not again."

Jamie chuckles.

"C'mon, you two, you know the rules," Margot says.

"I don't want to kiss him again," Brad groans.

"Well, I don't want to play anymore if it's gonna be like this," Margot says, pouting, her hands pooled in her lap. "It's boring." I study Margot and it seems as if that former air of distraction now frosts her face again. She's half-in, half-out of the game.

"But I didn't even get the chance to kiss Miss Sophie," Brad says, his half-lidded eyes skittering between me and Margot. He's clearly trying to get a rise out of her.

My cheeks blaze. I look at Margot. Her face hardens but I sense she's not angry at Brad's loosely flung comment; instead, she's still simmering about their earlier quarrel.

"Keep playing if you want, then." She plants both palms on the ground, pushes herself to standing. "I don't give a shit," she says over her shoulder as she vanishes down the pitch-black hallway.

33

Brad studies the backs of his hands, then sweeps his hair out of his eyes. His strong jaw clenches and unclenches.

"Guess I need to go see about that," he says, now staring at the floor.

Jamie's smirking, clearly enjoying every second of Brad's punishment.

"Mama's boy. Always have been, always will be," Jamie says.

Brad punches him in the shoulder on his way down the hall.

The gilded clock on the wall says it's midnight.

Fuck.

After draining the rest of my martini, I grope in my bag for my keys. They feel heavy in my hand, like a weight. I'm drunk. I've got to get out of here before I make anything worse. What am I still doing here?

"You look very pretty in that dress," Jamie remarks, his voice floating from across the room. He comes over and sits next to me on the sofa. His leg brushes mine and I can feel the heat from his body radiating through his jeans. He places a hand on my bare knee. My whole leg tingles as I stare down at his hand, perfectly manicured and sprinkled with freckles. After a moment of sitting like this, deciding if I want to lean over and kiss him, I stand.

"I've gotta go. And I've gotta say bye to Margot first." I turn away from him and creak down the hall.

I pass by the guest bathroom and pause at the master bedroom. The door is almost completely shut, but a beam of dim light slashes across the wooden floorboards.

From inside the room, their voices are muffled as if they're pitched along the far wall; I can picture Margot standing in there, arms crossed against her chest, staring out the window at the lake.

I strain to listen but I can only hear the shards of their argument, a few well-slung words.

"You *told* me you were going —" Margot says, her voice heated and volatile.

Brad cuts her off. "I am *trying*. You don't get it. You don't understand —"

"The fuck I don't!" she says, and her voice is now aimed toward the door, so I slink back down the hall into the bathroom.

I flip the switch, and the vanity lights lining the mirror momentarily blind me. I blink hard, sit on the toilet, and pee for what seems like days. I wash my hands and splash water in my face, which is beaded with sweat. I stare at my reflection. I look soused. From inside my bag, my phone dings. A text, from Graham.

> Heading to bed now. Feel free to wake me up when you get home, which I'm hoping will be soon. xxx

Good. He's not mad, at least not yet, but it's twelve fifteen and he's clearly waiting up for me. He's the best; he doesn't deserve this.

I need to go. I just played freaking spin the bottle with a pair of eighteen-year-olds; this is not who I am. I need to go *now,* I try to convince myself.

But when I open the door, Jamie is on the other side of it, his arm resting on the doorframe, a sly grin slung across his face. I move to step around him but he doesn't budge. Instead, he leans in and kisses me. Takes me by the shoulders and steers me down the hall. Past the master, past another series of rooms, all the way to the back of the house.

We step into what looks like Margot's son's room. Dark blues and whites. A small lamp glows from the nightstand, and next to it rests the bottle of vodka and two shot glasses.

"I brought gifts," he says, guiding me over to the side of the bed.

He sits but I remain standing until he reaches for my hand, pulls me down next to him.

"Do you have a curfew or something?" he says, his whole face crinkling with a smile.

"No, but I *do* have a husband and young son who are at home waiting for me," I answer weakly.

He pours us two shots. I sip at mine while he slams his.

"Ummm, it's a shot. The idea is to drink the whole thing."

"But I'm already drunk. And this isn't a good idea, I need to be —"

"Going, yes. You keep saying that," he says as he slides a hand around the back of my neck and brushes my lips with his thumb.

He kisses me again. This time I kiss back, my tongue darting in and out of his mouth, my stomach clenched with longing.

I break away, stand up.

He's right behind me, though. His hands

are on my neck, massaging it. He slips a strap off my shoulder, lips grazing my neck. His hand moves down to my breasts and he stops on my nipple and traces it with a finger. I exhale, grab his thigh.

He pulls up my dress. Slides his hand down the front of my panties. I grasp his forearm. Stop him.

"I just want to touch it," he says. "Please."

So I part my legs a little and let him. He knows exactly what he's doing and before I know it, I'm grinding against his hand and I know what's going to happen next and I want it. I can imagine how he'll feel inside of me, hot and urgent, and I'm about to give in but then I think of Graham and his belief in me, all alone in our darkened house with Jack, and I bat Jamie's arm, twist away from him.

"Sorry, I just can't," I say, and push the door open, stride down the hall before he can stop me. I'm still turned on, though, but it's not Jamie I really want, it's Margot.

I think of her in the master bedroom, anger surfing through her. If she's still mad at Brad, maybe we can finish what we started earlier. I remember trailing my fingers down her neck, I hear her moan all over again in my mind, and I want to kiss her neck all the way down until I reach her breasts. I know she wants it, too; I think her earlier kiss was a signal, so I stop at her door, place my palm on it, and softly open it.

The room is empty.

I scour the great room and kitchen but they are empty, too.

I have to find her.

I burst out the back door and head out into the damp night, the hem of my dress clinging to my thighs as I wade down the grassy slope, slick with dew.

I hear sounds coming from near the water, so I walk along the pier, the boards squeaking beneath me. A symphony of bullfrogs croaks all around, but as I get closer to the lake, the sounds get louder.

I step toward the boathouse and gasp.

Brad's back leans against it. I'm still a good twenty feet away, but in the yellow glow of the boathouse lights, I can just make them out.

The front of Brad's shirt hangs open, his jeans ride low on his hips, and his arms are wrapped around Margot, who is bent over and naked, groaning with pleasure as she bucks against him.

His hands are massaging her breasts, and as he leans in closer, she arches her head back, groaning louder. He cups one breast, lifts it, and cranes his head down to kiss her nipple.

She grunts and moves against his hips even quicker until they're both moaning, their raw, jagged sounds skidding across the calm of the lake.

I turn and stagger away, walking as quickly as possible. Jealousy shrieks through me, and something else: foolishness. For thinking Margot wants me. For thinking I'm anything but a pawn in her attention-grabbing scheme. And rage at her for leading me on.

But also this: blinding lust. Because seeing her in that primal, savage moment only makes me want her even more.

34

The soles of my boots are slick from the wet grass, and I almost slip heading up the hill. I bang open the screen door, which slaps behind me as I stumble inside.

The house feels empty, and after surveying the rooms, I find that, indeed, it is.

Jamie's gone.

The bottle of vodka rests on the kitchen counter, and even though I shouldn't, I pour myself a shot and slam it back, crashing the shot glass down with a thud.

My hands are shaking and I'm rattled by the evening.

The clock on the microwave shouts that it's twelve forty-five. I *must* leave. Plus, I want to be gone before Margot and Brad return from their fuck fest.

I walk over to the sofa, dissolve into it. Fumble through my bag for my keys and cell. My vision is blurry and the lights in the room seem to flicker. I'm smashed. I sink farther into the cushions and rest my head on the arm of the sofa.

A loud noise rattles me awake. It seemed like a boom or a blast, something that my whole body felt. I sit up, check the clock on the wall. Two forty-five. Fuck, fuck, fuck!

I peer in my bag, claw around for my phone. No texts from Graham, thank god. Hopefully he's asleep. My tongue is thick in my mouth, and my pulse jitters through my body. I'm both hungover and still drunk. I fish in my purse for my bottle of water, slug half of it.

I stand. A mistake. My stomach lurches and I feel like I'm going to be sick. But I've got to get out of here.

I've got to get home to my stable and truly good Graham, my center of gravity.

I've got to get home to my honey-skinned Jack, who deserves far better than this.

I've got to stop this thing with Margot: Anything else will lead to madness.

I stand again and the room wavers, but I walk the few steps up into the kitchen. I'm filling my water bottle at the tap when I hear a loud banging at the front door.

I go to the door and wrench it open. It's Callie, wild haired and sweaty, a searing look in her eyes.

"Have you seen Margot?" she asks, her words slurring as if she, too, continued to drink this whole time.

"She's not here," I simply say. "I just woke up."

Callie narrows her eyes at me and sighs before pushing the rest of the door open, stepping around me.

She scans the kitchen and great room, then heads down the darkened hall. She's obviously been somewhere stewing this whole time about me staying behind with Margot alone; she can't handle it.

I remain standing in the doorway, unsure of what to do with myself. After an apparent sweep of the back rooms, Callie weaves her way through the great room, eyes cutting me before she slides past me again.

She bolts back to her car, which I notice is the only one in the driveway other than mine. Her tires grate against the gravel as she tears away.

I shut the front door behind me, not bothering to lock it, and climb inside the Highlander.

35

It's well after three a.m. by the time I turn down our street. It's still pitch-black out, dark as an unlit hallway, but instead of heading straight home, I park at the entrance to the jogging trail.

I know it's not the smartest move, my being alone on the trail at this hour, but I've got to clear my mind. I need to sort myself out before I face Graham and Jack.

I change out of my dress and boots in the front seat and into some jogging clothes and sneakers I always keep stashed in the back.

The night has cooled away the dank heat from earlier and it feels refreshing to be out here with puffs of sharp air pinging my face as I run.

Fingers of moonlight leak through the pines, and as I jog up a steep incline, I see a pool of fog beneath me, hovering over the dips in the trail. I run. I run and drift through the fog like a plane dipping into low-hanging clouds. I run until the sweat leaches out of every pore, until my whole body smells like it's been bathed in booze, until my calf muscles burn as though they've been zapped by cattle brands.

I run farther on the trail than I ever have, until it dead-ends on a quiet street. My lungs are stinging as I take in huge breaths of early-morning air, but my body is flooded with endorphins, and for the first time in what seems like weeks, I can step outside of Margot's hold and think clearly.

I crossed a line tonight. I know I did, and it was so stupid of me. And more than that, dangerous. What if Graham were to ever find out? I can't even hold that thought in my head because if I were to lose him, I'd lose everything. I'm disgusted with myself, but at least things didn't go any further with Jamie or Margot. They certainly could have.

I turn and head back to the house, and it seems as if I can't run fast enough. Even though I'm hoping Graham's asleep, I can't get home quickly enough.

And when I step through the back door, I know what I'll do.

I'll leave the boys asleep while I shower in the guest bath, so as not to wake them. I'll turn on the waffle iron and make batches of cinnamon waffles with berries and a heaping side of bacon. I'll make Jack's favorite drink — strawberry milk — and I'll somehow slip out of Margot's narcotic grip over me and be a part of their lives once more. It will be as if this whole thing never happened.

36

Saturday, April 14, 2018

It's afternoon. Sunlight beams through the kitchen window, warming the square of countertop where I stand smashing garlic heads with the blunt back of a kitchen knife.

I'm making one of Graham's favorite pasta dishes: toasted garlic tossed with cherry tomatoes and a coating of lemon zest on top.

This summer, I plan to grow a yard full of cherry tomatoes so we can pluck them straight from the vine onto our plate.

I powered through the day, chugging multiple lattes and luxuriating in the simple, dramaless company of Jack and Graham. Well, Graham hasn't been exactly drama-less. He's been distant and icy all day but he didn't mention anything this morning about my coming in so late; I'd hoped he'd slept straight through it and hadn't noticed. And I'm not about to be the one to bring it up. That's why I'm making his favorite pasta, hoping my offering will be enough to defrost him without having to get into things.

We went berry picking earlier this morning at a nearby farm. Jack played hide-and-seek through the thick rows of blueberry bushes while Graham and I filled wooden baskets to the brim with plump, sugary berries.

"I never knew fruit could taste this good," I said to Graham, grabbing a mouthful of blueberries from the basket, a trail of purple-blue juice streaking down my face. He didn't say anything, just nodded.

"Seriously, these are so much better than the frozen ones we ate for breakfast," I said, angling for more of a response from him. But he just kept on picking berries, methodically yanking the fruit off the bush with a businesslike air about him.

"Yumm-ee! Yumm-ee!" Jack echoed me, scooping up fistfuls and smashing them into his mouth.

His hands were stained blue by the time we buckled him into his car seat, his belly round and full with the mountains of berries he gobbled up between more rounds of hide-and-seek.

■ ■ ■ ■

I thought Jack would drift off to sleep in the car but he fought his nap until we got home. He's still sleeping now as Graham sifts through sketches of a new bid at the kitchen table. He sighs, takes his glasses off, rubs the bridge of his nose.

I uncork a bottle of white and take a long sip. It's exactly what I need right now. Even though I've made it through most of the day, my head is throbbing with the remains of my vicious hangover, and my nerves are shot from tiptoeing around Graham.

I drag another glass down, fill it to the brim, and take it over to Graham. His jaw is set and a look of disdain clouds his face as he takes it from me. I can't take it anymore; I have to say something.

"What *is* it?" I ask, my stomach doing cartwheels.

He folds his drafting papers up, thin as onion skins, and pushes them across the table.

"I heard the shower come on this morning," he says, his eyes not meeting mine, "and I realized you'd only just come in. While you were showering, I went through your phone."

Dread grips my gut, a vise squeezing my insides while I listen.

"I looked through your texts with Margot," he accuses, spitting her name out as if it's an object of disgust. "What exactly did she mean, a few weeks ago, when she said, 'Looks like you were having fun anyway'?"

I gulp. It feels like a rock is in my throat, and my hands shake as I set my wineglass down on the countertop. How much should I tell him? That's what I'm trying to decide when he continues.

"From her text, it sounded like you were at her lake house during a weekday. And there were other people out there. Who? Who, Sophie?" he says. This time his eyes are on me, his open stare a mixture of anger and bewilderment.

"Look. I told you these women are crazy. Margot especially." The words pour out, and I realize it feels good to say this out loud, to share this with someone else.

"But what does that *mean,* exactly?" he asks, his head cocked toward the fireplace.

I decide to come clean. At least, part of the way clean. I don't, I can't, tell him about my obsession with Margot. And I stop short of telling him about Jamie.

"She cheats on her husband."

Graham leans back, lets out a sharp sigh.

"Go on."

"And some of the other women do, too. Well, not all of them; there's this nice woman, Tina, who doesn't. And they don't sleep with other men, or at least they're not supposed to, they just sort of flirt and make out," I offer, my face boiling with shame. I'm instantly filled with regret from telling him this; I've crossed a line. "And it's not like it's all the time. We really are just out there shooting guns and drinking for the most part."

He's nodding, biting his lower lip as if he's working out a complex problem in his mind.

"And you?"

"Graham! Who do you think I am?" I say. Even though I try for indignant, I can hear the desperate screech in my voice, a telltale note of guilt.

He crosses his arms across his chest, tucks his hands into his armpits.

"I would never do that to you. To us," I say as hot tears prick my eyes.

It's a lie, but only a half lie, I tell myself. At least I haven't fucked anyone else yet.

"Why did you wait all day to talk to me about this?" I ask.

"I didn't want to bring it up in front of Jack; he doesn't need to hear all this."

I go over to him, place a hand on his

shoulder, but he just sits there, square-jawed and solid in his chair, his hands digging farther into his armpits.

I lean down and place my hands on his face. Stare directly into his hazel eyes.

"You have to believe me. Margot's text meant nothing. She was with someone that day and the man brought a friend but I promise, nothing happened between us."

"I hate this," he says, the words hissing out of his mouth.

"I do, too," I admit. "I won't hang out with them anymore, if that helps."

"You do what you want. You know I'm not controlling like that," he sighs. "But don't turn me into the type of person who feels as though they need to snoop through their spouse's phone."

His chair scrapes the floor as he pushes it back from the table. He stands and slams his glass of wine, wiping his mouth with the sleeve of his shirt.

"Honey," I say, my voice quiet and demure, "I love you. I wouldn't do anything to mess us up." I stand on my tiptoes and plant a kiss on top of Graham's head, grab his hand and give it a tight squeeze.

He simply nods, but the gloominess in the room is slowly beginning to evaporate. He steps out onto the back patio, and I know him well enough not to follow him out there. Whenever we fight — even after we've made up, as I hope we have just now — he always needs a little space.

37

We're finishing the last of dinner. Jack is parked on my lap, his tanned hands resting on my arms as I drag the last piece of spaghetti through a puddle of olive oil.

He's been extra clingy tonight, as if he can sense our discord, so I'm trying to flood him with attention, erase those pinched lines of worry that are stamped along his forehead. When I set my fork down, he grabs my hands and brings them to his chubby neck so I'll tickle him. Which I gladly do over and over.

Graham has the television on. Normally, we don't watch TV while we eat, but the Spurs are playing against Golden State and he wants to see the outcome. But really, I think he's just trying to burrow further into his cocoon and ignore me for the evening.

I'm actually relieved, and as soon as Jack bounds off my lap and toddles down the hall toward his room, I split the remainder of the wine between our two glasses.

It has warmed by now; I prefer it cold, but it's so soothing I don't bother to refrigerate it and wait for it to chill. The last of my hangover is slowly melting away, and I slide an empty chair toward me and throw my feet up in the seat.

I'm not paying all that much attention to the game, but I sit up and take notice when the local news cuts through and a picture of a teenage girl fills the screen.

It's a photo of Abby.

And beneath it, a headline beams out at me like a scream: LOCAL GIRL MISSING SINCE LAST NIGHT.

I set my glass down, grip Graham's arm. Grab the remote and stab at the volume button to raise the sound.

"A Mapleton teenager, Abby Wilson, aged seventeen, has been missing since late yesterday evening," a tiny, blond reporter says. She's parked behind the news desk while her co-anchor, a broad-shouldered man with graying hair and concerned eyes, delivers the rest of the news, which I can hardly hear with the blood roaring in my ears.

"Abby was last seen by her boyfriend, Brad Simmons, late last night when he dropped her off in her driveway after a date. The couple had dined earlier in the evening with Abby's parents, Marcie and Bruce Wilson, who report never having heard Abby come home. When they woke early this morning, at around five a.m., Marcie peeked into Abby's room and discovered her daughter's bed was still made."

A picture of Brad in his football uniform is flashed across the screen next, followed by a picture of Abby's parents.

Marcie, Abby's mother, is short and fresh-faced. Pretty but plain-looking, no makeup on, wispy blond hair pulled into a ponytail, and dressed simply in pale pink sweats. Her husband, Bruce, looks like a science teacher, with black-rimmed glasses and a button-down, short-sleeved oxford shirt.

Marcie is a stay-at-home mom, the anchor tells us, and Bruce is, in fact, a schoolteacher. Not a science teacher but rather algebra at the local middle school.

"Oh my god, Graham," I say, my voice wobbly. "I know this girl."

He starts to respond but I shush him so I can hear the rest of the story.

"Police aren't assuming foul play at this early stage," the male anchor continues, "and are hoping that Abby returns home quickly and safely. But please, if you have any information at all, call the number on the bottom of the screen."

The number to the Mapleton Police Department flashes below before the coverage segues into the weather report.

My head swims and I feel like I'm going to be sick.

Graham slides the remote from my hand and punches the mute button.

"That's terrible," he says, his voice almost a whisper. He's staring at me as if I'm something fragile that may break.

He places his hand on top of mine, rubs it softly. "How do you know this girl?"

I let out a long, ragged breath and keep staring down at the table.

How am I supposed to answer?

I take a moment, then explain that I had met Abby just last week at Jill's swim party. That Brad, the boyfriend in the news clip, is Jill's son.

"How awful," Graham says, his face scrunched up with concern. "Well, hopefully she'll show up soon. You know how teens are."

I don't tell him that Margot is sleeping with Brad.

And I don't tell him about Margot's text

to Brad, which comes flashing back into my brain like neon:

Get rid of her.

38

Monday, April 16, 2018

It's midmorning, nearly ten o'clock. I'm parked behind my laptop, where I've been since Graham left this morning with Jack. I'm unable to move, unable to pry myself from the screen, from searches of Abby. Unable even to go to the kitchen to warm my latte, which has grown cold and sits untouched on the corner of my desk.

Yesterday was pure torture.

Over breakfast, Graham spread the Sunday paper out in front of him — as is his habit — feeding me only bits and pieces about Abby's story. No new details, no new leads, only glimpses into her life, some of which I knew already through Jill: Abby is a junior, a cheerleader, on the honor roll. An only child, beloved by all, with a large circle of friends, steady boyfriend. Wholesome Abby, now missing Abby, and I wanted to snatch the paper from him, read every word myself, but I couldn't act too overly interested.

I kept hoping all day that Tina would call with more info — out of everyone in the group, she'd be the one most likely to loop me in, but she never did. I had to fight the urge to call her, the minutes ticking by with slow-moving agony, my thoughts running rampant like a pack of wild dogs. Had Brad done something to Abby? Had he gotten "rid of her" as Margot had asked him to? Had Margot and Brad done something to her in the window of time when I was blacked out? Surely not. Surely I was being paranoid. Surely Abby would turn up safe and sound soon. But nothing about Abby suggested to me that she was the runaway type. Where the hell was she?

Inwardly, my stomach churned, but outwardly, I plastered on a calm veneer for Jack and Graham until bedtime. Until Graham finally clicked off his bedside lamp and roped a heavy arm around me, pinning me in place.

I stared up at the ceiling, Graham's hot, purring snores on my neck. That usually comforts me, but last night his ragged breathing only set my nerves further on edge.

An hour later I was still wide-awake when

my cell sprang to life, sending shards of blue light dancing along the wall.

Gently peeling Graham's arm off me, I rolled over and grasped my phone.

A group text, from the Hunting Wives, from Tina, who was clearly unable to contain herself one second longer.

Tina: Praying for sweet Abby! Have you guys heard anything at all? Jill, honey, please let us know if you need anything. Anything at all.

My face reddened on Tina's behalf and I hoped Jill wouldn't pick up on her outright thirst for gossip. I mean, Tina's a good person and all, but she can't help herself when it comes to juicy news. A few seconds later, though, a reply from Jill lit up my screen.

Jill: Obviously we're all sick over here.

Margot: Obviously! We're here for you, Jilly.

Callie: SO terrible!

My hand clutched the phone, and my thumb hovered over the screen as I thought of how to reply. I settled on: Sending love! And as I was hitting send, I saw that Callie was typing a fresh message.

Callie: Why don't we meet at my place tomorrow? At noon. I'll have Rosa make lunch.

Jill: That would be really nice, Callie. Thank you.

Callie: Sophie, my house is 11 Kensington Drive. Text me when you get to the gates and I'll buzz them open.

I was caught off guard by Callie's warmth — it seems as though it takes a tragedy for her to act even remotely human — and it took a minute for me to reply. And honestly, I wasn't sure how I felt about going over there and being around Margot. After Friday night, I really wanted a clean break. But I also knew I didn't have a choice: I needed to know the latest about Abby.

I typed back:

Me: Ok, sounds good, see everyone tomorrow.

Margot: See you soon.

Tina: Soon!

So here I am passing the time until I'm due at Callie's, scouring the net but finding nothing new. Abby's Facebook profile is predictably outdated, and like most teens, she probably uses a secret handle on Instagram, if she even has an account.

The only new piece about her is from the local paper, the *Mapleton Times* (which, as of this morning, I follow on Facebook — we only get the Sunday edition for home delivery), and it's a brief announcement that Abby's church, the Piney Woods Church of Christ, will be holding a candlelight vigil for her tonight. The article ends with the hashtag #prayforAbby.

I snap my laptop shut, and for the umpteenth time, pick through the article in Sunday's paper, which is littered over my desk, and scan it yet again for new clues, my fingertips turning gray and chalky from the inky pages.

My eyes rest on the photograph of Abby's parents, of Abby's dad in particular. He has a serious, almost forlorn look about him — a look that screams control freak — and I catch myself having the sick thought that

I'm hoping he's responsible for Abby's disappearance. That it's not Brad or Margot and Brad, that it's ten steps removed from them. From me.

But why would he harm his own daughter? And his alibi is airtight: He was with his wife all evening, the two of them together, unsuspecting, inside their home.

Abby never even crossed the threshold that night.

Folding the paper back together, I shove it to one side of my desk and head down the hall to get dressed for Callie's.

39

The outside of Callie's house is as cold and austere as she is; it's a massive modern contemporary, all glass and grays with slate-blue trim and boxy lines. The landscaping is similarly monochromatic. Even though it's spring, there's not a pop of color or a flower to be found. Only a dark carpet of Saint Augustine grass bordered by stark beds of charcoal-colored rock with cacti and other jagged succulents poking through.

It's at the end of the street from Margot's, and as I ease into the cul-de-sac at five minutes past noon (I'm purposely late; I don't want to be the first to arrive and have an awkward, one-on-one moment with Callie), I spy both Jill's and Tina's cars parked out front.

Margot will most likely just walk down from her place, I think to myself, and then I wonder if she will actually show at all.

My pulse is jittery as I head up the sidewalk, and as I approach the front steps, a dog howls from inside. Through the slim horizontal window that flanks the tall black door, I see a chocolate-and-white beagle pawing at the glass.

I press the doorbell, sending the beagle into more frenzied bellows until the door swings open and an older woman in a white linen blouse with matching slacks toes the dog and snaps, "Hush, Carter!"

She has silver hair pulled into a tight bun and her demeanor is chilly, her expression severe. She offers me a thin, forced smile before planting her bony hand on my back and ushering me into the sunken living room.

The interior of the house is as frigid as the outside: no family photos lining the walls, no personal touches as far as I can see; it feels like the set of a magazine shoot.

The entire back wall of the living room is lined with glass, overlooking a narrow, leafy, walled garden with more cacti and an enormous slate fountain that bubbles softly in the background.

As I step down into the living room, Callie shoots me a glare of irritation as if I'm interrupting, as if she hadn't just buzzed me in five minutes earlier. Her arm is wrapped around Jill, who sits between her and Tina on a sectional.

Tina turns toward me, gives me a quick smile, and I cross the room and sink into an ottoman next to them. Jill is dressed in all black, her hands twisting a wad of Kleenex in her lap. Her eyes are puffy from crying, and when she looks up at me, my throat tightens but I manage to squeak out, "I'm so sorry. I really, really am."

She sniffs and nods.

"I'm sure she'll turn up soon," I dumbly add, and at this, more tears gush from Jill's eyes, and to my surprise, she holds her arms out to me like a toddler. I lean in and hug her as sobs rack her chest.

A moment later we're interrupted by the housekeeper.

"Red or white?" she asks me.

Drinking in this situation feels slightly bizarre, but a shot of alcohol actually sounds nice. Something to take the edge off my jangled nerves.

"Red, thank you," I say, smiling. But she just swivels in her clunky sandals and clip-clops down the long hallway.

Platters of food line the glass coffee table. There are big ribs of celery stuffed with pimento cheese, tea sandwiches with the crusts trimmed off, small discs of quiche, and a mountain of chilled grapes.

"Rosa," Callie calls toward the kitchen, "would you bring me more red as well?"

Seconds later, the housekeeper appears with our wine. I take a small sip — it's pure velvet — and immediately take a longer gulp.

The front door opens, light spilling in, and there's Margot, sashaying through the entryway, blowing air-kisses at Rosa, who rushes over to her, gives her a tight hug.

Margot's in short, black dress shorts, and my eyes, as usual, drink in her exquisite legs. She's wearing a white boatneck shirt and strappy black heels. Her oversize sunglasses stay parked on her face, even as she coasts toward Jill and pulls her into her arms. The two stay locked together, swaying slightly from side to side as Margot speaks lowly in Jill's ear, stroking her hair while she talks.

They finally pull apart and Margot removes her glasses and plops down into an armchair.

Rosa is soon at Margot's side with a glass of chilled white.

"So, what's the latest, honey?" Margot asks Jill.

"Nothing. Nobody's heard from Abby at all. Brad's been texting her constantly, of course," Jill says, staring down at her hands. "Her family's heard nothing, the police have heard nothing. It makes no sense." She sighs, her breath blowing her bangs toward the ceiling. "Brad's distraught. We all are."

Rosa is now parked behind Margot with a hand on her shoulder, as if Margot's the one in distress. Watching Margot lap up Rosa's attention slightly grosses me out — she looks like an entitled child.

"That'll be all for now, Rosa," Callie says, dismissing her. Rosa slinks dutifully from the room.

I grab a celery stick and sneak in a few crunchy bites to put something in my stomach.

Margot leans back in her chair, swirls her wine around in the glass.

"I'm just so sorry, Jilly," Tina says, a hand placed over her heart. "We know how close they are, and I feel *so* awful for sweet Brad." She pulls her face into a frown but I can see that glint in her eyes, that flicker of excitement.

Jill drains her wine, parks the empty glass on a nearby coaster. "But the strange thing is, they evidently had a fight that night."

Her gaze is trained on her lap as she continues. "Brad has apparently been trying to end things with Abby. I had *no* idea, of course, so I'm absolutely shocked by that as well, but he told me he felt that their relationship has taken too much of his focus off of football, and college." She lifts her eyes, then looks around at each of us as if for confirmation.

I find myself nodding, because I don't know how else to react.

Callie rests her hand on Jill's knee, a gesture that coaxes her to continue talking.

"That night," Jill says, "Brad went to dinner with Abby and her parents. Afterward, he tried to break it off and she flipped out."

Jill dabs at her eyes with the remains of the Kleenex. Tina passes her a fresh one. "He said that Abby got hysterical, went ballistic on him, wouldn't stop crying, threatened suicide. He told me she'd threatened this before," Jill adds, sucking in a deep breath and then exhaling.

I remember Brad saying that in his text, that Abby had threatened to slit her wrists. I wonder if he's telling the truth. Abby seemed stable, grounded. But what the hell do I know? She *is* a teenage girl after all.

"I had no idea any of this was going on," Jill says. "She demanded that Brad drop her off at the top of her driveway that night instead of seeing her inside. He was so rattled afterward that he spent the rest of the evening with his friend, Jamie, driving around, blowing off steam. He can't imagine what's happened to Abby, and he's so mad at himself for not walking her to the front door."

I flick my eyes to Margot to try and read her expression, but she has her nose in her wineglass.

"If she doesn't come home safely," Jill continues, her voice cracking, "the guilt is going to eat my son alive."

The room falls silent except for the whishing of the outdoor fountain and the faint sounds of Rosa washing dishes in the kitchen. Jill looks depleted, all the makeup drained off her face from crying. She slumps back into the sofa, tucks her feet underneath her.

Margot sets her drink down on the glass coffee table and smooths the tops of her shorts with her hands. "Well, let's not get too ahead of ourselves. It's only been a few days."

Jill looks up at her, nods as if she's grateful, and fresh tears pool in her eyes. "You're right, I know. It's true. I need to keep it together."

"I'm sure Abby's just fine; I'm sure she'll pop back up in no time," Tina interjects, placing her hand on Jill's arm and briskly rubbing it up and down. "Breakups are hard, especially at that age. She could just be trying to sort things out."

Margot rises, goes over to Jill. "I've gotta get going, sweetie, but call me later tonight. And, please, let us know the second you hear anything."

They hug and Margot makes her way out the front door. Her sudden departure feels abrupt, but it doesn't seem to faze Jill, and I'm itching to get out of here, too, so I take advantage of the moment and stand up.

"I've gotta run as well," I say and lean down to Jill to give her a quick hug. She ropes an arm around my neck and rubs my back like she's trying to soothe me; my heart crumbles for her grief-ridden awkwardness.

Outside, I sit in my steamy SUV for a few minutes before starting the engine. I watch Margot fade smaller and smaller down the sidewalk as she walks toward home. But not so small that I don't see her sliding her cell from her bag. I don't even need to guess at what she's doing. The mounting unease in my gut tells me that she's calling Brad.

40

I've been home from Callie's for over an hour. I should be folding laundry, prepping dinner, but I'm back online, looking for Abby.

I'm sipping a strong cup of Earl Grey, hoping the pipe tobacco–flavored liquid will cut through my afternoon wine buzz. My fingers peck at the keyboard, wearing down the same online paths as earlier — the *Mapleton Times,* Facebook — but to no avail. Nothing has changed since this morning.

I arrow the mouse to the top of the screen, close the browser, and am staring at my latest screensaver — a pink-hued photo of the New Mexico desert — when I hear a car door slam.

I hop up and head down the hallway. Peer out a window to see a black Mercedes parked out front and Margot making her way up the front steps. The doorbell chimes and I suck in a quick breath before opening it.

"Heeeey," she says. She slides her sunglasses back on her head, leans toward me. She slips a hand around my neck, her lips grazing my cheek. Her skin smells intoxicating, and I have to stifle the urge to turn my face toward hers so that our lips meet. Before I can even react, she drops her hand, leans against the doorjamb.

"Wanna come inside?" My pulse pounds through my veins, and hot sheets of wind melt the air-conditioned chill inside the house.

"I'd love to," she says, her eyes direct and level with mine. "But I can't stay. Just needed to stop by."

"Oh?" I ask, not sure of what to do with myself, so I cross my arms in front of me. Of course she didn't come over here to make out with me, and given everything that's going on, I'm repulsed by my desire. And it's achingly obvious that her pull over me hasn't dimmed one bit.

"Listen, if anybody asks you about Friday night," she says, "just tell them I was with you."

Now my pulse is pounding in my temples and I shift my weight between my feet. And as if she can sense my wariness, she quickly adds, "I'm sure they won't, but if they do . . ."

She reaches down for my wrist, takes it in her hand. Heat rises along my arm as she holds it; her eyes are trained down at the ground between us, and an almost sheepish look spreads across her face.

"Look, I can't have anyone finding out about me and Brad. No one needs to know. Especially Jed." She locks her eyes onto mine. "*You* understand, I'm sure."

And she doesn't even have to say Jamie's name because it hangs in the air, suspended between us. A clear threat.

She drops my wrist, and before I can answer, her lips are on mine. A quick peck before she spins around and floats down the steps to her car. "Gotta run and grab the kiddos from school," she calls over her shoulder, blowing an air-kiss my way.

Back inside, I slump against the entryway wall. My entire body is shaking; I don't know what to do.

Of course I know what I *should* do, and that's pick up my cell and call someone, tell them everything I know. But who would I tell? Graham? The police? And what would I say? "Hi, this is Sophie O'Neill. Last weekend I was at a spin-the-bottle party with two teenage boys and I read a text message I shouldn't have."

I pace to the kitchen to make a shot of espresso. I need something stronger than the tea, something to wake me up, something to help me think more clearly.

My hands clatter as I scoop the grinds from the silver tin, fill the basin with filtered water.

I need to get a grip. Maybe Tina is right, maybe Abby is just sorting things out. Maybe she's just fine.

But why would Margot stop by to try and hush me unless she knows something? Something about Abby. Something bad.

As the espresso sputters into the bottom of a shot glass, Margot's words creep back into my mind: *No one needs to know.* You *understand, I'm sure.*

The thought of Graham finding out about Jamie makes me double over, grab the counter, and fight to catch my breath.

I don't know what I'm going to do, but for now, I know that Margot is right: No one needs to know.

41

Wednesday, April 18, 2018

It's one in the morning and the sky outside my window is pitch-black, crammed with a quilt of rain clouds blocking out the moonlight.

I'm wide-awake, staring through the slats of our plantation blinds, unable to sleep. I haven't slept well since Saturday night, since the news about Abby broke.

The rain is starting to drum again against the window. It's been like this all day — short bursts of showers followed by longer stretches of cloying humidity.

It turned hotter this week, and for most of the day, I sat in my office, staring out the window, watching raindrops hit the scorching pavement, hissing against the patio like an iron sizzling against a moistened shirt. Instead of a release from the relentless heat, the rain has made it even muggier, the atmosphere of a soup cauldron.

I couldn't focus on anything all day. I can't turn my mind off of Abby. Or Margot or Brad. Or off the what-ifs. What if she's never found? What if she *is* found and something's happened to her?

My stomach is sick with worry, eaten up with guilt over where she might be and what I know and am not telling anyone. Especially Graham.

He walked through the back door when he came home from work tonight, chipper and clutching a grocery sack filled with steaks, spinach, and potatoes, and offered to cook dinner.

As Jack and I sat at the dining table dipping paintbrushes into discs of watercolors and jars of water, Graham grilled the rib eyes in his grandma's old cast-iron skillet, wilting the spinach in the steak's juices.

"Any word about the girl?" Graham asked as he topped the steaks with butter, slid the potatoes from the oven.

Without meeting his eyes, I shook my head. "No, nothing, unfortunately."

I hadn't told him anything about going to Callie's on Monday and, of course, didn't tell him about Margot stopping by. And these lies — not lies exactly, but omissions — expanded in the back of my throat like a sponge and I could barely choke down my dinner; I focused instead on cutting Jack's steak into tiny bites so that he'd eat it.

Later, in bed, Graham pulled me on top of him, nibbled on my ear. I kissed his cheek but the effort was lackluster and he picked up on it.

"Is there something wrong?" he asked.

I didn't feel like getting into anything about Abby; he can't know how all-consuming it's become for me, so I dragged my fingers through his hair, kissed his lips.

"I'm good," I murmured, "but I started today." Another lie. (But only a small one. I should have my period by tomorrow or the next day and I'm rarely in the mood while I'm on it.) I didn't want to turn him down, but I couldn't bear to allow myself any pleasure when all I can think about is Abby, about where she might be.

"Ooooh, well that explains it," he said, twirling a lock of my hair through his finger.

"Explains what?"

"Oh, nothing. Just the moodiness at dinner. The long silences. The, um, you know, general vibe of impending doom." He was grinning as he said this, and I elbowed him in the gut.

"Guess it's just me and *Dwell* tonight, then," he said, fake pouting. He slid the architecture and design magazine off the nightstand and shifted two pillows under his neck.

I laced my arm around his stomach, planted a kiss on his cheek. "I love you so much, honey."

"I love you, too, Soph. So very much." He rubbed the top of my head with one hand as the other flipped through the magazine.

Feeling his fingers trace along my scalp relaxed me, and I actually dozed off for an hour or so, but now it's the middle of the night and I'm wired.

I peel back the hot sheets and creep down the hallway to my office, where I power up my laptop and log on to Facebook. One of the first posts I see is from the *Mapleton Times.* A photo from earlier this evening, from the candlelight vigil for Abby at her church. Hundreds of faces are illuminated by candlelight, and a banner that reads PRAY FOR ABBY hangs outside the church. My eyes blur with tears as I scan the sea of faces until I find her parents, clutching candles and each other, their eyes gazing back at me, grief-stricken and dimmed of hope. It's now been five days since she vanished, and we all know the statistics: The first forty-eight hours are the most important, holding the greatest hope for finding the missing person.

It's also the most critical time for people to come forward with pertinent information, tips, but here I sit, parked in my cozy house, afraid to share what I know. And what makes me feel even guiltier is knowing that, yes, I'm gut sick over Abby, but if I'm being honest, I'm equally worried about what keeping this secret might do to me.

42

Thursday, April 19, 2018

Abby is no longer missing. Abby is dead.

I got the call from Tina last night, just as Graham was pulling red snapper from the grill, the pink skin charred and seasoned to perfection.

Yesterday morning, the rain finally broke and a cool front swept in, so I threw open all the windows and let the fresh breeze energize the stuffy house.

I stayed off my laptop for most of the day, spending the whole morning working in the garden, tugging out a nest of weeds that was threatening to choke all my newly planted herbs and veggies.

I pruned the basil and rosemary, piling the cuttings into a colander to rinse and later air-dry from strings of twine in the kitchen window. Because I'd neglected the garden these past few weeks, most of the tomatoes had been pecked by birds, shot through with black holes and drained of their juices. But I managed to harvest a sink full of cherry tomatoes, slicing them in half and tossing them in a salad for dinner.

The work in the garden helped lighten my mood, so before I changed my mind, I called Graham on his lunch break, asked if we could grill and eat dinner outside. I almost texted Erin and invited them over, but didn't want to push it. I felt slightly better, but only slightly, and I certainly wasn't in the mood for light chitchat.

Just before dinner, I was swinging Jack in the tire swing we hung from a gnarled branch of our oak tree when I heard my phone chiming.

"Be right back," I said, crossing the patio and lifting it from the bench.

A group text from the Hunting Wives pinged across the screen.

Tina: Oh, Jill honey, I just heard. I don't even have words. Praying for you all.

I felt my throat constrict, and I gripped the side of the bench, steadying myself.

Callie: I can't believe it. So awful.

I looked over to Graham. He had just

lifted the lid off the grill and smoke gushed out, creating a screen between us; I was grateful he couldn't see the alarm on my face. My cell rang. It was Tina.

"Mommeeee!" Jack cried, pink-faced from the swing. "More! Swing me more!"

"Just a second, honey!" I called to him, stepping inside the back door.

Clutching the phone, my palms slick with sweat, I answered on the second ring.

"I *just* got off with Callie." Tina's voice was shaky and she was talking too fast. "She called like five minutes before I sent that text. I honestly didn't even know what to say . . . I—"

But I cut her off before she could finish her rambling. "What's going on?" I glanced out the glass door, flashed a tense smile at Graham, who was staring at me as he lifted the fish from the grill onto a platter.

"Abby. It's Abby. They found her body." Her voice dropped a register. "She's dead. Shot to death."

The phone nearly slid from my hand, and all I could hear for a moment was the coursing of my blood in my temples. I opened my mouth, closed it. Opened it again to speak but couldn't form words.

"Sophie," Tina continued, sounding spooked. "They found her body on Margot's land, right at the clearing where we shoot."

The word *clearing* was cut in half by the ding of an incoming call. I glanced at the screen. Margot.

My vision swam and I staggered back from the door a few steps so I could lean against the dining table. I could feel Graham's eyes on me, so I looked up at him, lifted an index finger, and turned toward the living room so I could take it all in without him scanning my face.

"Oh, god," I managed to exhale out. "That's . . . that's terrible. Her family must be in shock. Jill must be in shock."

"We were out there the night she went missing. It's too creepy to think about what else could've happened. To any of us! I hope they catch the bastard that did this," she hissed.

My phone kept chiming in my ear, dicing up Tina's sentences. "I gotta go, call you back ASAP," I said and pressed end. I set the phone on the table and clutched my stomach. Bile surged up my throat, and sweat needled my armpits. This was worse than I could've ever imagined. I'd thought of Abby dead, many times since Saturday, but had hoped beyond hope she'd still somehow magically reappear, sparkling with life and unharmed.

I certainly never imagined she'd be found, shot dead, on Margot's land.

A shudder passed through me and I twisted around just enough so I could peer outside. The sky was darkening and Graham was pushing Jack in the swing, Jack's laughter echoing through the night air, his tangle of golden locks lifting off his forehead with each shove, and I wanted to squeeze myself into this happy frame, shrink the world down so that it was just the three of us. I squinted my eyes, tried to take a mental snapshot of the moment because the dread creeping over me told me that no matter what was coming next, things would never be the same again.

I stared down at my cell as if it were a snake coiled to strike. Three missed calls from Margot. Fuck. I needed a second to process everything Tina had told me before calling her back, but my phone started blaring again and the screen sprang to life, flashing her name.

"Jesus, Sophie," she started in before I even had the chance to say hello. "Where the hell have you been?"

"On the phone with Tina; she just told me everything, she —" I said, my voice rattled with nerves.

She interrupted me. "It doesn't matter. Look, I can't talk long." It sounded like she was standing outside; I could hear the whoosh of a car zipping past.

"It's *so* horrible what's happened. And on my land, no less," she added, letting out a jagged sigh. "But listen, what happens next is important. If we stick to our story, no one will find out about Brad or Jamie." There was a stab to her voice, and I could tell this was no request. It was another threat.

I stood there clasping the phone to my skull, feeling like I was becoming detached from my body, like my mind was floating upward toward the ceiling.

"Sophie," her voice purred in my ear. I parted my lips to speak but before I could, she said, "Gotta run," and ended the call.

She didn't even have to wait for my reply; she knew I was going to stick to the script. I have no other choice. Graham can never find out about Jamie.

A sheen of sweat coated my body. It was nearly pitch-black outside now, and I could just barely make out Graham's and Jack's darkened figures at the tire swing. The dining room suddenly felt too bright, like I was onstage under a spotlight. I opened the back door and stepped out.

The platter of snapper rested on the wrought-iron table, and a team of flies was already dive-bombing the fish before I could swat them away.

"Everything okay?" Graham asked. The tire swing creaked and groaned as he waited for my reply.

I shook my head.

He shrugged his shoulders. "Well?"

"It's Abby. She's —" I ran my index finger across my throat as if to slit it, and immediately felt like I was playing a character in a television drama. "Talk about it later, okay?" I angled my head toward Jack.

Graham's hand flew to his mouth and his eyes filled with sadness. "Sorry," he choked out. "That's terrible. Yes, fill me in later."

We took our dinner inside, away from the hungry flies. Jack slung his dirt-crusted bare feet up on the table while he ate; I didn't stop him. My mind was racing but also a blank.

After a few moments I couldn't stand to sit still at the table any longer, so I told Graham I needed to be alone for a moment to call Tina back. His lips shone with olive oil and he nodded and said, "Of course."

I crept to the back of the house, to our bedroom, and gently shut the door. For safe measure, I stepped into the master bathroom and closed that door as well. I lowered the toilet seat and sunk down on top of it, bracing myself. The curtain was drawn back and a chunk of moonlight sliced through the bare window, casting shadows across the bone-white surfaces of the countertop and floors.

"So glad you called back," Tina said, almost in a whisper.

"I need to know everything." My voice halted and I caught myself. "I mean, what all do you know?" I asked more softly, hoping I sounded not as forceful, less suspicious, and more sympathetic.

She unloaded the rest to me, and as she spoke, I raked my bare toe along the cold tile floor, giving my body a calm focal point as my brain exploded with everything she spilled.

She got everything from Callie, who heard it all from Margot.

Abby was found. No, her *body* was discovered by the groundskeeper who tends Margot's lake house and in-town estate. An older gentleman who's been with the Banks family for decades. He was cutting the grass on a riding lawn mower at the clearing when he noticed Abby's body, facedown in a shallow puddle of leaves near the shoreline. He immediately phoned the police.

"Her back; her back was shot clean through," Tina said, clearly struggling with tears as she spoke. "Cops said it was a shotgun blast."

I inwardly gasped. A shotgun? How stupid could they be? And on the land no less. But I then reminded myself that I didn't know everything, that it might not be Margot or Brad at all. Oh, *please,* I thought, let them *not* be involved.

"The police are still out there, combing the property. Callie said Margot was seriously freaked out. Especially when the police told her and Jed to head back into town for the time being and not return to the lake for some time. For their own safety."

I didn't want to ask if she'd talked to Jill. I couldn't bring myself to think about Jill's bottomless grief yet.

"I'm so sad about sweet Abby," Tina said, "and I feel guilty for thinking this way but I just keep wondering — what if it had been one of us instead? I mean, they don't even have a suspect yet. It's just too creepy to think about."

I thought about telling her everything just then, about Margot and Brad, about Jamie, about the text I saw, but I swallowed my words.

"No, I know what you mean," I said, only because I had to say something. Tina's logic was not only selfish (like mine has been lately) but also screwy: According to Brad, he dropped Abby off that night at the foot of her drive. She wasn't *at* the lake at the time of her disappearance.

So how had she ended up there?

After Graham tucked Jack in for the night, he found me in the kitchen, washing the last of the dishes from dinner, and placed his steady hands on my shoulders.

"Okay, tell me what's going on."

I nodded and flicked newly formed tears off my cheek, pried open the fridge. I needed a drink for this.

I pulled out two Shiner Bocks, twisted off the tops, and passed one to Graham. He leaned against the counter, crossing his legs at the ankle.

"She's dead." My voice sounded detached, like it belonged to someone else.

I took a long pull of the beer, then folded my arms across my stomach, clutching the cold bottle to my chest.

"That's fucking awful. Do you know what happened?" Graham's face looked stricken.

"I don't know all the details just yet, only what Tina has told me."

I hesitated telling him about Margot's land, but there was no point in keeping it a secret; it was going to be splashed all over the news first thing in the morning.

"Her body was found this afternoon. She'd been shot. Blasted by a shotgun. A groundskeeper discovered her body in the woods."

"Oh, Sophie, I'm so very sorry." Graham set down his beer, walked over to me, held me in his arms. I felt despicable allowing myself to be consoled like this, so I only allowed it for a quick moment before I released his hold. I slid his arms down to my sides and clasped his hands in mine.

"There's something I need to tell you." I kept my eyes trained on the floor and gave his fingers a quick squeeze. "Abby was found on Margot's land. At the lake. Where I've been meeting the girls to shoot." I flicked my gaze to his.

His hands fell limp in mine; his eyes blazed with obvious fear.

"I don't understand."

"I don't, *either.*"

"Sophie, what the fuck? That's crazy." He pulled his hands away from mine, grabbed his beer, sipped it. I couldn't read his expression; I couldn't tell if he was mad at me or alarmed about all of our well-being the way Tina had been.

"Jesus," he continued, his head cocked back, his eyes staring up at the ceiling. "That could've been you."

I knew this was probably my last chance to come clean about all I knew; I wanted to tell him that there probably hadn't been a boogeyman lurking around Margot's land, that the real culprit was most likely Margot herself. Or Margot and Brad. Or just Brad. But the truth stayed lodged inside my chest, a stubborn, stabbing pain.

"I know," I said instead, and then felt guilty for playing along with this scenario, as if I were milking undeserved sympathy.

"Any suspects?"

I shook my head, drained the rest of my beer. *Brad. Margot. Margot and Brad.*

"Her poor parents."

I felt my shoulders relax when he said this; I was happy the focus was back off me. "And your friend, Jill or whatever — sorry, I can't keep them straight —" he said with genuine apology in his voice.

"Jill, yes," I said softly.

"She must be in shambles."

I nodded, bit down on my lower lip.

"Oh, Soph," he said, drawing me back into a hug. "I'm *so* sorry for your friend."

I buried my head in his chest, which

smelled charred and tangy from the grill, and this time, allowed myself to be folded into his arms while a rigid dam inside me burst and my chest began to quake with sobs.

Abby is dead. Abby is dead. Abby is dead.

43

Friday, April 20, 2018

It's Friday, late morning. The sky outside my window is stained with black storm clouds, but it hasn't rained yet and the air outdoors feels stuffy and oppressive.

I'm back inside just now from my walk on the trail. I couldn't bear to stay in the house this morning, waiting for the full story about Abby to drop, so as soon as Graham and Jack left, I bolted out the back door and headed up the quiet street. I couldn't even still myself long enough to sit behind my laptop and wait for it to spring to life — I needed to keep moving.

I woke up at daybreak this morning, my eyes puffy from crying, and powered up my phone. As of six thirty there was no news story yet about Abby. And even though I was itching to turn on the television or peek at my cell while the three of us ate a rushed breakfast of toast and overly cooked scrambled eggs, I held myself in check in front of Graham: I knew whatever I read would only make me crumble, and I didn't want that to happen again in front of him if I could help it.

Walking up the steep crest of our street, I slid my phone from my hoodie. At seven thirty, still no story. But midway through my walk, just as I was approaching the battered wooden bridge that crosses the stream, my phone pinged from inside my pocket.

It was Tina, the town crier. A text. No message, just the link to a piece in the *Mapleton Times,* which I promptly clicked on. It wasn't a long story, only a quick paragraph.

BODY OF LOCAL MISSING GIRL FOUND IN WOODS

The body of Abby Wilson, 17, was found yesterday afternoon in the woods on a parcel of private land on Cedar Lake, ending a near-weeklong search for the Mapleton teenager. The victim of an apparent homicide, Abby was last seen with her boyfriend, Brad Simmons, on Friday evening when he dropped her off at home after dinner. Authorities said that Wilson's body was discovered by a groundskeeper and that she is the victim of a shotgun wound. No suspects have been named yet and the Seminole County medical examiner will perform a full autopsy to determine time of death, but authorities are speculating that the preliminary findings show the time of death to be close to the time of Wilson's disappearance, possibly within hours. This story is still developing.

I stashed the phone back in my pocket without replying to Tina and ran the rest of the way home.

I'm pacing the hallway now, churning from room to room, my head spinning with this latest piece of news.

The preliminary findings show the time of death to be close to the time of Wilson's disappearance . . .

My mind chews on this tidbit, working it over and over; it brings me a twinge of relief. It doesn't absolve me, but at least I can tell myself that sharing my secret about Margot and Brad probably wouldn't have saved Abby; what happened to her most likely happened the same night she went missing. Even if I had told someone about the text, the terrible outcome would have still been the same.

Part of me wants to share this turn of events with someone, and I'm struck by the strange urge to call Graham. Not to tell him *everything,* but to share this latest update, to simply say that the search for Abby had been futile — it was over before it even started.

This won't exonerate me, of course, but somehow it might start to scrub away at the filthy shame I've been drenched in these past few days.

But I can't call Graham now because as I'm standing here in the living room, chewing on a frayed fingernail and staring out the window, I see a police car pull up in front of the house and park.

44

I watch them file out of the car and stroll up the narrow sidewalk toward the house. A square-jawed man with a tall, broad-shouldered woman. Both in plain clothes. He's wearing aviator sunglasses but the woman's eyes are unshielded, and as she scans the outside of the house, she squints them into an unfriendly expression. Dread seeps over me and I want to fall to the floor, hide beneath the window, and crawl, commando-style, to the back of the house and not answer the door.

But the knocking begins — sharp, quick raps — which sends adrenaline zinging through my body, giving me an instant headache.

I open the door.

"Sophie O'Neill?" the man asks with a quick flash of a smile. Dimples pool on both of his cheeks, and as he removes his shades, tucking them into the front of his white oxford shirt, smile lines crinkle around his pale blue eyes.

"Yes, that's me." I'm still in my jogging clothes, and my white T-shirt is pasted to my body, damp with sweat. I should've changed when I saw them approaching. I feel dirty, exposed.

"I'm Detective Flynn," he says, slipping his badge from a back pocket for me to inspect. "Mike Flynn. And this is my partner, Wanda Watkins."

He sticks out his hand for me to shake and I take it. His grip is strong and his skin is dry like cardboard.

"Good to meet you both," I say, my eyes now traveling to Wanda, who still has her face crimped into a tight squint.

"Pleasure, ma'am," she says. Her voice is brash and her accent is thick East Texas.

"Could we come in for a minute?" she asks, swatting a hand in front of her face as if to fan it, as if the sweltering heat outside is my fault. Her hair is a helmet of brassy blond curls and she's wearing a maroon skirt suit with honest-to-goodness shoulder pads. She looks less like a police officer and more like someone who would've given me a makeover at the Merle Norman counter in high school. And what kind of name is Wanda Watkins? I've already taken an instant dislike to her, and in my head I've now childishly renamed her "What the What."

"Of course," I say, ushering them into the living room. "May I ask what this is about?" I add, after they've both taken seats on the edge of the sofa, leaving me no choice but to sit in the armchair opposite them, which puts me on the defensive, the pair of them facing me down.

"We're sure you've heard about Abby Wilson," Detective Flynn says, brushing a speck of lint off the knee of his freshly pressed dress pants. He looks up at me with an expectant, warm smile.

"I have indeed," I say. My eyes fall to my lap. "And it's terrible. I feel just awful for her family," I bumble, casting around for something proper to say. "I'm sorry but I forgot to offer you something to drink." I suddenly feel cotton mouthed and need a sip of water. I rise from my chair and step into the kitchen. "Coffee? Tea?" I ask over my shoulder, sounding, again, like a character in a television drama. Doesn't everyone offer the police coffee in TV shows?

"No, we're fine," Detective Flynn answers.

My hands wobble as I fill a glass with tap water and take a few swallows before returning to the living room.

Wanda's eyes take in the surroundings —

framed pictures of Graham, Jack, and me resting on the mantel; a faded peach-colored ottoman that Jack loves to dribble his juice on; tacked-up, colorful masterpieces of Jack's art hanging on the wall — before returning to my face. Her gaze is cold, her eyes cast-iron black.

"Where *were* you the night of Friday, April 13?" she asks. A notepad flipped open on her lap, she grips a ballpoint, hovering it over the blank page.

"I —" I start, but my voice catches in my throat.

Wanda needles me with her eyes.

"I was here, at home, in the early evening, with my husband and son," I say.

"And after that?" Wanda asks with a huff of impatience in her voice.

Have I *ever* met a nice Wanda? My mind ticks back: Wanda Spears, second-grade teacher, stone-faced and stern, gripping her hand around mine to try and correct my messy handwriting. Wanda Klein. A friend's mother in Florida, forever complaining. No, no nice Wandas.

"Mrs. O'Neill?" Detective Flynn's voice cuts through my reverie.

"Oh, yes, sorry. After dinner I went out to Margot Banks's lake house."

"And what time was this?" Wanda asks.

"Let's see." My hands are now clasped together, my thumbs logrolling over one another. "I guess I left the house about six thirty p.m."

"And what was the nature of your visit to Mrs. Banks's lake house?" Wanda asks, hitching a burnt-orange, penciled-in eyebrow up her forehead.

If anybody asks you about Friday night, just tell them I was with you. Yikes. I'm not sure whether I'm supposed to mention that the rest of the Hunting Wives were out there, too. I venture into this line of questioning slowly.

"We meet out there on the weekends sometimes. To chill, to have a few drinks. Like a ladies' night," I say vaguely.

"Yes," Flynn says. "We've already talked to your friends. Jill, Callie, Tina, and Margot." I sense a note of disdain in his voice as he says their names. It's slight, but it's there. As if he can read my thoughts, he changes tack, offers a quick smile. "Just confirming some details." He leans back into the sofa and clasps his hands behind his head.

I suck in a deep breath, exhale. Thank *god* I didn't just lie to them about the other three being out there. I get the sense that Wanda is trying to trip me up, trick me into lying. I have to be careful here.

"Drinking, huh?" she asks, her mouth pressed in a flat line, her eyes following her pen as she scribbles in her notebook. She glances up at me.

"What else do you do out there, besides drinking? Fish? Swim?" Her eyes are now dancing with delight. She's getting off on this. Fuck. I opt for the truth.

"Well, we also shoot guns," I say, certain they can hear the hitch in my voice. "Shotguns. Just for sport. Skeet, to be exact. I — I'm not that into it. I've only been out there a few times and I've only shot twice; I'm a total rookie," I add, hoping this makes me seem all the more innocent.

The sounds of Wanda's pen scratching across the page sets my already threadbare nerves on edge. I look up at Flynn, who leans forward, forearms resting on his knees. I hope I'm not the first one who's told them about the guns.

"Yes, your friends mentioned that to us as well," Flynn offers.

A sigh of relief oozes from my lungs.

"What time did you leave the Bankses' lake house that night?" he asks.

"Gosh, it was late," I say. My hands are clammy and I keep wiping my palms on the sides of the armchair, trying to dry them.

Flynn and Wanda both stare at me, waiting for me to cough up an answer.

"Honestly, I had a bit too much to drink." I feel Wanda's eyes narrow at this admission. "And I thought it might be best if I waited to drive home until I sobered up," I add, hoping this paints me as responsible. "But I actually passed out on the sofa."

"And what time was *this*?" Wanda asks brusquely.

"What time did I pass out?"

"Bingo." She's grinning again.

"Ummm, let me think." I rack my brain, try to remember.

"Look," Flynn says, "we know that Miss Wilson was with her boyfriend, Brad Simmons, until about ten thirty p.m. And we've confirmed that Brad was with a friend after that for the rest of the evening."

A friend.

I shift in my seat, pray he doesn't see me swallow the hard lump that has formed in my throat.

"What we're trying to figure out is what could've happened to Abby after Brad dropped her off."

He looks at me encouragingly, as if to imply I'm not under any suspicion.

"Our working theory is that someone followed Miss Wilson to her door that night.

That someone was possibly stalking her. There's no shortage of gun-crazy, deranged sickos around here, so we're telling everyone to steer clear of not just the actual crime scene but also the Bankses' lake house in general for now. So I have to advise you not to go out there for a while. Until it's safe."

I can feel Wanda's gaze trained on my face, can feel her sour smile even though I refuse to glance in her direction.

"It's also possible that Miss Wilson was murdered elsewhere, and that her body was later dumped on the Bankses' land," Flynn says, then clears his throat. "Sophie," he says, switching from the more formal Mrs. O'Neill, "I'm not trying to scare you, but for all we know, you ladies were also in grave danger that night."

I feel my eyes widen and I nod my head as if in agreement.

"And anything you can tell us about that night would really help. Did you notice anything at all out of the ordinary? While you guys were out on the land or once you were back inside the lake house? Anything suspicious? Cars that might've passed by? Unusual sounds?"

I shake my head, narrow my face into a mask of concern as if I'm deeply pondering something.

"No, nothing comes to mind. It was just a normal night. Except for the fact that Margot wasn't feeling great, so we cut the night short. I mean, the others left just before nine, which is kind of early for us. But I stayed."

"And why's that?" Wanda asks.

"Margot asked me to," I blurt out before I can stop myself. Their attention seems to prick at this admission. "I mean, she wasn't up for a full-on girls' night but she wasn't ready to call it a night, either. So I stuck around and we chatted and drank wine. Too much of it, obviously."

A nervous giggle escapes my lips but then I immediately put my serious face back on.

"I can tell you for certain that I was awake until midnight. I remember that very clearly because I knew I should've been heading home." I straighten up in the chair, fold my hands together in my lap.

"That's good. That's very good," Flynn says. "And about what time did you finally leave?"

"Just before three a.m. I remember that clearly, too, because it was *so* late and I knew my husband would be worried about me."

"And was he?" Wanda asks, her mouth

pressed into a smirk.

"He was actually asleep when I got home," I say triumphantly.

"So he didn't hear you come in?" she asks.

"Not when I first came in, but I took a shower almost immediately and that woke him up."

Wanda nods, flips a page, and begins filling it with fresh notes.

"And just to confirm, everyone else left by nine, you say?" Flynn asks.

"I think around nine, yes."

The image of Callie banging on the door, yanking me out of my middle-of-the-night blackout, flashes in my mind but I don't offer up this bit of information. I feel like at this point it's best to stick to Margot's story.

"And Mrs. Banks" — Flynn looks up at me as he asks this — "was she passed out, too?"

I blow a stream of air out of my cheeks. Think about how I should answer. Fuck, fuck, fuck. Margot didn't prep me on how to answer this question. Fuck.

"I'm not sure, to be honest," I say, as if I'm being anything *close* to honest.

"So it was just the two of you out there. No one else?" Flynn presses me.

No one else except for Brad. And Jamie, who later fingered me.

"Yeah, it was just us," I manage. "Kind of creepy to think someone else might have been out there, too, though."

Flynn gives me a clipped nod.

"What was the last thing you remember before *blacking* out?" Wanda asks.

"Stretching out on the sofa, drifting off."

I hope Margot has told them the same thing.

"And when I woke up, I didn't take note if Margot was still around or not. I saw the time and bolted. I knew I needed to get home. I just assumed she was asleep in her bedroom."

Flynn considers this, nods again.

I glance at Wanda, but her face is a blank and she's busy writing down everything I say.

At his hip, Flynn's cell buzzes and he silences it, but the buzzing persists.

"It's headquarters. Mind stepping outside and calling them for me?" he says to Wanda, who sighs but rises and strides out the front door.

With Wanda out of the house, the very air inside my living room feels different. Lighter. If Flynn did that on purpose, it's worked. I instantly feel more relaxed with her gone.

"I could use some more water," I say to him. "Sure you don't want anything, Detective Flynn?"

"A glass of water actually sounds nice," he says. "And please call me Mike." He slings a foot over the tattered ottoman, stretches his arm behind his head.

I grab a tumbler from the cabinet, pluck a few ice cubes from the freezer, and fill it with tap.

"Here you go." I pass the glass to him and sink back into the armchair.

"Thanks." He takes a few small sips and sets it down on the red-lacquered side table. "Sophie, if I may ask, how long have you lived in Mapleton? Your friends said you were new to town."

My *friends.* Are they really?

"Not very long. Eight months or so."

"Where are you from?"

"Chicago; well, just outside of Chicago."

"Yep, thought so," he says with a sheepish smile.

"What do you mean?"

"I mean, you're *clearly* not from around here." His blue eyes lock onto mine. His gaze is kind and under other circumstances — say, if I were single and we had met in a bar and he wasn't interrogating me on my whereabouts — I think I'd feel the slightest stirring of attraction take hold. My eyes sweep to his hand and I note the lack of a wedding band.

"I'm not, either," he says, his smile spreading into a wide grin as if we're sharing an inside joke. His hair is closely cropped into a buzz cut, the blond stubbles tipped with gray. I wonder if he's ex-military but he seems way too warm and easygoing for that. "I'm from Dallas. Oak Cliff area. Been here two years. Believe me, I know what a shock to the system this place can be."

"So why did you move?"

He rubs his jaw, which is freshly shaven. Pauses for a second before answering. "Divorce."

I feel my face grow hot. My tongue is thick in my mouth; I don't know how to respond. I mutter, "Sorry," and bring the water glass to my lips, shielding my face.

"Life," he says, tossing his hands in the air. "What ya gonna do?" The same grin spreads across his face. He wags his foot back and forth on the ottoman and I feel a closeness to him; I feel like we could indeed be at a bar together, sharing a drink.

"So how'd you meet them?" he asks, still smiling.

"Who?"

"Margot, Callie —"

"Oh yes, of course, sorry." I set my glass down, lean back into the chair. "At a fund-raiser. An old friend of mine . . ." A sting of emotion pricks my chest as I think of Erin. "Is involved in that sort of thing."

"Got it," he says. "And Margot." He drawls out her name and his eyes stay steady on mine. "You two have become close?"

He doesn't say it but I can tell he doesn't like Margot. I can imagine him trying to interview her, and how she probably came off to him. Snooty, icy. I bet he doesn't like the others, either. He can tell I'm different from them, and he likes me, I decide.

Am I close to Margot? *I'm obsessed with her. We're not close but we played spin the bottle Friday night.*

I raise my hand to my mouth, plant my chin in my palm. "I mean, we just met a month or so ago, so we're not like super close or anything, but yeah, we hit it off, I guess you'd say." I'm stammering now, dancing around the truth.

"Sophie, is there anything else you're not telling me?" His eyes search mine. "You don't have to protect anyone."

The sun outside has torn through the clouds, and light spills between us. And I trust him, I do. I think of Margot and Brad, and I want to tell him everything I know.

It's right here, dangling from my lips, begging to be yanked out. I want to come clean, spill it all to him. I can't believe I'm lying to the police. But I think of Graham, and my stomach lurches and I can't say the words. I can't tell him the truth. I would lose Graham forever and that's a risk I'm not willing to take.

"I wish there was," I say, my gaze meeting his, my hands now steady on my lap. "I wish there was some way I could help, but honestly, I've told you everything I remember about that night."

His head hangs down and I register his disappointment. But he quickly recovers his sunny demeanor and stands. Fishes in his pocket and hands me his business card.

"My cell's written on the back. Please do call me if you think of anything. I know this has been nerve-racking, and something might come to you later when you're not being put on the spot." He offers me his hand again and I shake it.

"Detective —"

"Please, it's Mike —"

"Mike. Thank you," I say, but I don't even know what exactly I'm thanking him for. For being nicer than Wanda? For pretending to accept my lies? For not pushing me any further today?

"My pleasure, Sophie." He gives my shoulder a pat with his broad hand before turning to leave. It smells woodsy and clean like soap. I follow him to the front door and watch as he steps out into the humid morning and climbs into the cruiser with Wanda, who cuts her eyes toward the house.

45

It's nighttime. I'm in the dimly lit kitchen, muddling bitters with sugar cubes for old-fashioneds. Graham's second of the night and my first, after a glass of brisk chardonnay.

I need something stiff after this day, and also, before I spring the news on Graham about the cops stopping by today.

As soon as Wanda and Flynn left, my phone was lighting up with a call from Tina.

"Did the police come over to your house, too, today?"

"They just left actually."

"What all did they ask you? What all did you tell them?" Tina's voice was a rapid-fire assault weapon in my ear. I relayed everything I told them.

"This is getting seriously freaky."

"I know." I couldn't muster more than two-word answers for Tina after being drilled by Flynn and Wanda this morning.

"Sophie," Tina said, then lowered her voice. "Don't you think it's strange that Brad was the last one with her? I mean, do you think he killed her?"

Yes. Yes I do. Either alone or with Margot's help.

"It is strange, I agree," I offered. "But the detective confirmed to me what Jill told us, that Brad was with his friend Jamie for the rest of the night after he dropped Abby off."

"The male detective?"

"Yep."

"He was kinda hot," Tina said, her voice growing devilish.

"Yeah, he was."

"I dunno, I would never say anything to anyone else, so *please* keep this between us, but I just think it's strange about Brad," she said, her voice settling back into a near whisper. "I mean, I hope to god that's *not* the case — and it's probably not — and Jill would kill me for thinking this, but I dunno, isn't the boyfriend always a suspect?"

"Have you talked to anyone else? Callie, Margot? How is Jill?"

"Callie says Jill's too distraught to come to the phone. She stopped by her house for a minute, told me Jill was a mess."

"That's terrible." I plopped onto the sofa,

felt my stomach form into a tight knot thinking about Jill.

"It really is, and I'm terrible for saying that about Brad."

"Keep me posted," I said, hoping to end the call. It worked.

I carry the two cocktails into the living room and nestle next to Graham on the sofa. He's in a playful mood and after he takes a sip, he leans over and kisses me, slides a hand under my shirt and rests it on my stomach.

"Mmmmm," he says in a low voice in my ear, "you taste so good."

I'm always shocked at how handsome he is, but here in the maple-colored, lamp-lit room with bourbon dancing through my veins, he looks especially delectable.

I brush my mouth against his, trace his velvety lips with the tip of my tongue. "Not as good as you." I run my finger down the front of his shirt, stop at the top of his jeans. I kiss him again while fiddling with the button. My arms are covered in goose bumps and I want him so bad.

From the side table, my phone jumps to life. We both freeze.

"Ignore it," he moans.

I want to, I really do, but I can't. "Gimme a sec," I breathe into his ear.

It's a text. From Tina.

You need to call me. As soon as you can.

I let out a sigh and set the phone down. The mood is blown. I wanted to tell Graham about Detective Flynn stopping by in my own time tonight. I wanted a normal moment with Graham, a break from thinking about all of this. But now that moment is punctured and the inky sickly feeling spreads over me again.

"What is it?" Graham asks.

"So, the police came by today."

"The police? Here?" He fastens his jeans, straightens up on the sofa. "Why did they come here?"

"It's no big deal, honey," I say, without a trace of conviction in my voice to back it up. "They just wanted to ask me some questions. Abby was found out on the land, you know."

"Guess so, but what would *you* know? And why didn't you say anything about this earlier?"

"I was waiting for the right moment. And they just wanted to know if I'd seen anything suspicious out there. Like you said, it could've been me." My voice rises and I'm in danger of sounding indignant. "Anyway, that's Tina texting. She wants me to call her. I told her to keep me posted about Jill."

"Oh, yes, of course, I'm sorry. Make the call."

"Thanks. Sorry, honey." I swipe the phone from the table, step into the dining room, and angle myself away from Graham.

"What's up?" I ask, with more annoyance in my voice than I intend.

"Sophie." Tina's voice is tinged with what sounds like fear. "I just hung up with Callie. Jill just called her."

"And —"

"The full details of the autopsy are in."

I suck in my breath and hold it, steeling myself for what I'm about to hear.

"And Abby . . ." Tina's voice sounds more spooked than I've ever heard it. "Abby was pregnant."

46

Saturday, April 21, 2018

It's Saturday afternoon, nearly four o'clock, and I'm driving over to Callie's. The sky is cloudless and the heat is unrelenting. It's pizza-oven hot inside my SUV, and sweat pools on my chest. I blot it with the top of the cotton camisole I'm wearing and blast the AC.

Last night I stayed on the phone with Tina for another ten minutes while she told me all she'd heard: At the time of her death, Abby was approximately two months pregnant. Presumably Brad's. And Jill is falling to pieces, of course.

"She needs us," Tina explained, so we're gathering again at Callie's house this afternoon.

Graham isn't too happy about it, especially after our interrupted date last night, but in the end, I convinced him that I needed to make an appearance.

"I know this sounds awful, but you're not even really that close to them, are you?" he asked, nursing a third old-fashioned, the alcohol seeming to numb his usual sensitivity.

"Does that matter? I mean, Jill's whole world is crashing down!"

And, of course, I want to comfort Jill in any way I can, but also, I *have* to find out the latest. I need to know everything and I need to know it now.

"I'm being a dick; I'm sorry." Graham folded his hands between his legs.

I scooted closer to him, rubbed his back. "Thanks for understanding, honey."

Tina also told me that Jill had no idea Abby was pregnant, and that according to Brad, he didn't know, either. I find it difficult to believe that Abby would've kept this from Brad. Surely that's the real reason he was trying to dump her. And, most likely, the reason he killed her. I no longer wonder if Brad did it; I'm certain he did. And I'm positive Margot helped him. After Graham slid into a bourbon slumber last night, I panicked and almost called Flynn. I sat at the kitchen table with my cell parked in one hand and the detective's business card in the other. I flicked the edge of it with my thumbnail, so much so that I tore it, but in the end, I couldn't force myself to make the call.

Margot, Callie, and Tina are all gathered on the sectionals in the living room, clutching tall glasses of iced tea. Like last time, Rosa greets me at the door and shows me in. She strolls to the kitchen and returns with a glass of iced tea for me. It's sweetened with sugar and it's exactly what I need after the blast of afternoon heat.

Margot lifts her chin to me when I walk in and Callie gives me a deadpan "Hello."

"This is tasty, Rosa, but please, I need something stronger," Margot pleads. Rosa disappears and returns with a chilled bottle of Ketel One vodka, plants it in the center of the glass coffee table.

Margot twists the lid. "I know I'm bad, but this shit is stressful," she says, pouring a layer of vodka on top of her tea. "Any other takers?"

Callie, as usual, copies Margot precisely and tops off her own glass and Tina follows suit.

I decline. "Mommy duty for the rest of the evening, I'm afraid," I say. But really, I'm in no mood to get soused while being here. I can feel Margot's disapproval beam at me from across the room, but I won't look in her direction.

"Where is she?" Margot asks, twisting a thin silver watch around her wrist.

"She just texted me," Callie says. "She's heading over now."

Naked sunlight beams into the back garden and bounces off the water feature. The effect is blinding and makes me squint. I feel uneasy being here. I feel off center, as if the whole world is about to tilt into an uncomfortable direction.

Jill opens the front door and stands in the entryway for a moment, fanning herself. She's dressed in a black wrap sundress, and giant, rounded sunglasses cover her face. Margot crosses the room, envelops her in a hug.

"Here, have a sip." Margot passes Jill her tea, once they're seated.

Jill takes a long, slow sip. She sets down the drink and removes her glasses. Her eyes are as swollen as used tea bags, and she pats the lids with her ring finger.

"They, they —" Jill starts to say, but then her voice cracks. Margot slides closer to her, reaches out to pat her arm. Jill exhales, then continues: "They ransacked Brad's room this morning. The police. *And* his car. He's the primary suspect now." She's shaking, and when Margot tries to put an arm around her, to console her, Jill shrugs her away.

"I mean, he didn't even *know* Abby was pregnant!" Jill's voice rises into a shriek. "He would've told me if he did, I know he would've. I mean, I'm his mom, and he keeps things from me, but he would've told me this. Bastards. He's heartbroken over Abby and now he has to deal with this. It's all so unfair."

"Wasn't he with Jamie all night? Isn't that enough for the police?" Callie asks.

At the mention of Jamie's name, my face flushes.

"You would think so, but apparently not," Jill says. She picks up Margot's tea, slams the rest of it. "They're saying there's no one else to verify the boys' alibis. They haven't arrested Brad, but after they tore through his room, they confiscated his phone." Jill sighs. "His texts were all deleted. He always erases them; he doesn't like me combing through his business, but it's not like they'll find anything anyway. But the cops told me they'll get access to all of it in a day or two from the cell company. I can't believe this is happening to us."

I risk a look at Margot and see that she's fidgeting and visibly uncomfortable.

Get rid of her.

Flynn will see the text and then he'll know. He'll know about Brad and Margot, and before long he'll know about me and Jamie, too. It will all come out. I feel nauseated. Like I'm on a runaway train.

"That's seriously fucked up. I'm *so* sorry, Jill," Callie says. "You guys have a good lawyer, right?"

Jill waves a hand dismissively. "Of course we do. And we'll get through this." She rattles the ice around in the empty tea glass. "Brad isn't perfect, but he's also not a killer."

47

In the car on the drive home from Callie's, the iced tea crept up into the back of my throat; I felt like I was going to be sick. Just before I left, Margot had locked her eyes onto mine as if to say, *Stick to the story.*

I'm back at home now, busying myself in the kitchen, dishing up bowls of rocky-road ice cream for Jack and Graham. I have no appetite, but I spoon myself a fist-size amount into a dish, just to play along. As I lick the back of the metal ice cream scoop and drop it into a glass of water in the sink, there's a knock at the door.

Before I can turn to answer it, I hear Graham already opening the door and greeting someone. Detective Flynn. I know this because I hear Jack's excited voice, pealing down the hall. "Police guy! Police guy!" Which is what he calls the cops. He must've clocked Flynn's cruiser.

Graham's face is flushed as I step into the

entryway.

"Detective Flynn, this is my husband, Graham," I say, even though I'm quite sure Flynn has already introduced himself.

"Pleasure to meet you," Flynn says, smiling to Graham, his dimples winking. "And this little guy must be —"

"Our son, Jack," Graham says, protectively slinging an arm around Jack's shoulders.

"What can I do for you?" I ask. The inside of my mouth is filmy with ice cream.

"Do you mind if I come in and have a word?"

"Not at all, of course. Honey," I say to Graham, "ice cream's up in the kitchen if you wanna . . ." I motion with a flick of my head for Graham to take Jack into the dining room.

Flynn steps inside but we remain standing in the entryway, out of earshot of Jack and Graham. He fiddles with his keys before slipping them in the pocket of his dark dress jeans.

"I'm not sure if you've heard about the autopsy report, but it was determined that Abby was pregnant at the time of her death."

I nod. "I have indeed. It's terrible. I don't even know what to say."

"I have to let you know," Flynn says, dropping his gaze to the floor, "that this pivots our investigation considerably."

"Meaning?"

"The boyfriend, Brad Simmons, is now our lead suspect," Flynn says, pasting his eyes on mine.

I swallow. Try and take a measured breath. Swipe the back of my hand along my hairline, which is damp with sweat.

Flynn looks at me expectantly, and I feel my eyes widen as if I'm oblivious.

"Your friends," he continues, "mentioned that you all were at the Simmonses' lake house a week before Abby vanished."

"Yes, that's right. I was there." My voice sounds foreign to my ears, faraway and robotic.

"So, you met Abby. And you met Brad, and saw them together?" His blue eyes trace my face, searching for clues.

I nod.

"What did you think of him? Of them as a couple? Of Abby? Everyone keeps telling me how normal they seemed, how caring and attentive Brad was, but I thought you might have a different perspective. I mean, you haven't known them all that long, so you might not be as invested in covering for Brad."

I'm aware of how pin-drop quiet the rest

of the house has become. I can imagine the scene on the other side of the wall: Jack has discarded his empty bowl and padded down the hall toward his room to his iPad. And I can sense Graham standing stock-still in the dining room, straining to hear our conversation.

My hands have taken on a life of their own, and I realize I've been twisting the bottom of my camisole with them; Flynn clearly notices, too.

This is yet another chance to part ways with Margot's script, to tell him all I know. But I can't. I might be bulldozed for it soon but I can't be the one driving the bulldozer.

"Honestly, I have to agree with what everyone else is saying. They just seemed like normal teens to me, and yes, Brad did seem genuinely caring toward Abby. So, I'm shocked, of course, at this latest turn." I raise my eyes to Flynn's, stare at him unflinchingly.

He exhales so sharply it sounds like a whistle.

"Sophie." His voice is kind but edged with impatience. "I can't shake the feeling that you're not telling me everything. That you're holding something back. Now why *is* that?"

Because I am.

I swear I can hear the creak of the wooden floorboards in the next room, of Graham shifting his weight in his sneakers. The thought of him absorbing every word of this conversation makes my stomach tighten.

"I have no idea what you're talking about." I keep my voice calm and measured. "I wish I could help you more; I really, really do. But I've told you all I know, which isn't much." I look up at him, risk a brisk smile.

He crosses his arms in front of his toned chest, taps his lips with an index finger. He stands this way for a long, uncomfortable moment and my hands resume their twisting of my shirt.

"Then I guess I ought to leave you alone," he finally says, "for the time being."

"Sorry, I really wish I could've been of more use." My hand reaches for the knob on the front door, and when my arm leaves my side, I can feel that my pits are drenched with sweat.

"You've got my card, Sophie, if you have second thoughts," he adds before heading to his vehicle.

I don't even wait for him to close his car door before I shut the front door and blow out a huge sigh.

I turn around. Graham is standing right in front of me, which causes me to flinch.

"Jesus, you scared the shit out of me." My voice sounds like air hissing from a balloon, spraying all my anxiety from Flynn's visit all over Graham.

"Sorry," he says. But he doesn't look sorry; he looks tense and flustered.

I move to step around him so I can go and check on Jack. Graham touches my arm. "Don't you think we need to talk about this?"

"There's nothing to talk about."

"Don't you think it's weird he keeps coming by?" Graham's voice veers on hysterical.

Yes, I do. "Maybe? But I guess he's just covering all bases."

"*Are you hiding something?*" His normally soothing hazel eyes dart over my face, scanning it.

"What the hell, Graham," I practically yell. "Why would you even suggest that?"

"I don't know." His shoulders slump as he lets out a huge sigh. "But something feels off. You didn't sound like yourself when you were talking to that detective."

Pressure builds behind my eyes and I pinch the bridge of my nose. He's right, of course, but I can't keep the snippiness out of my voice. "You try talking to the police. It's nerve-racking as hell!" I storm down the hall toward Jack's room.

48

Monday, April 23, 2018

Digging, digging, and more digging. That's all I've been doing this morning. Plunging my shovel into the earth and scooping out spongy soil. Sweat streams down my back as I tear into the ground, digging deep troughs for a stand of fig trees I'll buy later this afternoon at the local nursery.

I had to find something to do to keep my hands and mind busy so I don't go insane. It's like I'm pitching a tent, claiming space, and saying, "Here is my little plot of sanity." It's the only way I can function, the only way I won't crack in front of Graham or, worse, in front of Jack.

It's nearly eleven o'clock and the sun is perched overhead, set to broil. I need to call it a day. I can feel my skin beginning to redden, and I need to go inside and refill my water glass. But instead, I plant my foot on the edge of the shovel and keep carving away at the trench. As the blade of my shovel strikes against a stubborn root, I hear the clapping of a car door.

I stand and circle to the side of the house and see Detective Flynn striding toward the front door. Fuck.

"Hi, Mike. I'm out here," I call to him, motioning to the backyard.

He climbs the hill, and when he reaches me, he flicks a line of sweat off his brow with the back of his hand.

"Sophie," he says, dipping his head in deference. "Hard at work, are we?"

"Yep, but I need a break. What's up?"

We're standing in the shade of the house, but it's still too sweltering, so I invite him in. He takes a seat at the dining table and I bring us each a glass of ice water.

Flynn takes a sip and cools his hands on the sides of the sweating glass.

"Let's try this again," he says. "Are you *sure* you've told me everything?"

Sunlight dances off his water glass, sending sparkles across the wooden table. My eyes trail the scattered light as it hits notches and grooves on the scarred surface.

What does he know? What has he found out?

He's probably gotten all of Brad's texts by now; he's probably seen the text from

Margot. He could know about Jamie and the fact that I've lied to him about it just being Margot and me out at the lake house that Friday night, but who knows?

"Look, this is your last chance to tell me everything. Your last chance with just me around. I want to help you, but you need to tell me exactly what went on Friday night and you need to tell me now."

I study the backs of my hands, which are stained with dirt, despite my elbow-length gardening gloves. My mind is racing. I should've gotten a lawyer by now, but how would I have explained that to Graham? I have no idea how to answer Flynn, so I decide to call his bluff.

"I have nothing new to offer you," I say as I keep staring at the backs of my hands.

He edges his water glass away from him, props an elbow on the table. "I was really hoping to break through here with you, Sophie, I really was. I like you. But I'm afraid we're going to have to do this differently now. I'm going to have to ask you to come downtown to the station with me."

"I don't understand."

Flynn drums his thumbs on the table, fidgets again with the water glass before finally saying, "We got an anonymous tip late last night." He trains his gaze on the water glass as if peering into a Magic 8 Ball.

"And?"

"And the murder weapon, a shotgun, was discovered in the woods on Margot's land. Not far from where Abby's body was." He looks up and fixes those sky-blue eyes on me expectantly.

Confusion clouds my brain. If they found the weapon, then why does he need to bring *me* into the station? I guess because he knows I know more than I've told him, and now it's glaringly clear that I have to fess up. This is horrible. But maybe there is a way I can still keep it all from Graham.

"I just need to change into something fresh and I'll head that way," I say, standing up and gulping down the rest of my water.

"You're free to change but you're going to have to come with me." Flynn rises also, scraping his chair against the floor as he stands.

"Why?"

"Sophie, please," he says with thinly masked exasperation. "When they pulled the shotgun from the woods, they were able to recover fingerprints."

I stare at him, dumbfounded.

He jangles his keys in his pocket, cocks his head to one side while he delivers the rest. "And the prints on the gun are an exact match to yours."

49

The inside of the interrogation room is meat-locker cold, so I'm grateful for the steaming cup of coffee that Flynn has placed in front of me. The room is bare, but the walls are painted in a warm shade of yellow, calling to mind a preschool classroom instead of a police station. It must be a small-town touch, but it makes the experience of being here even more disorienting, not less so.

The drive to the station was wordless, with me in the back of the cruiser, my mind racing as trees blurred past. How could my prints be on the gun? And how could they have already matched them? But then I remember: being fingerprinted at the DMV to get my driver's license when we first moved back to Texas.

I squeezed my cell, thought about calling Graham, but couldn't bring myself to do so. I thought about calling a lawyer, but I don't know any in Mapleton, or anywhere else for that matter. Why would I?

My thoughts went back to that final Friday night at the lake house, and I heard Margot's voice in my head.

We brought Daddy's gun; it doesn't kick as hard. Promise.

It all suddenly became clear to me. Margot. That bitch. She framed me. She must have. It had been her plan all along. Her text to me: *I want you, to stay,* the kiss we shared during spin the bottle, her insistence that I not leave, that I use that particular gun, all of it was premeditated.

By the time Flynn wheeled the cruiser into his dedicated parking spot, I was shaking with rage and bursting at the seams to tell him everything.

And that's exactly what I do.

I retell him every moment of that night, only leaving out the part about playing spin the bottle and the fact that Jamie and I were together.

I tell him about the gun and how Margot had prompted me to use it. He advises, though, that while there were other prints on the gun, it was my prints and mine alone that were lifted from the trigger. I then tell him about Margot's text to Brad: *Get rid of her.* I tell him all I know about their relationship, and even about catching them having sex on the boat dock. Each revelation feels like a tiny stab, like I'm digging a knife deeper into Margot's back. It feels good. My hands are shaking but I'm filled with the righteousness of someone setting the record straight.

The whole time I'm talking, Flynn listens, nods, and scribbles notes on a pad while the tape recorder whirs between us.

But one thing I notice as I spill everything to him is that his face doesn't register surprise. It registers the same look of exasperation I saw back at my house. And when I finish, he pauses the recording and stands.

"I'm going to get more coffee. Refill?"

I hand him my paper cup and he exits the room.

I felt puffed up and strong from telling him everything, but now I feel small and deflated, and even though I can't see behind the pane of glass that lines the wall opposite from where I'm sitting, I can imagine Wanda's eyes boring into me from the other side.

Flynn returns, sets my coffee down on the table, and plops into the chair directly in front of me. When his eyes meet mine, they're hard, drained of their usual warmth and care.

My stomach clenches.

He just sits and stares at me, as if waiting me out, only dropping his gaze to blow a curl of steam off his coffee.

"Well?" I venture.

He sighs and folds his arms across his chest. "Sophie, I need to let you know that Mrs. Banks, um, Margot, came into the station this morning of her own volition. With her lawyer."

My stomach clenches even tighter. Margot remains one step ahead of me.

"And she preemptively confessed to us all about her relationship with Brad. She told me everything." He pauses and lets the word *everything* dangle between us.

I have no idea what *everything* means, but based on the sense of dread that washes over me, I'm assuming he is referring to Jamie.

Not only has she framed me for Abby's murder, she set me up to lie to the police.

"Before we go any further, I'll remind you that this is a criminal investigation. A murder investigation." Flynn reaches forward, punches the pause button, and the tape begins whirring again.

"Now, let's go back to Friday night. We are most interested in the hours between midnight and four a.m." His face darkens as he says the rest. "That time frame where you claim to have been passed out."

My mouth is dry as chalk, so I take a small sip of coffee.

"I *was* passed out." My hands tremble, so I drop them to my sides, jam them under my legs, which are pumping. I can't seem to still my body.

Flynn turns the pages in his notepad. "And it says here that you told us, when we first questioned you, that you left the Bankses' lake house just before three a.m.? Is that correct?"

"Yes, yes it is."

"And you went straight home and showered, waking your husband? Can he verify the time?"

My throat constricts at the word *husband.* Oh, Graham.

"Yes. But I didn't head straight home."

Flynn's eyebrows shoot up in pricked attention.

"I — I went to the jogging trail near my house and ran for a few miles." Even though I'm telling the truth, my face grows warm, and I feel as though I'm lying. It's the same feeling of having a cop trail behind your car and you start to believe you're doing something illegal.

I take a deep breath, steady myself.

"Why is this important?"

Flynn's mouth turns into a sour line. "Another thing I need to let you know is this: The results of the autopsy came back, and the coroner is placing the time of death between the hours of midnight and four."

This is so much worse than I could've imagined. So much worse. I feel like someone has knocked me across the chest with a bat and the wind is kicked out of me. The coffee burns my stomach, makes me sweat. What the fuck. But I *was* passed out, and then I was on the trail, and then I was at home.

"That's what I keep telling you!" My voice has turned sharp but I can't help it. "Margot has *framed* me. Don't you see? She and Brad must have killed Abby after I passed out, knowing full well that I wouldn't have an alibi. By the way, what's *her* alibi?"

"Mrs. Banks was with Brad just after midnight at an all-night diner on the outskirts of town. They stayed there for a few hours, drinking beer and eating breakfast. Arguing some. We have an eyewitness to back it up. And after that, Margot was home with her husband."

I stare into Flynn's eyes. Any trace of camaraderie we had before has now vanished. He thinks I'm lying; he thinks I'm guilty.

"Look, Sophie," he says with a puff of irritation, "you're still hiding things from me. And this is getting old."

Jamie. Now is the time to come clean about Jamie.

And I do. I tell him that we kissed, that we played spin the bottle, that I made a huge mistake and left at three a.m. to go home to my family. Flynn lets me know that Margot already told him about my fling with Jamie.

"You have to believe me. I'm being set up." My voice is a strangled cry.

"I want to, I really do, but you lied to me."

"Only because Margot asked me to. And threatened me. Not in actual words but she implied she'd tell my husband about Jamie if I didn't tell the police that she and I were together Friday night."

This stops Flynn in his tracks for a second, but only for a second.

"Sophie, you're *still* not telling me everything."

I guess he wants me to tell him that I shot Abby, but I didn't.

"What do you mean?"

"From what I understand, you're quite obsessed with Margot." He flicks his eyes on mine. I feel my cheeks burn; I can't hide my expression if I wanted to.

"Where did you get that from? Who told you that?"

"It doesn't matter."

Margot. It had to be. Unless my fixation is more apparent than I thought. But no, no one else would know except maybe Callie, who was clocking my every move.

Flynn's voice snaps me out of my reverie. "And *you* were the only one present at the scene. And it's your prints on the weapon."

I drop my gaze to my lap. This is so fucked up. I feel like I'm trapped in a giant ball of yarn and every time I try to escape I just get more tangled up.

"But —"

"So what *I* think happened is this: Maybe you thought you were doing something Margot would've wanted you to do." His coffee cup is empty and he flips it upside down with a twist of his hand. He drums his fingers on the bottom of the overturned cup, waiting for my response.

My mind casts back to that night, searching, thinking. *You were the only one present at the scene.* No, no I wasn't. The image of Callie wrenching open the front door and asking for Margot floods back into my brain again.

I straighten in my chair, meet Flynn's direct stare. "I know how this all looks, and you're right, there's something I left out. Something important. When I was blacked out, I heard a loud noise that jolted me awake. A pounding at the door. It was Callie, looking for Margot, and she seemed frantic."

Flynn narrows his eyes at me. Shakes his head. "Mrs. Jenkins returned home just after nine o'clock, where she remained all night with her husband."

"That's not true! She was there!"

"You're reaching, Sophie, you really are. And before you point the finger at Jamie, he was home with his parents just after midnight. Look, even with all this evidence, I still don't have enough to arrest you. But I have to advise you that you're our main person of interest at this point."

My skin grows cold. My posture slumps from the adrenaline draining from my body. I'm numb. I can't do anything other than stare at the table.

"You're free to go now," Flynn says with a dismissive flick of his hand. "But you shouldn't even think of leaving town."

I push my chair back and stand. Turn and head to the door. As I clasp down on the metal handle to open it, Flynn fires a parting shot at me.

"And, Sophie, I would highly recommend you get a lawyer."

50

I'm parked outside of Graham's office. I need to tell him what's going on and I don't want to wait until tonight.

I texted him a few minutes ago.

Me: Can you come outside? I'm here . . .

Graham: Ooooh, a surprise visit. I like it. Be right out.

His enthusiasm pierced my heart, making me feel even worse about what I was going to tell him.

I watch him stride to the car, sandy blond hair being licked by sunlight, his hands jammed in the pockets of his khakis.

He climbs in, curves a hand around the back of my neck, and moves his soft lips against mine.

"Couldn't wait till tonight to see me, eh?"

He rests his hand on my thigh, delight twinkling in his eyes.

Placing my hand on top of his, I stare straight ahead. It will be easier to deliver this news if I'm not locked in his dreamy gaze.

"I'm just going to come out and say it."

I feel his fingers twitch underneath mine.

"I just left the police station. I've been framed for Abby's murder."

He yanks his hand away. "Sophie, what the fuck are you talking about?"

"I know it sounds insane, but just hear me out."

I turn and meet his eyes and tell him all about shooting the gun — how Margot urged me to use it — how she framed me. And about how Margot is banging Brad. And her ominous text to him about Abby.

"Wait," he says, with true disdain clouding his face. "Margot's sleeping with her best friend's son? Sophie, how old is he? Is that even legal?" He shudders as he asks this.

And, of course, I know the answer. It's legal. In Texas, consensual age is seventeen. Brad and Jamie are eighteen. I googled it late the other night when my mind was spiraling out of control, wondering if I was going to get locked up for being with Jamie.

"I told you these women were crazy. Especially Margot."

He gnaws on his lower lip, thrums his fingers against the seat.

"So this Brad — he was out there that night with you and Margot, and you were okay with it?"

I was going to tell him about Jamie next, but my courage has now evaporated.

"No, I wasn't okay with it." The indignant tone I've adopted during our recent conversations has crept back into my voice. "That's why I told you I would stop hanging out with them. Only, Abby went missing and I needed to be there for Jill, who genuinely seems nice. It's honestly Margot and her shadow, Callie, who are nuts."

"But why would Margot frame *you*? Why would she single you out?"

I don't tell him that it's because I became entranced by her and, therefore, was the easiest prey.

"I guess I was the new, dumb girl."

"And you really think she killed Abby? With Brad's help? You think they're capable of that?"

I nod.

"I can't fucking believe you've got yourself tangled up in this mess."

"Well, I didn't do it! It's not like it's my

fault. And nothing's going to happen to me, Graham. I'm innocent. Don't panic," I say, while my own voice rises with panic.

"Well, we need to get a lawyer. Like right now. Sounds like Margot's dangerous *and* powerful. I'll ask around the office —"

"Are you crazy? I don't want everyone knowing about this."

"Okay, okay, I'll find out quietly. But we need to deal with this. The right way."

His whole body is now contorted against the side of the door, as if he's intent upon putting as much space between the two of us as possible.

The urge to tell him about Jamie comes over me again.

"Graham," I say, my voice trembling. I glance over at him, and the look of concern on his face is so strong that my voice melts in my throat.

"What is it?" His eyes are lasers drilling over my face.

"Nothing. I'm just — I'm so sorry."

51

Tuesday, April 24, 2018

The holes I dug for the fig trees yesterday are filled with rainwater, a pair of black, blank eyes reflecting back at me. It poured last night and I'm now standing over them, trying to decide what to do with myself. Go to the nursery to buy the trees and actually plant them? Or do what I should be doing and pick up my cell to call the lawyer whom Graham found?

Instead, I stay outside and pace the length of the backyard, eyeing the herb beds for signs of new weeds and scrutinizing the flower garden to see if it's time to deadhead the roses.

I'm procrastinating and I know I should step inside and get the call over with, but I'm not ready to talk to a lawyer just yet; there's an irrational part of me that believes this will all go away. That Flynn will call and tell me there's been some mistake and he's sorry and I'm off the hook.

But even the most stubborn part of me knows this isn't true, and even though it's only ten o'clock in the morning, I'm already coated in sweat, so I cease my pacing and go inside.

I'm in the back bathroom washing my hands and freshening up when I hear the back door open and slam shut. My heart lurches as I wonder who the hell is in my house. But then I hear Graham's voice.

"Sophie? Where are you?"

He sounds steamed; I tread down the hall and find him in the dining room. His hair is mussed and his cheeks are mottled red as if he rushed getting over here. He's clearly in distress.

"What the *fuck* is this?" He slings a newspaper from under his armpit and thuds it against the dining table.

I step over to the paper and peer at the headline.

TEENAGE SEX TRIANGLE WITH PROMINENT SOCIALITE LINKED TO MURDER OF LOCAL GIRL

My stomach coils into a knot. I scan the article and see my name. And then Jamie's.

Fuck.

I scan further, my eyes roving over the print as fast as possible. Even though I'm not named specifically as a suspect — most likely thanks to some shred of decency in Flynn — the article does go into the fact that my prints are on the murder weapon and that I'm a person of interest. It also goes further than I'd like into the heady night of spin the bottle.

Reading it, I wince. The paper makes it sound as if Jamie and I slept together. The vague term *relations* was used, leaving the rest up to the imagination. And it hints at my obsession with Margot. "An unnaturally close friendship quickly formed between Mrs. O'Neill and Mrs. Banks."

A picture of me, ripped from my Facebook profile, is parked next to a sleek shot of Margot in her signature, oversize sunglasses. I wonder if it's even legal for the paper to have used my image without permission, but I decide I have too many legal problems already to care.

I look up at Graham. His jaw is tense and his fists clench and unclench. He's shaking. "Did you know this was all over the papers this morning?"

"No, I've been outside all morning. I'm so —"

"So *this* is what you've been hiding all this

time?" His eyes are darting over my face and filled with such hurt I can't even hold his gaze. "Un-fucking-believable, Sophie!"

"Graham, you have to listen to me." Tears fill my eyes.

"I'm done listening to you. You lied and lied to me, Sophie. And I forgave you over and over and bought all of your horseshit excuses." He shakes his head in disgust. "I even apologized to *you* once! Here I was, trying to be the cool, evolved husband that lets his wife blow off steam with the girls, and all the while you've been playing me. Un-fucking-real." He's practically yelling at me now.

"Please, listen! This is so overblown; this is *not* what happened."

But he turns to leave. I catch his arm and my fingernails accidentally graze his skin.

"You have to believe me that this is *not* what happened; what happened meant nothing." My voice squeaks out of me. "I promise I can explain everything. I've been too afraid to tell you the truth, but I —"

"I'll pick Jack up today. You have until then to collect your things and get out."

"You're throwing me out?"

The vein on his neck bulges and throbs. "Pack a bag and leave."

"But you can't just banish me! I need to

see Jack!"

"Sophie, I honestly can't think straight right now, so you just need to go. I need space."

"But go where?"

"A fucking hotel! Or your fuck mate Margot's house! I don't know and I don't care. I just don't want to lay eyes on you right now; I don't know what to think of you. You make me sick. Stay the fuck away from us for now. And if you don't realize that I'm not fucking around here, you could push me so far that you might lose your son."

He could've kicked me in the face and it would've hurt less than hearing these stinging words. My throat constricts and I feel like I might faint. I can't believe he just said that about losing Jack.

"But you don't think I hurt Abby, do you?"

"Of course not. But I also don't believe that what you have going on with that kid, and with Margot, means nothing." He grasps the handle on the door, flings it open, and slams it behind him.

Everything in me wants to follow him outside, to yell and plead for him to come back to me. But I can't. I need to let him go for now.

My body is numb with shock. I don't know if I'll ever recover from the look of betrayal pitched on his face. I go over to the sofa and lie down. Drawing my knees into my chest, I wrap my arms around them while I convulse with sobs.

Graham is gone.

52

After an hour of sobbing on the sofa, I unlatch my knees from my chest and stand up. I can't believe Graham is kicking me out, but I can hardly say that I blame him. And I know I need to do what he requests if I want any chance of salvaging things between us and saving our family. I can't work him over anymore, I can't fix this, and who knows what he could do with Jack if I push him. The term *unfit mother* creeps into mind.

I walk down the hall toward our room, pausing at Jack's door along the way. I step inside and go over to his unmade bed, lift his Thomas the Tank Engine comforter, and bring it to my face, breathing in his little boy smell. Juice and baby shampoo. Tears flood my vision, so I drop the comforter and make his bed, tucking his favorite stuffed bear next to his pillow before leaving. I need to do this quickly, before I lose my nerve and Graham comes home to find me here.

Even though it kills me, I go into our closet and pull down my pale pink duffel bag from the top shelf. I yank a few shirts off their hangers and stuff those in the bag with some shorts and pajamas. I swipe my toothbrush and toiletries from the bathroom and toss in a pair of sandals. I'm not packing a lot; I'm determined to get back home in a few days, no matter what I have to do.

Before leaving, I grab a few bottles of water, some bags of chips, and the sticky note with the lawyer's number scrawled in Graham's handwriting; then, I head out.

I coast all over Mapleton. Not many choices here. A shabby, one-story motel on the east side of town that looks like a halfway house. As much as I want to punish myself and check in, I can't bring myself to do it.

I keep driving until I settle on a chain-run extended-stay motel. The sign out front advertises free breakfast and, more importantly, a pool.

I'm harboring the hope that Graham will let me bring Jack over to swim. He loves the water.

I step into the lobby and am immediately assaulted by a rack of newspapers parked next to the check-in desk. The sordid headline screams out at me, but as I walk to the desk on wobbly legs, the hotel clerk greets me with a smile. Clearly, she doesn't recognize me from the picture in the paper. And even as I slide my driver's license across the counter, her face registers nothing other than Southern hospitality.

"Here's your room key, Mrs. O'Neill. You're in 203. It's the second floor toward the middle of the building." She waves her hand to indicate the location.

The room is nice and clean enough, done up in buttery beiges and pastels with a beachy vibe. But still, the carpet holds the antiseptic odor of all hotels and there is an AC window unit, already droning noisily, instead of central air and heat. I know I won't sleep well here.

I toss my bag on the luggage rack and sit on the edge of the bed. Digging in my purse for my cell, I fish out the number to the lawyer and dial it.

"John Gunther and Associates!" a bright, female voice chirps on the other end.

"Hi, I need to speak with Mr. Gunther."

"May I tell him who's calling?"

"I'm, um, yes, this is Sophie O'Neill."

"Oh, yes!" I hear her tongue click with delight. "We've been expecting your call!" She pauses as if she wants me to respond.

I don't.

"Well, please hold the line. I'll get John for you right away!"

Cheery hold music fills my ear, but only for a second. I end the call. Cradling the cell in my hands, I let my arms flop between my legs.

I need to talk to somebody, but I'm in no mood to talk to an eager-beaver attorney.

I go to my contacts, to the people I have saved as "favorites." Erin's name is the third one. I tap it. It rings once but then the call goes straight to voice mail, as if she dismissed it. Surely that's not the case, I think, so I punch it again and listen as it rings four times and then rolls over to voice mail. I'm just about to leave a quick message for her to call back when my phone dings in my ear. With a text, from Erin.

Erin: I'm sorry, Sophie, but you're not who I thought you were.

Heat rises to my face and it feels like my body is being filled with liquid shame. I can hear my heart pounding in my ears. I'm frozen by her words. And stung. But honestly, I'm not surprised. Erin could forgive me, possibly, for keeping the Hunting Wives a secret from her, but she can't overlook my involvement with Jamie. It's a line she would never cross.

My phone nearly slips from my hands they're so clammy, so I wipe my palms on the thin, cheap, seashell-print comforter and scroll through my phone log. I stop when I reach Tina.

She usually answers on the first ring, but it rings three times before she picks up. Her voice is tentative and wary. "Hi, Sophie."

"Hey — I just wanted to call —" I'm stammering because I really don't know what to say to her.

"Listen, Bill's here," she says. "And," she continues, her voice growing softer with each word, "please don't call or text me anymore. This makes me uncomfortable. I can't talk to you anymore."

My lips tremble and I press end before she can hear me cry. What a bitch. She was okay with Margot messing around with Brad; she thought it was funny, a scene to rubberneck, but she can't handle what I did with Jamie. Even though she doesn't know the whole story. But then it hits me square in the eyes — she probably *doesn't* care at all about Jamie. It's much worse than that: She thinks I murdered Abby.

I feel sick to my stomach and realize I haven't eaten all day. I scrounge in my purse for the bag of potato chips and tear them open, but can only force myself to crunch through a few. I have no appetite.

I should try and find Rox and call her no matter where she is in the world, but I can't; I'm too ashamed. Even my mom Nikki's face pops into my mind, but I know that telling her all this will somehow make me feel so much worse.

I set my phone down on the night table, stand, and cross the room. I grab the cord to the vinyl blackout shade and yank it, darkening the space. Creeping back to the bed, I crawl under the covers.

I startle awake. The boxy clock on the bedside table reads two thirty p.m. The time of day when I pick Jack up from preschool and he flings himself into my arms, molding his little boy body into mine, fingers twining through my hair as I carry him out to the car.

Jack.

I'm sad and destroyed over Graham, but just the thought of Jack, the grief of not being able to hold him right now, to tickle his chubby neck, to hear him say *Mommy,* threatens to swallow me whole.

I slide my phone off the nightstand and call Graham. Predictably, it goes to voice mail. I don't leave a message. I let ten minutes pass and then I text him.

Me: Do you have Jack yet?

He lets five excruciating minutes pass before replying.

Graham: Yep.

Me: Where did you tell him I was?

Graham: Working. I told him you had to go back to Chicago for work. That way he won't be looking for you every five seconds.

A cry bubbles up in my throat. I cannot believe I can't see my own son. He is less than three miles away and I could just drive over, drop in, but that would be cruel.

Me: Okay. I love you.

I know I shouldn't have typed that last part but I couldn't help myself. I wait five minutes for Graham to text back, but he doesn't. Why would he? What could he possibly have to say to me right now?

I flick the bedside lamp on and sit up. Slipping my feet into my sandals, I grab my keys off the coffee table and head outside into the blinding sunlight. The leather seats in the Highlander seal themselves against my bare legs, but the heat feels good after the frostiness of the motel room. I'll need a strong drink tonight if I'm going to stand any chance of sleeping, so I turn the key in the ignition and head to the nearest liquor store.

53

Wednesday, April 25, 2018

I wake with a sharp pain in my temples, my breath still reeking of last night's bourbon.

I hadn't planned on drinking as much as I did, but with only the remainder of the potato chips for dinner, the alcohol hit my bloodstream, fogging my judgment.

I found myself refilling the plastic cup with ice and bourbon more times than I can remember.

When I arrived back at the motel from the liquor store, bottle in hand, I strode through the lobby and nabbed a copy of the newspaper. I wanted to grab them all, hide them from the rest of the motel guests, pitch them in the trash, but I lifted just one from the rack, slipped it under my arm, and hurried to my room.

Even though I kept it on the corner of the desk, far from the bed, Margot's picture peered out at me, taunting me. Every time my eye caught sight of her, rage pulsed through me. At one point, I nearly drunk dialed her to unleash my fury, but luckily, I stopped myself.

I'll have to confront her in person.

I'm still weighed down by grief, but in addition to being sad this morning, I'm something else: mad. Furious. Pulse poundingly so.

Creaking from bed, I step into the bathroom and am immediately assaulted by the sharp fluorescent lights. I flick the light switch off and run a hot shower, washing my hair in the dark.

I dress and head downstairs to the breakfast room. The sun-filled room is gloriously empty, except for an elderly man reading the paper (oh god!) and nursing a cup of coffee. I grab a Pepto-pink tray and spoon a helping of what looks to be powdered eggs on my plate, along with a jelly-filled croissant and a healthy stack of charred bacon. I need to fortify myself. My mouth is still pasty from the hangover, so in addition to the gallons of coffee I'm sure to guzzle, I also fill a large glass tumbler with orange juice.

Taking a seat at the window table, I snap a piece of bacon in two, shovel it in my mouth. Margot's image from the newspaper creeps back into my mind. Fucking Margot. I'm sure her husband is livid, but I bet he hasn't thrown her out. She's handling and being handled by her lawyers. Insulated from being under suspicion for Abby's murder by framing me. I can picture her now, lying out by the lake, sipping a chilled glass of wine without a care in the world.

And that's exactly where I plan to head to next.

54

It's Wednesday, Margot's lake day, and I'm hoping to catch her out there by surprise.

I'm at the edge of town now, turning on the country road that leads me to the lake. I don't have a real plan of attack, of what I'm going to say or do, but I can't sit by one second longer and allow her to destroy my life.

Easing onto the lake road under a dome of bright green trees, my hands practically shake on the steering wheel. It's probably partially the bourbon hangover, but it's mostly my rage. I think of Jack, waking up this morning, walking sock toed to our bedroom, looking for me, and the fury that's been simmering all night now turns to a boil until my whole body is quaking.

I'm going to call her out, ask her what the fuck she thinks she's doing to me, and let her know she's not going to get away with it. No matter what I have to do. I'm done rolling over.

I turn down Margot's drive. The grass is usually shaved and sculpted like a golf course, but today it's nearly ankle-deep and it occurs to me that the groundskeeper's work was most likely interrupted when he came upon Abby's body.

I creep down the drive farther and spot Margot's black Mercedes. Parked right next to it is Callie's. Yikes. I hadn't anticipated Callie being here. I tense at the sight of the pair of cars, and suddenly the fury I was just feeling drains, replaced by dread and adrenaline, filling my mouth with the taste of metal. Slowing the car, I park and step outside.

Even though it's still early in the day, the heat has already called the cicadas out and their buzzing and hissing fills the steamy air around me. I'm wearing a T-shirt and denim cutoffs, and sweat rings the pits of my shirt. As I make my way around the wraparound porch, I'm hoping the footfalls of my soft leather sandals won't give me away. I don't want anything to tip them off. But when I round the corner, there is no sign of Callie outside, only Margot lying out on the dock.

She's on her stomach, face aimed toward the lake, sprawled on a chaise longue. She holds a magazine with one hand and a glass of white with the other. Her right knee is bent skyward and her foot lazily circles the air above her. Her skin is even tanner than I remembered, and she's wearing a canary-yellow string bikini with a dramatic thong that punctuates her toned cheeks.

My mind is jumping like a flea as I walk down the planks of the pier; seeing Margot out here like this, carefree, just as I'd imagined, sends the anger surfing through me again. My heartbeat thuds in my ears and even though I'm treading as softly as I can, the wood creaks and groans under my feet.

Margot sets her magazine down.

"Sophie," she says without even turning around to check that it's me. "I figured you'd come."

I stand over her wordlessly, unsure of where to begin.

"I've been meaning to call you, to check on you." She has now rolled herself up on her hips and is looking at me, an elegant curve of her hand shading her eyes.

"Margot, what the fuck?" I say, and am about to continue when she cuts me off.

"Look, I'm sorry, but I *had* to come clean to the cops. I know, I know I should've told you first, but it all happened so fast. I mean, they were going to find out as soon as they saw Brad's texts, so my lawyer advised —"

White-hot rage is splitting my head in two. I can barely process what she's saying, and when my voice comes out, it's shaking with disgust. "You think I'm upset about *that*? You're a real piece of work — you've gotta be fucking kidding me! Graham has thrown me out!" I'm yelling now and my voice bounds off the calm surface of the lake.

Margot swings her legs to the side of the chaise longue, stands eye to eye with me, and plants her hands on my shoulders. "Sophie, look, you need to calm down. I said I was sorry —"

"You fucking *framed* me." I swat her hands off my shoulders.

Behind me, I hear the floorboards of the pier squeak. And then Callie's voice, cold and detached. "You need to leave."

I'm about to tell her to fuck off, when I turn to face her and see she's holding a shotgun, aimed at my chest. I freeze. Hair rises on my arms, and my chest flutters with fear. I automatically raise my palms as if in surrender and take a step back.

"Whoa," Margot says. She steps between us and places her hand on the barrel of the gun, lowering it to the ground.

"Relax," she says to Callie. "I can handle Sophie. Better yet, why don't you go and refresh our drinks? And bring Sophie some wine while you're at it."

I'm still frozen in place, unable to move, even though the nose of the gun is no longer pointing at me. Callie's eyes scour my face. She's still gripping the shotgun, presumably trying to decide whether to follow Margot's orders.

"Callie," Margot says, annoyance flashing through her voice, "wake the fuck up and bring me more booze."

Margot laces an arm around Callie's lower back, kisses her cheek. "Play nice, please?" She grins up at Callie, snapping her out of her tormented trance.

Callie nods, and swivels toward the house. Margot playfully smacks Callie's ass as she walks off. "And leave that damn thing in the house!"

My shoulders slouch with relief as I watch Callie retreat up the grassy slope. I almost feel a flicker of gratitude toward Margot, but then remember she's the one who got me into this mess in the first place.

"Here," Margot says, tipping her glass of wine to me. "You've earned it."

I hesitate but she gives me a wink and clasps my hand around the glass. My throat is parched and my nervous system is still on overdrive from the gun, so I down the glass of wine in a few greedy gulps.

"Better?" Margot flashes me a sly grin, sinks down onto the chaise longue, and pats the area next to her thigh, inviting me to sit.

I pause for a second, but am so flummoxed by everything that I eventually cave. When I sit down, her knee grazes against mine, and despite everything, a jolt of attraction zaps through me. I dig my fingernails into the bottoms of my thighs to try and make myself focus, and the act of it brings my rage back to the surface.

I'm about to open my mouth and press her, find out what the fuck she did and what the fuck she's going to do to make things better, when Callie surges onto the deck, brandishing a fabric cooler with a fresh bottle of chardonnay chilling on a bed of ice.

She refills Margot's glass and then her own before fishing an empty wineglass from the cooler. She cocks an eyebrow at me. "Having any?"

"No," I say, and shake my head, dropping my eyes to my feet. I need to keep my wits about me. No more wine.

Margot swirls the chardonnay around in her glass, takes a healthy nip. "Mmmmm, second glass is always the best one."

My mouth waters.

"Try your fourth," Callie snorts.

"Oh, shut it."

It feels odd sitting down here, passively watching Callie and Margot calmly sip their wine as if nothing sordid just happened, as if I hadn't just been held at gunpoint, but I decide it's the best tactic. My strategy here is to try and fade into the background as they get tipsy, and in doing so, hopefully get Margot to admit everything to me.

But my nerves are shredded and I can't settle down; my heartbeat bangs in my chest. And the crisp apple taste of Margot's wine still lingers on my tongue; I'm thirsty for another glass. Just one, to help soothe my nerves and keep me on point.

"Actually, I'll have a glass after all."

"That's my girl," Margot says, pivoting her body so that her back rests against the chaise longue, which she raises to a sitting position. She slings her legs over mine as if we are little girls at summer camp and she's about to fill me in on how her school year went. It's so hot out that when a breeze passes over the water, it doesn't feel refreshing; instead, it feels like opening the door to a clothes dryer and having the heat blast your face.

With a stiff arm, Callie passes me a glass.

I take a small, tentative sip. And because

of the hangover, I chase it with a larger one. Margot's right about one thing: I *do* need to calm down, but not for her sake. I need to calm down so I can think straight, gather intel, and formulate my plan. Obviously, sheer anger will get me nowhere with these two conniving psychos.

Callie is parked on the opposite chaise longue, sunglasses lowered, facing the water.

"Trouble at home?" Callie asks me with the corner of her mouth lifted into a grin. She dips her ankle into the lake and traces a slow figure eight with her foot.

I want to shove Margot's legs off of me and plunge Callie into the water, but I stick to my game plan. Remain calm. Act unbothered.

"It hasn't been the best couple of days, but I'll get through it." I sip my wine, and for the first time in days, I feel my muscles relax.

Strips of sunlight comb through the tops of the willow trees lining the shore, and I watch as the shadows of leaves rake back and forth along the chaise longues. I haven't even finished my whole glass, but I'm feeling more tipsy than I should. Especially since I ate a pound of bacon for breakfast. Though the surface of the lake is still, without a boat cutting a wake in sight, I feel like I can see the water expand and contract. Expand and contract. I look over to Margot, and then to Callie, and it's as if I'm peering at them through a looking glass — my vision is fuzzy around the edges.

Something isn't right. And I've realized what it is after it's too late: Callie's drugged me again.

I cup Margot's ankles in my hands, gently pushing her legs to the side so I can stand. Floating up from the chaise longue, I feel like I'm on stilts with everything out of proportion.

I take a deep breath and steady myself.

"Feeling okay?" Callie's voice drifts over to me.

"Fine, just need to pee."

I walk along the pier toward the house and try not to stagger.

I have to get out of here. I have to get in my car and somehow manage to drive. No telling what they're planning on doing to me next, but I can't wait around to find out.

55

I pull down the handle to the glass patio door and step inside the lake house. The room is chilled from the blasting AC, but I welcome it; after the drowsy heat outside, the cold is helping to sharpen my senses.

I glance over my shoulder at the boat dock — Callie and Margot are still beached on their chaise longues. I release a huge sigh; I'm glad they haven't trailed me inside.

The great room seems to tilt a bit as I cast my eyes around it, but I'm nowhere near as drugged as I had been in Dallas. Sheets of sunlight throb through the windows and I can hear the motor of the AC unit humming as if I'm sitting on top of it, but at least I'm still mobile. Sort of. When I take the steps up into the kitchen, my shin strikes the final one and I crash to my knees on the wooden floor.

I push myself to standing. I have to outrun the effects of the drug; I have to escape before I'm fully bombed. I swing open the fridge and yank out a bottle of spring water, twist off the lid and down half of it.

I sway down the hallway toward the guest bath and flick on the lights. They pulse, filling the room with stuttered light. I stare at myself in the mirror. My cheeks are flushed pink, and dark circles rim my eyes, which are bloodshot and dilated. My hair is frizzy from the swampy heat, my T-shirt clings to my chest, moist with sweat, and I have the look of a woman tossed from her house and holed up in a dinky motel room.

The faucet gives way under my trembling hand, gushing out cold water. I cup my palms beneath it, splashing some on my face to try and make me even more alert. A lush, seafoam-green towel dangles from a hook and I use the corners of it to dab my face dry.

But the bottled water and the face bath in the sink have done little to sober me up. If anything, I'm growing more woozy by the second.

I step into the hallway. The light is muted here, and it takes a second for my eyes to adjust to the darkened space.

"Sophie." I hear Margot before I see her. She is standing at the entrance to the living room, leaning against the hallway wall.

My skin crawls at the sight of her, and I try and think of what to do next. But before I can make a move, she sashays down the hall toward me, her leonine legs working the floor as if she is a runway model. She's still only dressed in the yellow bikini, and it's hard to ignore her smoldering figure as she approaches me.

Without another word, she takes my hand and tugs it, leading me down the hall, to the master bedroom. I have no choice but to follow. Maybe without Callie around, I can finally unleash on Margot.

A sheer, lemon-colored curtain hangs in the window, bathing the room in yellow. It must be the roofie coursing through my bloodstream, but the light in here feels as if it's been refracted through a glass of lemonade.

As I stand in the room next to Margot, the sharp cold of the AC has dulled and it feels stuffy, overheated. I sink down on the side of the bed, feeling light-headed. Margot remains standing in front of me, near the doorway.

"Clearly, you're pissed," she says. "So, let's talk about it." She fans her palms out in front of her like she's laying out a deck of cards, and the air fills with the tropical scent of her suntan oil.

Anger pinches my chest. I can't believe she's being so cavalier about everything; she clearly believes she has the power to mindfuck me.

"Talk about it?" My voice cuts through the hazy air. "There's nothing to talk about! You *murdered* Abby. And then you framed me for it."

Her eyes flash up at me. Dark and probing. "Hold on a sec. You think *I* killed Abby?"

"I do. You *and* Brad." I spit the words at her. "Margot, I saw your texts. And then Abby turned up pregnant. It's so obvious — you're crazy about Brad. And his girlfriend — and unborn child — got in the way of that."

She sucks in a quick breath, briskly shakes her head. A look of distaste creeps across her face.

"I didn't kill Abby." Her voice is level and strong. "And neither did Brad. I can see why you might *think* that, but seriously? Brad's a good fuck and all, but I don't care enough about him to kill his girlfriend. In fact, I've ended things with him."

The sun outside escapes from behind a cloud, streaking the room with even more vibrant, buttery light. My back roasts in the heat from the window. I search Margot's face for signs that she's lying, but my vision is swimming and my body feels like it's sinking deeper into the mattress.

Even in my dazed state, though, something about Margot's words cut through the fog, and doubt begins to crack across my mind, splintering all my assumptions. Something about what she is saying has the ring of truth to it. I don't know if I fully buy it all, but it dawns on me: Margot *doesn't* seem capable of loving someone enough to kill for them.

But if Margot didn't kill Abby and frame me for her murder, who did?

My head is spinning with these thoughts when Margot closes the gap between us. She sits next to me, placing her hand on my knee.

"Look. I know you did it, Soph. We all do." She leans across and kisses my neck.

Disbelief and hot anger swell inside me. I push Margot off me and try to stand, but my legs turn to pudding so I slump back on the bed. My mouth is dry, so dry that I can barely speak, and I'm unable to shout, which is what I'm dying to do. "Why in the hell would *I* kill Abby?"

Margot leans in even closer, loops her hand around my neck. "I know you're in love with me. And," she says, sliding her hand up my leg, "I think I love you, too." Her lips brush against my ear.

"It wasn't me." I can barely breathe. I'm on the verge of blacking out — that dream-like state between awareness and unconsciousness — and my heartbeat is drumming in my ears as Margot moves her hand across my body.

"But you were the only one here," she whispers, fingers tracing the back of my neck.

No. No, I wasn't. Once again, the image of Callie wrenching open the front door in search of Margot comes roaring back in my mind.

"Callie came back that night." I turn and lock eyes with Margot. "She seemed steamed, jealous; she said she was looking for you."

Margot's eyes widen.

"She did?"

I nod.

Her fingers stop their trailing for a moment.

Then another vision from that night surfs through my brain: Callie delicately lifting the shotgun from me after I had fired it.

Callie. Fucking Callie. *Of course* it was her. She would kill for Margot if she thought that's what Margot wanted, and she would definitely want to frame me for it. She's had it out for me this whole time. And I'm positive she's the one who told Flynn that I'm obsessed with Margot. But my thoughts are cartwheeling, my mind is twirling, and I can't hold on to anything solid.

Margot plants her hands on my cheeks and turns my face toward hers. "Look, we'll get you out of this. I promise. Even if it means —"

"Turning on Callie?" I ask.

She nods.

She stands and I think she is going to leave, but instead she closes the door. She turns to face me and reaches her hands behind her neck, untying her top, exposing her perfect breasts. Triangles of bright white flesh outline where her tan lines are. She reaches around her back and unties the rest, and her top slinks to the floor.

A shiver ripples over me. I can't stop gaping at her. Those breasts, those dark eyes glinting with desire. And soon she's on me, rolling the bottom of my T-shirt up until it is over my bra, which she unclasps and tosses on the bed. She pulls me even closer so that our bodies are touching. Kisses my neck.

"Sophie," she sighs in my ear. "I've wanted this for a very long time."

She kisses my cheek, then her mouth is on mine and I want to stop her but I don't. I can't. I can barely think or see straight, but one thing is startlingly clear: My body has wanted this for a very long time, too.

I feel her lips and tongue trace my nipples while her hand cups my breasts. My own hands are rubbing her breasts, and she moans in my ear.

I move my hands down her stomach, but they're clumsy from being drugged and shaky from being nervous.

"It's okay," she says. "I wanna take care of you first."

A shadow pools around us. I think it must be the sun, gliding behind another cloud, but I also feel a presence with us. Eyes watching. I twist my neck to look out the window to check, but Margot pulls my face to hers, kissing me urgently.

She gets down on her knees and unbuttons my shorts. I wriggle out of them. She kisses the inside of my thigh and then slides next to me again on the edge of the bed. She pulls my panties to one side and begins touching me.

I'm shuddering. And moaning. She has clearly done this before. She rubs small, tight circles over me, and before I know it, I've shed all my inhibitions and my hips are bucking against her hand, and I hear my voice echoing off the walls as I shout her name.

56

I awaken in a square patch of moonlight, lying on my side in bed. Margot's bed. In Margot's lake house. Tangled in Margot's high-thread-count sheets.

Jesus.

I can't believe that happened. My pulse is speedy, live-wiring through my veins, and I desperately need a glass of water.

The room is dark except for the silver-blue headlight of the moon, and I'm alone in bed.

But I don't feel alone. The hairs on the back of my neck prick to attention and I creak over, rolling up on my other hip. I notice a dark figure leaning in the doorway.

I gasp.

I'm still in my T-shirt, thank god, but I'm bottomless and I clutch at the sheets, fully covering myself.

"Miss Sophie." Brad's voice slurs from

across the room. "Didn't mean to startle ya."

He is drunk, or, at least, he sounds drunk. An air of menace hangs over his expression, which I can fully take in now that my eyes have adjusted to the dark.

It hits me that he might think I killed Abby, and maybe he plans on doing me harm. I wonder where Margot is, if she's talked to him yet, told him our theory about Callie.

"Where's Margot?" I ask, trying to sound as parental as possible.

"I was gonna ask you the same." His eyes are glassy and they move over my body. I feel exposed and vulnerable, and his roving eyes are making me more uncomfortable by the second.

I want to stand, bolt from the room, but he's got me trapped, and worse, I know he knows it. I follow his eyes as they land on my cutoffs and panties, in a ball on the floor. His full lips spread into a grin. I wonder how long he's been standing there, watching me as I slept. Acid heaves in the back of my throat.

"How long have you been here?"

"Oh, let's see." He combs his fingers through his thick hair. " 'Bout half an hour. Margot texted me a few hours ago. Wanted me to come meet her out here tonight."

I don't believe him. Because if she wanted him to come out, why is she no longer here? I believe she ended it with him, and that's why he is acting off.

"Callie here?"

"Nope. It's just us." He takes a step toward the bed, his figure blotting out the doorway. He reeks of booze and sweat and his sharp cologne.

"I need to be getting home," I say, trying to sound forceful, but my voice just sounds desperate, fearful.

"Do ya now?" Brad takes another step toward me.

Adrenaline thunderbolts through me, and I grasp the sheets around me and spring from the bed. I nab my clothes from the floor and shove past him, a burning pain sparking at my shoulder as it connects with his.

"Hey, easy there, Miss Sophie," he calls out after me.

But I'm racing down the hall toward the great room, where I round a corner and quickly finish getting dressed. I grab my purse and keys and bolt out the front door.

In the glow of the moonlight, I see a black Benz still parked in the drive. I can't tell if it's Margot's or Callie's but I don't care; I just need to get the hell out of here.

I climb into the Highlander, slam the door, and punch the lock button. My breath is quick and rapid, and the keys nearly slip from my hand, my palms are so sweaty, but I manage to jab them in the ignition, start the engine, and pull from the drive just as I see Brad's figure appear in my rearview, standing on the porch, watching as I drive away.

57

It's pitch-black out when I pull into the motel parking lot; only a few stray stars dangle from the sky, and the moon has sunk below a rim of pines.

It's just past ten o'clock. Whatever Callie gave me knocked me out for a solid ten hours. That and the sex with Margot. My cheeks flame at the memory, which is cloudy and blurry, but also exquisitely vivid.

I can't believe I did that; I can't believe it happened. It never would have if I hadn't been so soused. Sure, I've wanted it for a long time, but still, with all that's going on with Graham, no way would I have risked further messing that up if I'd been in my right mind.

I know without a doubt that I will not, and don't want to, repeat it.

I want to be home with Graham and Jack. And, surely, it was a one-night stand for Margot, too. She doesn't *really* love me.

Again, I'm quite certain she doesn't love anyone but herself.

My body melts with relief when I finally crawl into bed. Relief from being back in my own domain, but mostly because Margot is going to help me.

In my mind's eye, I see Callie again, next to the glimmering lake, her blond hair glistening with sweat, lifting the shotgun from me, careful not to wipe off my prints. And I see her later that evening, inside the lake house, offering to clean the guns. No doubt everybody else's gun but the one I had fired. I think of her open disdain for me, and her clear and open obsession with Margot. *Of course* I was a threat to that, and, of course, I'd be the one she'd love to take out.

I drift under the covers and sleep for a few restless hours. When sunlight bleeds beneath the blackout shade, I run a steamy shower and prepare for the day.

First, I text Margot.

Hey . . . Call me.

With shaky hands, I fix a four-cup pot of coffee in the room's pint-size coffee maker.

After the machine's final hiss, I pour myself a cup and taste it. And decide to hit the Starbucks drive-thru instead.

The line snakes around the building, and while I'm waiting, I check my cell. No reply from Margot. She is probably sleeping off her hangover.

After I place my order at the window — triple latte with a chocolate croissant — and pay, I dial Flynn's number.

He answers on the first ring.

"Detective Flynn speaking." His voice is clipped and edgy. He must know it's me calling — how many calls does he get with Chicago area codes? — but I still have to go through the process of announcing myself.

"Hi, Mike," I say brightly, "this is Sophie."

Silence.

I pull the car over on the side of the road.

"Listen, I know this sounds crazy, but I really need you to look into Callie Jenkins further. You have to believe me; she returned to Margot's lake house the night Abby went missing. She's lying about being home all night with her husband. And he's lying, too."

"Is that all?" Flynn sounds annoyed.

A school bus trundles past me and I roll up my window so I can hear Flynn more clearly. My neck burns at his dismissive tone.

"No, that's not all. I believe, and actually, Margot now believes, that Callie is the one who murdered Abby." My voice rises in pitch with each syllable and I take a deep breath to try and steady my tone. "Look, I remembered something. Something important about that night. After I was finished shooting, it was Callie who took the shotgun from me — carefully, I might add — as if she were concerned about removing my prints from it."

While the words stream from my mouth, I keep waiting to hear that click of recognition from Flynn across the line, but all I hear is the hiss of a sigh being released.

"Sophie, I was going to drop by and pay *you* a visit later this afternoon actually."

My stomach curdles with anxiety as he says this. Why would he want to come see me? And god forbid he pays another visit to the house again.

"Well, I'm really glad I called, then, because I'm actually not at home at the moment. I'm staying at the Sunshine Inn."

Again, an awkward pause I wait for him to fill. He doesn't.

"Why were you coming by?"

"Callie Jenkins called me first thing this

morning, Sophie. And she let me know what happened yesterday."

What happened yesterday? Was she at the window, spying on me and Margot? Or did she tell Flynn she held me at gunpoint?

"So she told you she pulled a shotgun on me?"

"She explained, Sophie" — he says my name as if he's talking to a confused child — "that you drove out there and threatened Margot. And yes, she informed me she pulled out a weapon but only because you were raging and she felt Mrs. Banks was in grave danger."

"But — that's bullshit, Mike! Yes, I drove out there, yes, I confronted Margot about framing me, but I was nowhere *close* to being threatening! You know me, you know I'm not even capable of that —"

"Sophie, what I *know* about you changes. Your story changes *so* much. And I know that Mrs. Jenkins phoned me first thing this morning to see if I thought a restraining order needs to be issued —"

A wave of nausea rolls over me. I should tell Flynn about the drugging, but I don't want to get into all of that. I don't want to have to tell him about what happened next, with me and Margot.

"A restraining order?" My voice squawks

out of me.

"Against you coming near Mrs. Banks."

"I can guarantee you Margot does *not* want a restraining order put on me." I can feel her hands all over me again, her lips brushing against mine.

"Have you talked to *her* about this? Can't you see that Callie is setting me up here? She's setting me up to look insane —"

"I haven't reached Mrs. Banks yet this morning, but I'll keep trying. And in the meantime, I'm warning you to stay away from her, and also, from Mrs. Jenkins."

"But —"

"I'm telling you this to help you. You're in way over your head here, and you're already in deep water." A hint of concern leaches into his voice. I can't decide if it makes me feel worse or better. Worse, I think.

58

It's evening. Six o'clock. I've been holed up in the room for most of the day. Fretting, sweating, and pacing over the thin beige carpet, checking my cell incessantly for a reply from Margot.

Nothing.

By three I was climbing out of my skin, and against my better judgment, I called her. I know I shouldn't have, but I couldn't take it any longer, so I clamped the phone to my skull as it rang.

After four rings, it rolled to voice mail. I started to leave a message, but panicked and hung up; with Margot, it's better to be casual and not too needy.

And I'm trying my best not to overreact, but why hasn't she responded to my text or called me back?

My hangover hasn't yet lifted; in fact, it's gotten worse. A dull, persistent ache throbs behind my eyes, and even an earlier dash to get a cheeseburger and fries has done nothing to quell how ill I feel.

It's fucking Callie and the roofie she slipped me. If I could find a place in town that makes wheatgrass shots, I'd slam a dozen just to clean my blood, but that doesn't exist in sleepy Mapleton.

Instead, I uncork the bottle of merlot that I grabbed on the way back to the room from the burger joint. I roll the wine around the glass, inhale its jammy scent before taking a long sip. I dropped nearly forty bucks on it and feel guilty for it, but if I have to live in this dump for now, then I deserve at least something nice once in a while. Especially when I feel this low. But I'm sure Graham would disagree.

Graham. Jack. Fuck. I can't stand this. And I wish Margot would call me, tell me that she's going to Flynn to demand that he listen to her about Callie.

After I've downed my first glass, my chest relaxes and my headache starts to loosen its grip. I scroll through my phone and hit the Photos icon. Jack's sun-kissed face fills the screen, and hot tears sting my eyes.

I close out and head over to Messages. Scroll until I land on Graham. And punch out a text before I change my mind.

Can I call you?

Only a few minutes tick by before his reply comes through.

No.

A cry bubbles up in the back of my throat and I sit on the edge of the bed, sobbing for a moment. But then I get pissed. I understand his not wanting me to be around right now, but he can't keep me from speaking to Jack.

I type back:

I want to talk to Jack.

Fine. But give us five minutes. Finishing dinner.

I'm now crying and smiling at the same time. Five minutes is perfect. Enough time to sprinkle water on my face and pull myself together.

Four minutes later and my cell starts chiming. FaceTime from Graham. I nearly start to cry again but I suck in a deep breath and exhale before accepting the call.

It's not Graham's face that greets me, though, it's Jack's, his cheeks smeared with what looks like Hershey's syrup. His eyes dance over the screen, taking in my face and the background of the motel room.

"Mommeeee! Mommeee!" His mouth opens into a wide grin.

"Oh, baby! I miss my Jack-o-licious so much! What did you have for supper?" My hands shake and it's all I can do to stop the floodgate of tears.

"Grilled cheese samm-ich!" He lifts the crust off his plate and guides it through the air like it's a toy airplane. "And Dad-eee made me *ice cream* for dessert!" He shouts the words, and my chest seizes with longing.

"Mommeeee, when are you coming back?" A scared smile plays across his lips.

I suck in a breath, paste on my best grin. "Soon, honey, very soon. I just have a little more work to do." I can't help it, the tears start forming and I flick them away, but I know I need to end this call before I dissolve in front of Jack.

"Love you so much, honey!"

"I wuv you, toooooo!" He's still airplaning his crust around.

"Bye, sweetie!"

"Bye-bye!" He's waving now and I wave back until I see Graham's tanned forearm grab the phone and end the call.

I toss my cell on the bed and fall back into the too-soft mattress as a howl rips through me. Ugh. I've become a far worse mother than Nikki ever was to me. That was a mistake. And selfish of me. Kids are smart, and I can tell that Jack senses something is up.

I'm not going to do that again.

I'm going to get out of this mess and get back home.

59

Friday, April 27, 2018

It's noon. I know I shouldn't be doing this — Detective Flynn told me to stay away from her — but I'm parked outside the gates to Margot's neighborhood. A ruby-colored BMW approaches and I trail behind it, slipping through the gates before they close.

I haven't heard a peep from Margot. Nothing after my text and phone call yesterday, and nothing at all this morning. I called her again first thing when I woke up. It went straight to voice mail, which made me bristle, made me paranoid that she's avoiding me on purpose. I hung up without leaving a message.

I slow the car and roll past her house. A lone black Benz is parked in the circular drive out front, but I peg it as Jed's — a Piney Woods Country Club Golf sticker is plastered on the bumper.

I idle out in front of her mansion for a second, my eyes sweeping through the bare windows that gleam in the sunlight.

No sign of Margot. The leaves on the trees overhead shudder as a gust of wind sweeps through, and I shiver, even though it's bright and sunny out.

I hear him before I see him. The sound of Jed's loafers slapping the long drive on the side of the house as he hauls out bags of trash to the curb. His jaw is set and a sweep of dark hair falls across his forehead as he strides down the drive and stuffs the trash bin with bags, slamming the lid shut. He is practically scowling, and when he catches sight of me, he narrows his gaze.

Adrenaline sizzles through me, and even though I'm certain he doesn't recognize me (we've never met in person and my face is currently masked behind a large pair of sunglasses), I press my foot on the accelerator and speed off.

Back in the motel room, I dig my cell out of my bag and dial Margot again. Straight to voice mail. But this time, I leave a message.

"Margot, it's me, Sophie. Look, I don't know what's going on but you need to call me. You promised you'd help get me out of this. I talked to Detective Flynn and evidently Callie's trying to set me up even more than she already has. Destroy my life even more than she already has." Despite trying to keep my voice even, emotion seeps into it and I'm nearing the verge of hysteria as I spit out the next words. "I need you to help me; I need you to call me right away. Please."

Next, I send her a text.

> Just left you a vm. I really need you to call me back. It's important.
>
> XO, S

My cell feels like a dead thing in my hand and I'm sick of clutching it, waiting for her to respond.

I flop back onto the mattress and drift off into a nap.

It's evening now. Well past nine o'clock. I'm sitting on the edge of the motel pool, dragging my calves through the water. My skin is fluorescent white against the glare of the pool lights, but I'm the only one out here to notice how ghastly they look.

I couldn't stand to be in the room any longer, holed up like a caged animal, scanning my phone constantly, so I'm parked out here, nearly finished with the remainder of last night's merlot. I tip the nose of the bottle into my plastic cup, shaking it to get every single drop out.

The warm night air and the sound of chirping crickets would be soothing under any other circumstances, but nothing — neither the wine nor the balmy atmosphere — can calm me down tonight.

I'm losing my mind. Growing more agitated by the minute.

Margot still hasn't responded. I tried calling her one last time but it went straight to voice mail again and I couldn't bear to leave another message.

All I can think is that she's decided she's not going to help me; she's had second thoughts about turning on Callie. Callie *is* her best friend after all, and completely insane and vindictive to boot, so maybe it was foolish of me to ever believe she'd turn on her in the first place.

But what I know is this: I'm currently the main person of interest in Abby's murder, Callie has stacked the deck against me, and if Margot won't turn on her, I'm screwed.

My mind is leapfrogging over the varying possibilities, running rampant with different scenarios. The scariest one being this: What if Graham somehow finds out about what I did with Margot? I would most likely lose Jack forever and Graham would never forgive me. What if Callie *was* spying at the window watching us, and decides to tell him? What if that was their plan all along?

How could I have been so blindingly stupid?

What if Margot never had any intention of helping me? Maybe she was just trying to "handle" me, as she said to Callie. What if she had sex with me only to fuck me over even more?

Why is she ignoring me?

But surely I'm being nutty. Perhaps she's just on a bender out at the lake. Maybe she's even staying out there instead of at home. That would make sense. Especially given the scowl on Jed's face. I'm sure he wants as little to do with her as Graham does with me.

If I weren't half-drunk, I'd climb in the Highlander and speed out there right now, Flynn's orders be damned.

But I can't risk getting pulled over, so instead, I slam the rest of my wine. Pull my legs from the tepid water and towel them off. Inhale a huge breath of damp night air and tell myself I'm just being paranoid.

When has Margot ever operated under anyone else's rules? *I* may be in a hurry to get all of this settled and behind me, but that doesn't mean that she is.

I'll go out to the lake tomorrow and everything will be fine. She'll come forward with me and I'll start to untangle myself from this mess I'm in. I hope.

60

Saturday, April 28, 2018

I'm in the breakfast room sitting at a window seat, staring out at the gray sky. It's overcast today, and milky white light fills the breakfast room, which is empty save for me.

I've slept in; it's nearly ten thirty, so the breakfast bar has been raided and picked over by now, and the only sound in the room is the clink of my spoon as it strikes the side of my cereal bowl. Raisin bran and cold milk. Breakfast of champions. I hate living like this. I miss home and my kitchen and Graham's omelets and Jack's pudgy hands on my face. I miss my espresso machine, the comforting hug of my own bed, my own bath, but more than anything, I miss them. A red-hot pain surges in my chest just thinking about it, and fresh tears burn my eyes.

I push the bowl across the table and dig

out my phone from my bag. It just chimed and I have a new notification, but it's not from Margot. It's just a ping from my calendar, reminding me to craft a new blog post. As if.

I clear it and drop the phone in my bag. Dig out a five-dollar bill for a tip for whoever has to bus the tables here, and tuck it under the corner of the cereal bowl. The carafe of coffee across the room beckons, so I grab a paper to-go cup and nearly fill it, leaving an inch for milk. I'll take it on the road with me to Margot's lake house; surely it will perk me up.

I'm in the parking lot, heading for the Highlander, when I see Detective Flynn striding toward me. My heart seizes. Maybe he found out I went by Margot's house yesterday.

He's on me before I can even think of what to say.

"Morning, Sophie." He gives me a brisk nod but I can't read his expression; his eyes are cloaked behind his pair of aviator sunglasses.

"Hey, Mike," I say, my voice feeble and tentative. "What's going on?"

"I need to talk to you."

"Okay, what is this about?"

"It's about the other night at the lake.

Wednesday night."

My mind races and the coffee trembles in my hands. "What about it?"

"That's all I can say here." He looks around as if he's worried others are listening in on us, but the parking lot is deserted. "I'd prefer to discuss this at the station. So, if you'll come with me —"

My first thought is relief. Relief that I'm not busted for stalking Margot's house. And also hope. Maybe *he's* heard from Margot and she's turned on Callie.

"Sure," I say with a grin that he doesn't return.

As I step into the frigid interrogation room, I notice that Detective Watkins is banked behind the table. Ugh. I've clearly lost all footing and clout with Flynn if he's seen the need to have her present. She's dressed in a tacky purple pantsuit and lifts her eyebrows at me as I take a seat.

I'm still clutching my coffee from the motel, so I decline Flynn's offer for more and he rounds the table, taking a seat next to Wanda. I'm having my first sip when I notice Flynn punch the red record button on the tape recorder. I feel my stomach tighten into a ball. I have no idea what's about to happen here.

"So, Mrs. O'Neill," Flynn starts, leaning back in his chair. "I understand you were out at Margot Banks's lake house this past Wednesday?"

"Yes. As I told you, I went out there to speak with her —"

"And what time was this?"

"Is this about Callie and what we talked about?" I'm dancing around our previous conversation about Callie framing me, wanting to keep my guard up in front of Wanda.

Flynn waves his hand dismissively, shakes his head. "What time?"

I feel the hairs on my arms begin to rise. Why is he questioning me like this, under these circumstances, when I've already called him myself to tell him all of this?

"I guess it was about eleven?"

"And what time did you leave?" This time it's Wanda asking the question. She taps the tip of her pen along the table as she waits for me to respond.

"I'm — I'm not sure." I think back, try and remember exactly when it was that I left. "Must've been after nine?"

Flynn and Wanda exchange a look.

"You don't remember?" Wanda asks, her razor-thin lips curling at the edges.

"Well, I was passed out. I —"

"Again?" Wanda asks pointedly. "This

seems to have become a pattern of yours, Mrs. O'Neill. Drinking too much, blacking out —"

"But I hadn't had too much to drink, that's the thing, I —" I flick my gaze to Flynn. "I — there's something else I needed to tell you about that day, Mike, um, Detective Flynn."

He tilts his head as if waiting for me to continue, but I pause, hoping he'll grant us a moment alone. He doesn't.

I'm whittled down by Wanda's stare, but I manage to spit it out. "Callie drugged me. Again. She slipped something in my wine that day — I swear I'd only had a few glasses — and that's why I passed out. She's done it before to me, once when —"

But Flynn cuts me off with another wave of his hand. "What *we* understand, from Callie," he says, then clears his throat, "Mrs. Jenkins, is that you showed up out there and threatened Mrs. Banks. Is that correct?"

"No, as I explained to you, I went out there to find out why Margot *framed* me for Abby's murder. There was no threatening going on, other than Callie pulling a shotgun on me." My neck burns with anger. "And as I've tried to explain, Margot now believes that Callie is *actually* the one responsible for Abby's death. And for setting me up for it."

I chase my words with a big swig of lukewarm coffee.

Flynn's eyes are locked onto mine and I can feel the pinprick of Wanda's gaze, but I keep my face turned toward Flynn's.

"Have you talked to Margot yet?" I ask.

Flynn ignores my question.

"What time did you 'pass out,' would you say?" Wanda makes quotation marks with her fingers around the words *pass out.*

"I didn't take note of it at the time, but if I had to guess, around noonish." Whenever Margot was done making love to me.

"And what did you do before blacking out?" Wanda's lips are curled into that same insipid smile.

Am I on trial for getting it on with Margot? Do they know about that? I twist my hands in my lap, lower my eyes to the table. The hum of the tape recorder makes my nerves twitch and I wonder if I need to call that lawyer after all.

"Like I said, I had a few glasses of wine out on the boat dock and then went inside. And that's where Margot and I discussed everything." There. I'm not lying, just leaving out one very important detail.

"And when you came to," Wanda asks,

"who else was out there?"

I take a second before replying, carefully selecting my words. "When I woke up, Brad was there. Brad Simmons."

I feel a perceptible hitch in Wanda's line of questioning. I've stopped her in her tracks. She and Flynn bring their heads together and pass whispered words between them. Flynn scratches his pen across a notepad.

"You say *Brad Simmons* was there?" Wanda asks, with a note of surprise, and possibly doubt, in her voice.

"Yes. And he was the only one there. No Margot, and no Callie. I grabbed my things and left."

"Did he mention what he was doing there?" Wanda folds her hands together, plants them on the table as she leans forward.

"Um, yeah. He told me that Margot had texted him to come out. But, I'm pretty sure he was lying. Margot had ended things with him."

"And you didn't see Mrs. Banks at all after you woke up?" This time it's Flynn, and he chews on the cap of his pen as he waits for my reply, concern darkening his eyes.

"No. Have you talked to her yet? She'll

confirm everything I'm saying."

Again, Flynn doesn't answer me. Instead, he jots something down in his notepad and elbows Wanda to look at it. She heaves a huge sigh of annoyance and tosses me a withering look before standing and exiting the room.

I needle Flynn with my eyes. "Well? *Have* you talked to Margot?"

"No, Sophie, I haven't." Flynn leans back in his chair, scratches the stubble on his chin. "Because Margot, Mrs. Banks, is dead. She drowned."

The blood drains out of my face and hands, and my fingers feel like they've been plunged into a bucket of ice. My ears are ringing and my brain can't begin to process what I've just heard. I open my mouth to attempt to speak, but before I can, Flynn starts talking.

"Her body was found early this morning. Floating next to her boat dock. A neighbor, out for an early-morning cruise on the lake, noticed her body as he drove past in his ski boat."

Flynn's eyes scan my face as he says this.

I feel as though someone has punched me in the gut, knocking the air out of me.

"So, she's . . . dead?" What a stupid question, but I had to ask it for some reason. I can't imagine Margot dead. It's impossible. She seems too powerful. More powerful than even death.

"Unfortunately, yes."

"I don't understand. What happened?"

"That's exactly what we're trying to figure out." Flynn traces my face with his eyes, searching.

Well, this explains why she hasn't been answering any of my texts or calls. But it doesn't explain what in the hell happened to her.

"I really don't get it. Are you thinking suicide?" But even as I ask this, I know it's not true. Margot would *never* be capable of even entertaining thoughts of offing herself.

Flynn bites his lower lip, shakes his head. "No, this was no accident."

Margot was a good swimmer, so I agree; I can't see her drowning on her own.

Unless. Unless she had been drugged, too.

"How do you know? That it wasn't an accident, I mean?"

Flynn draws in a deep breath and hisses it out between pursed lips. He seems to be trying to decide how much to tell me. "I'll just say this for now: There were apparent signs of a struggle."

The back of my throat constricts, and even though I try to hold back the tears, they come gushing out. Flynn averts his gaze for a second, giving me a modicum of privacy, as much privacy as you can get when you're seated in front of a two-way mirror with a tape recorder picking up everything that comes out of your mouth.

"According to Mrs. Jenkins, you were the last one with Margot. And she never made it home after Wednesday out at the lake."

His eyes are back on me now, drilling into my own. And it finally dawns on me why I'm here: This is another murder investigation and I'm obviously a suspect. Again.

Fucking Callie. The lying bitch.

What *if* Callie drugged her, too? What if she had been watching us through the window? I wouldn't put it past her to go into a demented jealous rage and kill Margot.

I keep the part about being in the bedroom with Margot from Flynn, but I tell him my theory about Callie drugging us both.

He seems unfazed by it, batting it away with another flick of his wrist. I want to reach across the table and tear his hand off his body.

"You can't prove that anyway," he says with open exasperation. "The drug leaves your system after twelve hours."

My shoulders slump in defeat. I can't win here.

"Now tell me, were you, or were you not, the last person to see Margot alive?"

"I don't know if I was or if I wasn't," I say through clenched teeth. "Like I told you, Callie drugged me, and it sounds as if she drugged Margot as well. I mean, I only saw her swimming once, but Margot was a good swimmer. I can't imagine her drowning unless she *had* been drugged."

Or unless someone forced her underwater and held her down. The vision of a drunk Brad, leering in the doorway of the bedroom, comes back to mind. If Margot really *had* broken it off with him, no telling what he might've done to her.

I don't know what to think. Or what to say.

"Like I said, when I came to, there was no one else out there except for Brad." I stare evenly at Flynn as I speak. "And he was drunk, and acting strange."

This gets a noticeable pause from Flynn. Just like it had with Wanda. Quick, but noticeable.

"I'll follow up with him," Flynn says.

"Can't you see?" I seethe. "Either Callie has set me up — *again,* I might add — or Brad did something to Margot. I don't know. I was passed the fuck out."

"But why? Why would Callie murder her oldest friend?"

"Because she was jealous of my relationship with Margot!"

"And what exactly *was* your relationship with her?"

My heart thunders in my ears and I feel as though a thousand eyes are on me. I look to the sheet of glass hanging behind Flynn, but all I see is my pathetic, washed-up form in the reflection staring back.

"We were friends. But close. Closer than Callie wanted us to be. Just ask the others, Tina and Jill. They'll tell you that."

"You drove out there and confronted Margot. And then, later that night, you're the only one out there, alone with Brad. And your only alibi — once again — is that you were passed out. I must say, this doesn't bode well for you, Sophie."

I'm done here. I'm numb. I can barely lift my eyes to Flynn or think straight. But I still have sense enough to know I can most likely walk out.

"Am I under arrest?"

"No. Not at the moment."

"Then I'm leaving." My chair scrapes the floor as I push it back from the table, jangling my nerves even more. I cross the room and am at the door when I hear Flynn's voice again.

"But don't think this is the last time we're going to discuss this."

My back stiffens as he says this, but I don't turn around or reply. With unsteady hands, I twist the doorknob and step out of the room, brushing past Wanda — who smells of hairspray and loud perfume — as she hurries back to Flynn.

61

Sunday, April 29, 2018

The sputtering of the AC window unit rouses me from sleep. It's six thirty in the evening; I couldn't sleep a wink last night. A strange mixture of adrenaline and grief blanketed me, making it hard to shut my mind off but also hard to want to do anything other than lie in bed all night, twisting in the coarse sheets, my thoughts racing.

I peel myself out of bed and cross the room to open the blackout shade on the window. Buttery sunlight spills into the room, and it takes a few seconds for my eyes to adjust.

My mind is a whirring blender. I'm still reeling from the aftermath of Abby's death and the fallout from that, and now this: Margot is gone.

It's nearly impossible to wrap my head around that fact. I can still feel her lips on mine, can still smell her intoxicating perfume as if it's pressed on my skin right at this very moment.

I'm in shock, and the shock of it all has numbed me. My feelings are mixed, which baffles me. On the one hand, I was obsessed and entranced by Margot — locked under her glittering spell — but I wasn't in love with her. And part of me had even grown to hate her. So I don't feel the deep grief of losing someone close, say, a family member, or the gut-wrenching pain I feel from Graham's tearing Jack away from me.

But I am sad, and it's disorienting for her to simply be gone. Poof. Out of this world. And also, disturbing to think of her — this larger-than-life presence — as what she was in her final moments: a victim.

More than anything, the news of Margot's death feels surreal to me. And I can't, of course, quit thinking about who did it.

Callie is front and center on my list; I have no trouble believing that she caught us in the act, drugged Margot, and then killed her. She was the only one out there while Margot and I were together. Maybe seeing us, locked in each other's arms, was enough to finally drive her over the edge.

And then she quickly set the stage for framing me for it, by hurrying over to Flynn the next morning to see if he thought a restraining order needed to be issued against me, barring me from Margot.

I'm certain it's her.

But Brad also creeps back into my mind. The strange way he was behaving. The lie he told about Margot asking him out to the lake, when she had in fact ended things with him. He *was* acting like a jilted lover, and who knows what that could have driven him to do. Maybe he murdered Abby as well. But that doesn't explain the fact that I was framed for Abby's murder, most likely by Callie. I don't know what to think, don't know which way is up. The only thing I *do* know is that the one person who could've helped me out of this mess is now dead.

And there's Jed. I think back to that eerie post Margot put on Facebook after our night in Dallas, of Jed clutching her shoulder in front of the church, jaw squared, with menace on his face. And the scowl I glimpsed just last night.

There's no lack of people from whom Margot could've incited a crime of passion. I know I wanted to strangle her myself in the end.

I can't shut down my hamster-wheel mind, and the worst part of it is, I have no one to talk to about it. To my surprise, Graham texted me earlier this morning.

I heard about Margot. I'm sorry. I don't even know what to say.

Stupidly, I called him, thinking we could discuss it. But he didn't answer, only replying with a curt text.

I don't want to talk to you. I just wanted to let you know that I knew.

Such a dick text but I guess I deserve it. I nearly picked up the phone to call Tina, but my pride wouldn't let me. And in desperation to hash this out with someone, someone half-sane, I even thought about calling Jill. But of course I can't do that; I'm sure she thinks I murdered Abby just like everybody else does. And no telling what Callie has told them since. Everyone must think I killed Margot as well.

My mouth is dry and parched; I twist the lid off a bottle of sparkling water. It scorches the back of my throat but it's a good, refreshing kind of burn.

This morning, just after daybreak, I padded to the corner store to restock supplies — bottles of Perrier, bags of chips, packages of almonds, and cheap cans of chicken noodle soup. I paused by the rack of wines, draped my fingers over a bottle of red, but left it. Since yesterday, I've lost my taste for alcohol.

At the cash register, I saw a thick stack of Sunday's paper and added one to my purchase, spying Margot's name across the front page.

Back in the privacy of my motel room, I read the article. It was just a brief piece, really, giving scant details: Prominent socialite dead. Cause of death: drowning. Due to obvious signs of a struggle, police suspect foul play.

The wealthy, it seems, are immune from having their privacy invaded.

It did point out that Margot's drowning came on the heels of Abby's disappearance and murder. *And* they both occurred on the same piece of property. It wrapped up by saying the police are investigating to see if there's a connection.

I shuddered when I read that last part. In Flynn's mind, *I'm* the connection.

The walls of this small town are closing in and I'll most likely rot in jail here if I don't do something. So that's why tomorrow I'm going to go see the only person left in Mapleton who might talk to me. Jamie.

62

Monday, April 30, 2018

It's four thirty when I steer the Highlander into a remote spot in the Mapleton High School lot, careful to park as far away from other cars as possible. Little has changed about the school since I went here nearly twenty years ago. Same ivy-choked redbrick building, same pine tree–rimmed parking lot, and same football field, which I glimpse at a distance through my window. A carpet of green sunken into the hillside, encircled by first-rate stands and a fancy concession. No cost spared by Mapleton's affluent booster club. And from the looks of it, apparently the same, nearly year-round, after-school football practice. I can see tiny figures skimming across the length of the field, and even with my windows up, I can hear the shrill blast of the coach's whistle.

I step out of the car into the damp heat. Sunlight trickles through a net of treetops, but even in the shade, it's scorching and sweat pools around my neck. I pluck at my shirt to cool myself off.

When I left the motel earlier, I popped into the corner store and bought a Dallas Cowboys baseball cap, the only kind available. And while I feel downright ridiculous wearing it, I'm hoping the hat, along with my large shades, will keep me incognito.

As I near the field, I'm relieved to see that other than the football players and coaching staff, there aren't too many other people around. Just small clusters of what look like parents scattered in clumps near the bleachers and along the track.

I spot Jamie right away, his red hair catching the sun as his limber body streaks across the field. Brad is on the sidelines, bent over, sucking in huge gulps of air as sweat pours off his head. I position myself next to a tree and gnaw on a fingernail as I watch the players run drills.

Even though it seems as if no one has taken notice of me, I can't steady my breathing or slow down my heart rate, which stutters and pounds in my ears. I scan the faces of the adults, hoping I don't see Jill among them, and when I've confirmed she's not here, a pent-up sigh oozes out of me.

I don't have a real plan for how to catch Jamie's attention, so I bore my eyes into him hoping that he'll somehow pick up on my intent gaze, even though it's shielded behind my sunglasses. After a few minutes of this, I realize it's not going to work. I'm going to have to approach him. So when he heads toward one of the fluorescent-orange coolers, I stride across the track and close the gap between us.

He's slugging water — Adam's apple bobbing up and down along his throat — and I step to the cooler, lifting a paper cup from the metal sleeve. My hand shakes as I press the spout and fill my cup. He's about to step away, when I call his name.

He turns to me with a befuddled look, as if he doesn't recognize me (mission accomplished), before his confusion gives way to recognition.

"Sophie!" he says, too loudly, as his lips part into a warm grin.

"Shhhh." I give my head a brisk shake. Digging into the pocket of my denim shorts, I fish out the crumpled note I'd penned earlier and pass it to him.

I need to talk to you. Meet me at the Sunshine Inn, Room #203 today after practice. It's important.

Still smiling, he locks those absinthe-green eyes on me and arches his eyebrows suggestively. I give a tight smile back. I don't want to encourage him, but I desperately need him to come over; so be it if he thinks we're going to hook up.

I drink the plastic-tasting water and crush my cup, pitching it into the trash can before turning to leave and doing the walk of shame back up the hill toward the parking lot.

63

I've only been back in the room for half an hour when I hear the knock at the door. I open it and his figure darkens the doorway, blotting out the broiling sunlight outside. Like a celebrity hiding from the paparazzi, I poke my head out and sweep my gaze through the parking lot, making sure no one sees me, before yanking him inside.

"I ditched the rest of practice," Jamie says, leaning on the edge of the desk. His lips are parted and he trains his eyes on mine. He smells faintly of aftershave — a pleasant, crisp odor — and it's clear that he's at least sponge bathed in the locker room. His hair glistens with product, and his breath pops with mint; he's absolutely expecting that we're going to get it on, and I feel a prick of both guilt and shame for ever being with him in the first place.

I stand near the side of the bed, careful to keep a few feet between us. "Look," I say, dropping my eyes to the floor, "I'm really glad you came over. But this isn't what you think. I can't be with you; my life is already complicated enough as it is. But I do need your help."

He blows out a sigh and sinks into the corner armchair in defeat. Runs his fingers through his copper hair.

I sit on the edge of the bed, fold my hands in my lap.

"You must know that I'm under suspicion for Abby's murder."

He nods. "And I know you didn't do it," he says, raising his voice an octave.

"How do you know that?" I ask. I'm both relieved and genuinely curious.

He drops his eyes to the floor, and his long, bony fingers form a cobweb, fidgeting between his knees.

"Jamie, you need to tell me what you know. My life's not just complicated; I'm in deep shit here."

But his gaze is still dropped and his face has turned to stone. I have no booze of my own here to offer him, but I think of the untouched minibar across the room and pry it open.

"Wanna drink? Sorry I don't have a better selection —"

"Yes, especially if there's whiskey."

I lift a doll-size bottle of Crown Royal and snap the lid off.

Jamie sips it, his right foot thumping the floor as he seems to be working out how much he wants to tell me.

"Who do you think killed Abby?" I plead.

Sadness streaks across his face and I think about how he was around her, how I'd suspected he nursed a crush on her.

"I'm sorry she's gone; I know you liked her."

He doesn't try to deny it. Just nods his head.

"Look, when we were together that night at the lake, before you arrived, I scrolled through Margot's phone. I found a text she had written to Brad. Jamie, she told Brad to get rid of Abby."

He guffaws, slams the rest of the whiskey. "Well, I'm not surprised. Sounds just like her."

"What do you mean?"

"Nothing. Forget it."

"You have to tell me what you know."

He studies the backs of his hands, lets out another sigh. "Brad didn't tell the police everything, okay?" He rises from the chair and begins pacing the short length of carpet in front of the bed.

"Jamie, did Brad —"

"God, no. He treated Abby like shit, okay? But he didn't kill her. But what I'm about to tell you will make it seem like he did, so you can't tell anyone."

"Okay, I won't."

"I mean it, Sophie. You have to *promise* me. Brad's my best friend. Prick that he can be. And this could get him into real trouble."

Poor Brad, I think to myself. But I play along. "Of course. This stays between you and me. You have my word."

"I *did* like Abby. A lot. I always have. Known each other since grade school. She just never liked *me* in that way. But we were both kind of the same, you know what I mean?"

"No, I don't."

"We're both from poor families. Or at least, regular families. We're not rich kids, but somehow we get to hang out with them. So anyway, I hated what Brad did to her, how he made her feel."

"What did he do?"

Jamie's eyes flit over the bedspread.

"You don't have to keep protecting him, Jamie."

Late-afternoon sunlight pulses behind the drawn curtain, casting waves of light across his freckled face.

"Well, in addition to screwing Margot

behind Abby's back, he pressured her to have an abortion." His voice cracks and his neck blushes.

My stomach twists into a knot. Brad's official story is that he never knew Abby was pregnant. So if he's lying about that, what else has he lied about?

"So you're saying that he knew she was pregnant?"

"Of course he knew! He called me one night and was flipping out about it; he didn't know what to do. He didn't know whether or not to tell his parents. But he did tell Margot, who kept pushing him to force Abby to get rid of the baby."

Every nerve on my skin stands at attention. Margot knew, too.

"Brad wanted to keep the baby?"

"Hell no. No way. He was set to go off to college, leave Abby behind. He told me Margot had plans for them once he was away. That she'd come visit him on the weekends, as often as she could, and that they could finally be together once he was out of Mapleton. So he pressured Abby until she almost cracked. She even visited a clinic in Dallas, but she just couldn't go through with it. Her family is so religious, they would've disowned her."

"Did Brad drive Abby to the clinic?"

"I have no idea; I just heard them arguing about it. And this was a few days before —" His voice cracks again and tears form in his eyes before he flicks them away.

"Jamie, I've got to ask you this again. Do you think Brad killed Abby?"

"No, no, I fucking don't. I know he's not capable of that. But Margot . . ." His eyes rove around the room. "She's a different story."

"And she's dead," I say with a flatness to my voice. "She didn't love Brad, Jamie. I was with her earlier the day she drowned. She dumped him. Did you know that?"

He practically snorts. Then smacks the table with his hand. I flinch. "Is that what she told you?"

"Yes," I say softly, trying to defuse his molten anger.

"That's bullshit. The night before she drowned, I was at the lake with them. I didn't want to be. But Brad always gets his way. So we went out there. And believe me, they were still *very* much together."

My skin crawls and my mind reels.

If Margot and Brad were indeed still together, why did Margot lie to me about that? Obviously, to shut me down, to manage me. To cover something up. I think back to watching her with Brad. How steamed she was when he was late getting to the lake that night, how I could hear them arguing about something in the bedroom. How even earlier that week, at Jill's pool party, Margot couldn't handle Abby being front and center. She had to take her top off and wrestle the attention away from Abby. *Psychopath.*

Margot wasn't going to save me after all. How ridiculous for me to even have thought so. The truth has been staring me in the face this whole time: Margot lied to me. Margot had something to do with Abby's murder. And if Brad didn't help her — as Jamie insists he didn't — then I believe Callie did.

My mind trickles back to the beginning of the pool party, when we were all still inside Jill's lake house, and I hear Margot's voice, velvety and smoky in my ear: *Callie may seem like a bull, but she does everything she's told. At least she does for me.*

I can picture Callie, Callie with the condo in Dallas, Callie who always does what Margot tells her to do, driving Abby to the clinic with Margot, quite possibly by force.

64

I'm in the Highlander heading west. Even though I know nobody is tracking me this closely, I still peer into my rearview mirror and check the cars around me as I cross the city limits.

I'm heading to Dallas, defying Flynn's orders not to leave town. As soon as Jamie left, I tossed a change of clothes into my duffel and threw it in the passenger seat.

The sun is an orange fireball parked on the horizon, and I have to steer with one hand while I shade my eyes with the other. My thoughts are engulfed by Margot; even in death, she consumes me. Liar. Psychopath. I can't stop spitting that word out in anger, and I need to center myself, make a plan for what's next.

Sticking to the older highway, careful to dodge any toll roads so that my license plate won't be photographed, I'm wearing the silly Dallas Cowboys baseball hat again. My god; I've sunk so low. I feel like a fugitive, but a necessary one.

It's nearly six thirty, so by the time I arrive in Dallas, all the abortion clinics will be closed for the day. But I want to get there ASAP so I can get an early start in the morning.

Just before I fled the motel, my fingers flew across the keypad of my iPhone, researching abortion laws in Texas. If you are seventeen, as Abby was, parental consent is required. This can be done in writing, but most of the private clinics I found online in Dallas — the ones I imagined Margot and Callie dragging Abby to — require that an adult be present as well. So right before I left the motel, I dug out that awful piece in the newspaper about Abby's murder and stashed it in my bag. I took screenshots of both Margot's and Callie's Facebook profile pictures to bring to the clinics with me.

It's dark by the time I reach Dallas, and even with all my time in Chicago, as I curl around the freeways, the glittering lights of the city feel dizzying after the pitch-black nights in Mapleton. My GPS directs me to the Westin Galleria, where I'm going to stay. My stomach grumbles as I approach the hotel, but I resist the urge to pull through a burger stand — I'm going to eat something decent. It's been too long since I had something other than fast food and gas station snacks.

My flip-flops thwack against the mirror-like marble floors of the empty lobby, and I feel underdressed and self-conscious in my denim cutoffs and cap. Most other women who float through the lobby are wearing pastel summer dresses or elegant linen pants, their glossed lips plumped, no doubt, with Botox, their shiny hair bouncing behind their shoulders.

As I approach the front desk, I pull a credit card from my wallet instead of my debit card that's linked to my checking account. Graham routinely scans our bank account online, but I'm the one who always opens the monthly paper statements from our credit cards, so this way, there's less of a risk of him finding out I'm here.

Once in my room, which is on the ninth floor, I sweep back the curtains and take in the view of the Dallas skyline winking below. My god, it feels good to be out of Mapleton for a minute. Collapsing into a leather chair, I dial room service and order a sumptuous dinner. Caesar salad with grilled chicken. A side of steamed rice. A dish of vanilla Häagen-Dazs with chocolate syrup, and a pot of chamomile tea.

I take a scalding shower, slip into the plush hotel robe, and mindlessly bounce between HGTV and the National Geographic channel. It isn't even ten o'clock when my eyelids begin to droop, heavy as concrete, and I feel myself slipping into sleep.

65

Tuesday, May 1, 2018

My Highlander inches through the growing rush hour traffic. It's three thirty in the afternoon, and I've spent the whole day racing from clinic to clinic — five in all — to no avail.

At the first three I visited, all in upscale neighborhoods, the women in reception would barely even talk to me. I know there must be privacy laws protecting the patients, so I changed my tack at the last one, trying to find a workaround. Not only did I show the photo of Abby in the paper to the lady behind the desk, I told her that Abby had been murdered and that I'm investigating a possible link to a clinic in the Dallas area. I gave a made-up name of a blog and pretended to be a journalist, and this caught the woman's attention.

She studied the article, thin lips pursed, but shook her head. "I'm here every day. So if this Abby had come in, I'd remember her."

I was going to call it a day after the five clinics, but even though traffic is threatening to grind my search to a halt, I guide the Highlander toward another tony neighborhood, called Highland Park. Enormous, gilded mansions rise from jewel-green lawns. It's like Margot's neighborhood on steroids. And not far from Turtle Creek, where Callie's condo supposedly is.

After a few wrong turns, I locate the OB-GYN Group of Highland Park. It sits back on a high lawn; I creep along the hedge-lined drive toward the parking lot. Just as I'm killing the engine, my cell rings. Glancing over at it on the passenger seat, I see Flynn's name flashing across the screen. Fuck. How the hell did he find out I left town? I'm certainly not going to answer it, not right now. It rolls to voice mail and I silence the ringer.

The white marble building looks less like a doctor's office than a day spa. Stepping to the front door, I'm stymied when I find it's locked. I'm about to turn away when I see a small gray box on the side of the building with an array of buttons. I press the one for main reception and, without any questioning, the tall glass doors swing open and I rush through them before they close behind me.

Sweat rings my underarms, and my hair is a hot mess under the ball cap, but I stride purposefully to the long bank of reception desks lining the far wall. A young woman with chestnut-colored hair and a dimpled smile greets me.

"Hello! Checking in for an appointment?"

I'm grateful that each receptionist has their own cubicle, so I lean in as close as is socially acceptable and drop my voice to soft and low.

"I'm actually looking for your help." I stare straight into her downy eyes, hoping to reach her, human to human.

"Yes, of course." Her already soft face softens even more, and it occurs to me that she most likely thinks I'm here for an abortion and need someone to talk with about it. "Let's step into the greeting room," she says, lifting a hand and motioning toward the right wall.

The room is cozy and softly lit. She clicks the door shut behind us and gestures for me to have a seat.

"How can I help? I'm Heidi, by the way." She extends her slender hand and we shake.

I cut to the chase, deciding that being direct with Heidi is the best possible tactic.

"I'm investigating the murder of a young woman. Abby Wilson. I'm a journalist. Abby lived a few hours from here, and I believe that she was murdered because she was pregnant." My voice warbles as I speak this truth out loud.

Heidi's eyes grow wide and she nods her head as if she's eager to cooperate. I show her the newspaper clipping, careful to keep the section with my photo and name folded under.

"Oh, this is terrible. So sad."

"Yes, it really is. Look, I have reason to believe she visited an abortion clinic, here in Dallas. So I'm making the rounds, trying to see if anybody remembers her."

She squints and reads beyond the headline, studies Abby's face more intently.

"I'm so sorry, but I can't say that I remember her."

I'm crestfallen. And getting nowhere.

"But that doesn't mean much. I'm only here two days a week. And the paper said that she was underage?" Heidi looks up at me with hope in her eyes.

"Yes, she was a minor. Just seventeen."

"Well, if that's the case, the person you really need to speak to is Stacey. Hold on, I'll go get her."

I stand in the room, fidgeting. After a few

minutes, I dig my cell out of my bag and check it. There's a text message from Flynn.

Sophie, you need to call me.

A wave of anxiety crashes over my chest and it suddenly feels as if the room is too small. I try and steady my breath and my hands, but it's impossible. Jamming my cell back in my bag, I begin to walk in tight circles around the room.

A tall, striking blonde opens the door and enters the room, with Heidi behind her.

"Hi, I'm Stacey," she says, flashing me a blinding white smile.

I smile back but don't offer my name.

"Heidi's filled me in; can I see the picture?"

I pass it to her, and as soon as her eyes land on Abby, her hand flies to her mouth. "Oh, god. I remember her." She nods her head quickly and her eyes mist with tears. Stacey hands me the paper back and sucks in a deep breath, presumably to collect herself.

"Look, I'm not supposed to be sharing any of this, but this one really bothered me, stuck with me. She came in one afternoon. Late. Like just before closing. It was strange because there were two women with her.

One was a blonde who sat in the lobby like a statue, but the other one — I just keep remembering how pushy she was."

Callie. And Margot. I knew it.

"The girl had an appointment lined up and everything in advance, so I assumed she didn't need any counseling about her decision. But when she approached me at reception, she was shaking and crying. I kept asking her if she wanted to go through with it, but she wouldn't answer me; she just kept looking down at the floor. Then the other woman — she said she was her aunt — came up to us and put her hands on the girl's shoulders."

My stomach is coiling into a ball as I listen to Stacey. I can picture the whole thing.

"So her aunt, a dark brunette, kept saying to her, 'You know we already talked about this; you know it's what's best. So sign the paperwork, sweetie. We need to get this taken care of.' " Stacey sighs and twists her long hair around her fingers. "I thought it was so odd that she was being so pushy. The girl clearly wasn't ready to go through with it, and here was this stern woman coaxing her into it. I mean, when we have cases like these, we normally will counsel both parties, but when I tried to suggest it, the aunt put her hand up to me and told me to leave them alone. And then the girl bolted out the front door without going through with anything."

"Do you think you could remember the women who were with her? What they looked like?"

"I can try."

I fish out my cell, tap on the screen until the photos of Margot and Callie appear. I show her Callie's picture first.

She's nodding as she studies it. "Yes, that was definitely her. Definitely."

A warm feeling spreads across my body. I feel so vindicated I could cry. I show her the picture of Margot next.

Her face scrunches up as she scrutinizes it. "I *think* that's her. But I can't say for sure. The whole time she was in here, she was wearing huge sunglasses and a baseball cap. I remember that clearly because I always think it's so rude when people indoors won't take off their sunglasses to speak with you — it's so snooty — and that's exactly the air she was giving off."

Oversize sunglasses. Definitely Margot.

I beam at Stacey and I can't help it; I pull her into a hug.

"I'm just sorry," she says, her voice breaking, "that I didn't do more for her."

I squeeze her, and tears prick my eyes as I

think about Abby and what she went through. "You've helped me so much. And now, I can help the police with finding out exactly what happened to her."

I stash the newspaper back in my bag, and we head out into the lobby. Scanning the ceiling for cameras, I spot a few near the front desk.

"Do you know if these are closed-circuit cameras?" I ask Stacey.

"That's exactly what they are."

"Great, I'm stepping outside to call the detective now. And I'm sure he'll be in touch."

66

I wait until I'm back on the freeway with the AC blasting before I call Flynn. I can't get out of Dallas fast enough, but even with the slow crawl of traffic, I should hit Mapleton long before sundown.

He answers on the first ring.

"Sophie. Took you long enough."

"Mike, listen, I've had a —"

"Hold up, there's something I need to tell you first; it's why I've been trying to reach you." His voice sounds warmer than it has lately, so I let him continue.

"Okay, then you go first."

Even with my windows up, the sound of traffic creeps inside the cabin, making it difficult for me to hear him. I raise the volume on my cell, press the phone to my ear more tightly.

"I understand that you know a man in your neighborhood by the name of Harold?"

Bloody hell. Is he dead, *too*?

My mouth is dry but I manage to answer Flynn. "Yes, yes I do. I mean, I don't know him all that well, just the occasional wave or quick chat from the trail. Why are you asking me?"

A black Suburban in front of me blocks my view of traffic, so I swerve around it, moving into a faster lane.

"He came to the station this morning. With a photograph of you."

The hairs on my arms rise, and an unsettled feeling washes over me.

"Okay, this is sounding creepy."

"I'm not gonna lie, it *is* creepy, but in this case, it works in your benefit. Evidently, Harold was out on the trail in the early hours of that Saturday morning when Abby went missing. He snapped a picture of you, jogging. On his phone. It was taken at three fifteen a.m., which confirms your alibi for that portion of the night. He said he had read about you in the paper and hated to see you mixed up in all of that, so he wanted to try and help clear your name."

I'm speechless. And relieved. It takes me a second to find my voice again.

"Does this mean that you believe me now?"

He sighs on the other end. "It helps, Sophie. But I need you to know that this in no way exonerates you. Again, it just confirms your alibi for that portion of the night."

The freeway is opening up now and I lurch into the far left lane, pressing the accelerator until the needle on my speedometer inches to eighty miles per hour.

"There's something I need to tell you, Mike. I'm in Dallas. Well, I'm not in Dallas anymore, I just left the city, and I know I wasn't supposed to leave town but I had to and when you hear me out, you'll know why."

"I'm listening." I hear the faint tap of what I assume to be his pen striking the edge of a desk, or maybe the console in his patrol car.

"First, Brad knew that Abby was pregnant."

"And how are you going to prove that —"

"Just listen to me. Jamie told me — I'll explain how and why later — but he also told me that Abby had visited an abortion clinic in Dallas, caving under pressure from Brad to get rid of the baby."

"Go on," he says. I hear the crackle of his CB before he lowers the volume on it.

"So, on a hunch, I drove to Dallas last night and hit a bunch of clinics today. Mike, I just left the one that Abby went to."

"What's the name of it?" he asks, his attention fully pricked.

"OB-GYN Group of Highland Park. I had a feeling that Margot, with Callie's help, drove Abby there, and possibly by force. And guess what?"

"Go on."

I exhale, slow down, and tell him every detail. About Stacey ID'ing both Abby and Callie. And possibly Margot. About how upset Abby was, and about how pushy Margot was. And finally, about the CCTV cameras in the lobby.

Flynn grows silent, and I wonder if he even believes me.

He finally speaks. "Sophie, if what you're telling me is true, if we can verify it with the footage from the cameras, then this, of course, changes everything. I'll need you to come in and give us a written statement first thing in the morning, but for now I'll get my team on it ASAP. I still have friends on the force in Dallas and can call in a favor."

"I'm telling the truth." Even as I say it, I can sense that he believes me. Or, at least, that he really wants to.

"Let's take this one step at a time. And in the meantime, stick close to your damn phone and answer it if I call."

I let out a chuckle and swear I can feel him grinning across the line.

I end the call and relief floods over me. I call Graham next. But predictably, he doesn't pick up. I don't leave a message. It's four thirty and I know he's knee-deep in taking care of Jack after school, so I decide I'll try him later, after Jack's bedtime.

I take a sip of water and focus my eyes on the highway that's now blissfully clear of traffic.

I want to talk to somebody else about this, and before I've even fully thought it through, I dial Jill's number.

To my surprise, she answers on the second ring.

"Hello?"

I'm not certain if she even knows it's me who's calling, and suddenly my neck grows hot and I'm having trouble stringing words together.

"Jill? Hey, it's Sophie, I —"

"I know who this is." She sounds detached, icy.

So I cut to the chase.

"I think I know what really happened to Abby," I blurt out.

I hear the drag of a sigh on the other end.

"Margot was involved."

Jill sucks in a quick breath. "How do you know?"

"Listen, I'm driving back from Dallas. I

can explain everything in person. Can you meet me at your lake house in about an hour? I want to talk in private."

"I don't know, Sophie." Her voice has grown cool again.

"Jill, I believe that Brad is innocent in all of this. And you have to believe that I am as well. And what I'm going to tell you will make everything clear. Everything."

Silence. Silence so long that I fear she's disconnected the call.

"Jill, you still there?"

Another long sigh.

"I'm trusting you. I'll leave town now. See you out there." She hangs up.

The flat stretch of highway begins to roll and dip over hills tangled with soaring trees, and I'm again back in the pine forest of East Texas. The mile marker to Mapleton reads eighty miles, but it's twenty more minutes to Cedar Lake on the west side of town, so I should make it in an hour.

The clock on my dash reads five thirty. I'll arrive at Jill's well before sundown, which is perfect, because once I've told her everything I need to tell her, I'm heading home. To Graham. I'm not naive enough to think he'll scoop me up with open arms — I'm not even sure he'll invite me inside — but I want to see his face when I tell him, gauge his reaction and whether I have a chance in hell of ever making things right with him. I can't even really think about that right now; it will crack my heart open so wide I won't be able to function at Jill's.

At the next exit, I veer off the highway and fill up my tank at a truck stop. While the gas is pumping, I text Flynn to let him know I'm headed to Jill's. I certainly don't have to, but now that he's on my side again, or seems to be anyway, I want to keep him in the loop.

Back on the highway, eighteen-wheelers coast by, rattling the Highlander, and after half an hour of gripping the wheel, I'm grateful when I see the turnoff to the lake.

I lower my windows and breathe in the damp, sticky air. Even though it's only six fifteen and the sun won't set for another few hours, the skinny lake roads are engulfed by mammoth pines, dimming the sunlight, so that it already feels like dusk.

I curl around the final stretch of road leading to Jill's and glimpse her white Lexus in the drive. My heart strikes against my ribs, and my hands shake as I kill the engine. I know I have been through a lot, but I can't imagine what she's been going through as well. To learn that Brad had indeed been screwing Margot, to have to deal with the pressures of the police suspecting Brad for Abby's murder — I'm sure she wants to crack as much as I do.

67

As I approach the front door, Jill's already in the entryway, opening the massive door for me. I'm not sure if I should lean in and hug her, so I don't. I simply thank her for hearing me out. I trail her to the living room, which is dimly lit, save for the stream of sunlight pouring in through the bank of gleaming windows.

Her eyes are puffy, but other than that, there isn't a hair out of place. She's dressed in a white jumper with delicate brown leather sandals. Her hair is glossy and hangs just beneath her shoulders, and she twines her fingers through it as if she's handling rosary beads.

"Wine?"

I notice that a bottle of red — open and half-empty — is resting on the glass-topped coffee table.

"Yes, thank you. That would be nice."

She glides into the kitchen to fetch a glass.

Returns shortly and pours us each generous amounts. A little wine dribbles down the bottle, and she sops it up with her index finger, licking it.

"I have to tell you, Sophie," she says, her voice slurring at the edges, "that I'm sorry."

I have no idea what she's talking about, but I look up at her expectantly as I sip from my glass.

"I need to apologize for never calling you. Especially after that piece in the paper. And you being under suspicion. I *never* thought you were responsible for Abby's death, in any way, for the record. But I guess I was just mad that you knew about Brad and Margot and failed to tell me." She narrows her eyes at me and I feel my neck burn with shame.

"But I didn't know, not at first anyway. And shortly after I found out, Abby —"

But she cuts me off. She nods and says, "I get it, and I believe you. I know how Margot could be. And how easy it is to get swept up in all of her bullshit. But I shouldn't have shunned you."

I stay silent, unsure of how to respond.

"So, what exactly is it you want to tell me?" She tilts her head to one side, pushing her dark-framed glasses farther up her nose.

I take a healthy gulp of wine and set my

glass down on the coffee table. "First of all, I'm not sure if you know this, but Margot was still sleeping with Brad, up until the night before she died."

Jill grimaces, but doesn't respond.

"I found out from Jamie. And no, I'm not seeing him, but I had to go to him to try and get some information. Also, Jill, I don't know if you know this" — my stomach clenches as I get ready to tell her this next part — "but Brad knew that Abby was pregnant."

Jill gives a tiny shake of her head, as if this is all too much to believe. So before she decides to toss me out, I spill the rest to her — about my theory that Margot was in cahoots with Callie and murdered Abby because she wouldn't go through with the abortion. How Jamie told me Margot had plans to continue seeing Brad once he was away at college. And how Stacey at the clinic had ID'd Callie and all but ID'd Margot as well.

Jill's face turns crimson. She pours the rest of her wine down her throat and crosses her arms over her chest. She gazes out the window and releases a pent-up sigh. "You know, this is all too much to take. I just —" She removes her glasses and wipes away a tear. "It's a lot to hear. A lot to process. I do want to talk some more, though, but can we go out on the lake? Take the boat for a spin?"

Her sapphire-blue eyes are pleading, and even though I'm anxious to head home and talk to Graham, how can I refuse her request?

"Absolutely; of course."

The lake is an empty pane of glass reflecting the sinking sun, pink-orange smearing the water's surface. Jill is deft in the captain's chair, starting the engine straightaway and backing out of the boat lift. She takes a slow cruise in front of the shore, gliding past one mansion after the next. When we're a good six houses down from hers, I hear the sound of my cell chiming. My heart leaps; it must be Graham. But when I claw my phone from my bag, I see that it's a text from Flynn. As I'm reading it, Jill guns the engine and speeds from the shore.

Got CCTV footage back and it wasn't Margot at the clinic. Sophie, it was Jill.

68

My blood goes cold. I'm about to respond when Jill kills the engine, leaving us moored in the middle of the lake. She glares at me, so I slide the phone back into my bag. I can't risk her seeing Flynn's message.

"I need you to stop looking into this."

Sunlight pulses off the lake, hueing everything — the polished surface of the boat, the polished lenses on Jill's glasses — with a surreal quality. I give Jill a tight smile and struggle to appear confused.

"But you seem to hate Margot more than anyone. Why are you covering for her?" My breathing is constricted and I'm sure the barely masked fear on my face is a dead giveaway.

The wake from our engine clops against the sides of the boat, gently rocking it. I plant my feet on the dark gray turf that lines the floor.

"I *do* hate Margot. That's why I held her

underwater."

My head spins, and alarm rises in my chest.

"She didn't even put up that much of a struggle, but, of course, she was soused as usual." Jill laughs with a searing scoff. "And that's also why I tried to frame her for Abby's murder, but I grabbed the wrong gun."

The rocking of the boat, the sunlight bouncing off every surface, the crazy words spewing from Jill's mouth — all of it makes me feel like the world has tilted on its side and is trying violently to shake me off the edge. I stare at Jill, trying to work out if she's truly as insane as she sounds. If she's truly capable of everything she just divulged to me.

"Oh, don't look at me like that," she hisses. "The little bitch was standing in my son's way; I had no choice. Both of them were, actually. Don't act so goddamned surprised."

She smooths her hair back, twists the key in the ignition, and guns the engine again, this time, speeding toward the opposite shore, toward Margot's land. She lowers the lever on the boat, increasing the speed, her forearm muscles flexing as she grasps it.

We're now traveling so fast that the front of the boat lifts off the water and bangs against the surface of the lake over and over as we speed across. Jill is laser focused on steering, so I carefully creep my hand into my bag and grope around for my phone, keeping my eyes on her as I find it. I glance down and find a second message from Flynn, then look back up at Jill.

En route to the Simmons lake house. Sophie, please confirm your location.

Jill's still staring straight ahead, guiding the boat. I quickly type to Flynn, letting him know I'm on her boat heading to Margot's land. My heart is palpitating as I press send, but I manage to do it before Jill cuts her eyes back at me.

The sun is beginning to sink behind the pines as we reach Margot's shore. Jill eases up on the lever, guiding the nose of the boat to a stump. She tosses a rope around it, anchoring us in place, then turns and stands over me.

Her figure blocks out the sun, casting shadows along the leather seats of the boat.

"I didn't want to frame you for Abby's death, Sophie; that wasn't part of the plan. Believe me, I wanted Margot to go down for it. I really, really did. Bitch has been messing with my son for *far. Too. Long.*"

Her neck and head shake with rage.

"But I don't understand. You weren't even there anymore; you left early that night," I say, trying to engage her in a more calm and rational manner.

"Yeah, and I was happy to leave early. I was tracking Brad. I watched as Abby stormed out of his Jeep. She stood in front of her house after he left, weeping for a while on the curb. I eased up next to her in my car and told her to get in."

She sinks down again in the captain's chair, lets out a huge breath, and keeps on talking, as if in a psychotic trance, her gaze trained toward Margot's land.

"I drove her out to my lake house and told her we could talk about Brad. She was all upset because he had just tried to dump her. And Brad told her that if she told her parents about the baby, he would refuse to admit it was his. She was all out of sorts, and becoming unmanageable," Jill says with a look of distaste on her face.

"She kept crying about how she couldn't give up the baby, and how she would die if she lost Brad. I couldn't reason with her, and I didn't know what else to do. She said she was about to tell her parents and the entire school everything. Which would spell certain ruin for my Brad. And I couldn't have that. Not after everything we've worked so hard for.

"I told her to sit tight at the lake house while I went to find Brad. That's when I went and got the gun. It was so easy; the front door was unlocked and you were the only one there, passed out on the couch. I thought I had the right gun — Margot sometimes uses her daddy's gun — but I'd forgotten *you* used it that night," she says as if it were somehow *my* fault.

"And, of course, when it turned out to be your prints," she sighs, "well, that was collateral damage. And it was unfortunate." She licks her lips, gives her head a quick shake.

"I wanted to kick myself later for not paying more attention. I wanted to get Margot back so badly for all she had done, sleeping with Brad and everything. When I got back to the lake house, I told Abby that we were going for a boat ride. That Brad was out on the Bankses' land, drinking beers with Jamie. That I had spoken with him and that he told me he didn't want to break up with her after all, and that we were going to work something out."

Jill's eyes finally meet mine, as if she suddenly remembered that I'm here, that she's talking to a real person. They narrow into slits and she snorts out an ugly laugh.

"And, *of course,* I knew Margot was still seducing my son, even after Abby's death. Are you dumb enough to think I wasn't watching his every move after that? I installed spyware on Brad's phone, monitoring every text that came through. So when Margot had the *nerve* to keep banging him, I had to intervene. *Again.* I intercepted her text — the one she sent Brad the night I drowned her — and that was it for me. The fucking slut. I knew I had to take her down.

"And now, I'm going to have to take care of you, aren't I? It will look like a suicide. And everyone will believe it. Especially you offing yourself on Margot's land. Everyone now knows how in love you were with her. It's *so* perfect. And this way, everyone will really believe you killed Abby. And probably Margot as well."

She clasps her hands together, and a smile creeps across her mannequin-doll face. Blood is thundering in my ears, and my vision swims. I keep hoping that my phone will ding, but so far it's mute. I think of Jack, curled up in Graham's arms, having his bedtime story being read to him, and hot tears sting my eyes. I flick them away and when I do, I notice the glint of something silver peeking out from underneath

Jill's seat. A revolver.

Jack. Graham.

I lunge for the revolver, but Jill is swift and grabs my right arm. And she's strong. She squeezes it hard, so hard I feel like she might snap the bone. With her free hand, she slides the gun out and aims it at my head.

Fury overtakes me, and I use my left hand to strike against her wrist. She fires a shot but it lands in the water, and with as much strength as I can muster, I elbow Jill square in the nose.

"Bitch!" she screams, her voice echoing off the lake.

And before I can duck, she socks me in the lips with the butt of the revolver, the taste of blood filling my mouth, before holding me at gunpoint and ordering me off the boat.

With one hand gripping my shoulder and shoving me forward while the other one holds the gun at my temple, Jill steers me to the clearing where we used to shoot skeet.

"Get down on your knees," she orders.

I obey. Jill releases the gun from my temple and circles me until she's standing directly in front of me, aiming the nose of the revolver at my forehead.

I can't believe I'm going out like this. Red-hot grief rips through me, and I silently say Jack's and Graham's names over and over again in my head while Jill stands over me, looking demonically possessed.

"You don't have to do this. I won't tell anybody, I promise. I'll move away from here — you'll never hear from me —"

But she whips the gun across my face again, hitting my jaw this time, sending scorching pain up the side of my head.

"Shut up!" she screams.

Just underneath the sound of her screams, I hear another squealing sound. Sirens in the distance. Jill freezes, her face a mask of terror, and she momentarily takes her gaze off me. I plant my hands on the ground and get on one foot, but she turns back to me, hands shaking as she trains the gun again on my forehead.

C'mon, Flynn, get here. Just get here.

Jill still seems to be sorting out what to do when I catch a glimpse of a figure moving through the forest behind her. I'm hoping beyond all hope that it's Flynn, but then I see the mane of frosty blond hair, the skinny jeans tucked into knee-high boots.

Callie.

Callie walking toward us with a shotgun. And I know that this is now the end. I get back down on both knees and brace for the shot. Images of my baby and my husband flood through my mind — our lives together in an insta-reel — and my heart lurches. My body is rigid with adrenaline and I look up at Callie, expecting to see her customary sneer, but to my utter surprise, she lifts a finger to her lips. She slows her pace until she's just upon Jill. Then she jams the nose of the shotgun into Jill's back.

"What the fuck?" Jill says.

"Don't move an inch," she says to Jill through clenched teeth.

Somehow, she knows Jill killed Margot.

The sound of blood coursing through my temples is overridden by the loud screech of sirens and tires skidding and the crackling of CBs and the blissful sound of Detective Flynn's voice as he calls out through a bullhorn for us all to remain still.

69

Two Months Later
Sunday, July 1, 2018

It's morning. I'm out in the garden, or what's left of it.

These past couple of months have turned brutally hot and the sun has torched all my plants, turning them into Shrinky Dinks.

It's my first time out here since moving back into the house, and I'm crouched over the scrunched-up plants, digging their limp bodies from the parched soil that crumbles in my gloved hands.

Today marks the two-month anniversary of when it all happened, when I was down on my knees, bracing for a shot to the head.

When Flynn's voice bellowed out over the bullhorn, ordering us all to stand still, that's exactly what Callie, Jill, and I did. We all froze until he reached us, with backup in tow, and pried the revolver from Jill's white-knuckled hands.

An officer placed an arm around my shoulder and led me up toward the back of an ambulance that was apparently waiting to receive me, dead or alive. The EMT wrapped me in a wool blanket, which I was grateful for. Even though it was still warm out, my body was racked by shivers; I couldn't stop shaking. They cleaned the wounds on my face as we rode to the hospital from where I'd soon be released with a few bandages and instructions to take Tylenol for the pain.

Flynn had phoned Graham and he was there, in the lobby, waiting for me. He'd dropped Jack off at Erin and Ryan's place (I still haven't heard from Erin but I'm determined to make amends with her and hopefully restart our friendship) before heading over.

My knees buckled at the sight of him, and even though there was a wariness to his face, he held me tightly when I crashed into his chest, letting me cry until I couldn't possibly cry anymore, and when we pulled apart, his eyes were wet, too.

He led me to the car and drove us home. I think it had less to do with wanting me around, and more to do with the fact of me being Jack's mom and how close I had just come to death.

He slept on the couch that first night, and for several nights after that before renting a small one-bedroom apartment across town.

We still haven't talked about us, about whether or not there still *is* an us. He hasn't wanted to discuss anything about what I did or didn't do with Jamie, or with Margot. He tells me he needs more time and still doesn't want to be around me.

We were worried about how Jack would react to Graham living away, but he actually finds it funny; he thinks of it as having two playrooms now. As much as it tears me apart — the not knowing what will come of Graham and me when all I want is for us to be back together again — I'm giving him time. He deserves it.

Detective Flynn comes around every so often to check on me and to keep me updated about the case. Or cases.

According to Flynn, as soon as they slapped the handcuffs on Jill and led her to the patrol car, she repeated to them everything she had just said to me verbatim, as if she were a robot. He said that she was most likely in her own state of trauma and shock.

I haven't seen Callie since that night, but Flynn told me that since Margot's death, which almost killed her, she had been spending nights out at the lake as a way to be closer to Margot, to cope. She had been sitting out on the back porch when she heard the shot from Jill's revolver, so she ran inside and grabbed a shotgun before heading down to investigate.

She confessed to Flynn that she had indeed driven Jill and Abby to Dallas to the abortion clinic — of course, she was on film, so there was no sense in lying about it — and that she had felt some apprehension when they left the clinic with no abortion having been performed and Jill continually verbally abusing Abby.

She had her suspicions, evidently, that Jill might have had a hand in Abby's death, but with my prints being the only ones found on the trigger, she'd thought it must've been me. Especially because when she returned to the lake that night, I was the only one there.

As for the night Margot drowned, Callie told Flynn that the last time she laid eyes on Margot was when she stood watching us together through the window. My mouth went dry and my face turned scarlet when he relayed that, and I begged him not to tell a soul, especially Graham, about it. So far, he's kept his word.

And when Callie saw Jill holding me at gunpoint, she told Flynn that everything just clicked — Jill's long-simmering rage against Margot, Jill's overprotectiveness of Brad — and she got close enough to hear the tail end of my exchange with Jill, my promise not to tell anyone what I knew.

I shudder to think of what would've happened if she hadn't been out there. I keep going over ways in which I want to thank her for saving me, but I haven't hit upon the right one just yet. But I know I will.

Tina, predictably, has reappeared, trying to worm her way back into my life, most likely to get the latest dish on things, but I've so far ignored all her texts. I don't want to be friends with her, and also, I'm leaving that part of my life behind.

The toughest part to leave behind, so far, has been Margot. I think about her all the time. Mostly because even though I have some answers — she didn't frame me, she wasn't trying to screw me over — I also have lingering questions. Who was she, really? She was obviously fucked up and, at times, dangerous, and, of course, she outright lied to me more than once, but she wasn't out to get me, and now I have a feeling she was a lot more vulnerable than she ever let on. I hate to admit it, but even after everything that happened, I do catch myself sometimes wondering what might have been if she'd lived.

Did I ever really know her? And did we really have something? I'd like to think we did, that the connection I felt wasn't all in my head, but she's as elusive to me now as she was when she was alive.

What did I mean to her? And more importantly, what did she mean to me? How did I lose myself so wholly when I was around her?

I've been FaceTiming with a therapist up in Chicago, trying to piece together why I risked everything with Graham and Jack, and how I can become more whole moving forward; so far, it's helping.

I've thought about moving back to Chicago — if Graham would agree to it — but then, I'm sick of running. And mainly, I'm sick of running from myself.

So here I am this morning, sweat streaming down my back, surrounded by a sea of green plants — watermelon, summer squash, okra, and tomatoes — having no idea if I'm going to be here in a few months when they come to harvest, if Graham will have decided to throw me out for good or not, so in addition to planting these, I guess I'm also planting something else.

Hope.

ACKNOWLEDGMENTS

I've had enormous support during the writing and publishing of *The Hunting Wives*, and my gratitude is due to many.

This novel simply would not exist without the championing of my valiant, straight-out-of-a-dream agent, Victoria Sanders. You changed my life with one phone call, and I'll be thanking you until the end of time. Your rock-solid guidance, endless support, and friendship continue to mean the world. "In Victoria we trust."

Big thanks as well to the rest of the fabulous team at Victoria Sanders & Associates: Bernadette Baker-Baughman, Jessica Spivey, and Diane Dickensheid. I can't thank you all enough for your tireless work, wit, diligence, and fastidiousness on my behalf. I'm honored to be represented by such a dream team.

Massive thanks to my wonderful and brilliant editor, Danielle Perez, for your infectious passion for *The Hunting Wives.* I'm so very grateful to be in such careful, capable hands. Thank you so much for your hard work, dedication, and extraordinary, razor-sharp edits, which vastly improved the novel. It's been a thrill to bring this "nest of vipers" to life with you, and I can't wait to work on the next one together.

To Benee Knauer, Book Goddess and lifeline, what can I say? Thank you so very much for pushing me, encouraging me, and coaxing me to make *The Hunting Wives* what it truly wanted to be. Your incisive early edits helped transform the manuscript from a skeleton to a living, breathing being, and I cannot fathom writing a book without you.

To the entire team at Berkley, thank you for being such an incredible publishing home. Many thanks to Ivan Held for such an enthusiastic welcome. Big thanks as well to Jenn Snyder, to Angelina Krahn for such great copyedits, and enormous thanks to Christine Ball, Jeanne-Marie Hudson, Craig Burke, Claire Zion, Loren Jaggers, Jessica Brock, Bridget O'Toole, Elisha Katz, and the sales team. I'm so fortunate to be working with all of you.

A huge thanks is also due to my amazing

film/TV agent, Hilary Zaitz Michael at WME.

My writing career would be nowhere without the support of family, and I must first thank my best friend, my mom, Liz Hinkle, one of the best storytellers I know. On a backcountry drive one afternoon, she told me a story about a hunting party that would go on to inspire this novel. Mom, you remain my biggest inspiration and my biggest cheerleader, and I can't thank you enough for all of the critical support — emotional, financial, spiritual — that you've given me since day one. I love you.

To my fabulous sisters, Beth and Susie, who are always there for me. Thank you, Beth, for insisting that everything would work out, in its own time, and for your unshakable faith in my writing — it's seen me through some hard times. Susie, I don't know what I'd do without you. Thank you so much for always — ALWAYS — believing in me no matter what and for talking me through things in such a wise, calming way. My life would be so different without you both in it.

To my BFF, Amy Thompson. Whew — I cannot thank you enough for being the first reader of *The Hunting Wives* and for demanding that I drop everything and go in my office to finish it immediately. Your early, wise notes and insistence that "this is gonna sell for sure" are what inspired me to write like a madwoman and send it out into the world. Also, thank you for being the best BFF for these past forty-plus years; I'd be so screwed without you!

To my sweet father, Charles, I cannot thank you enough for your endless support and encouragement! And especially your nudge that I should be writing thrillers. You've seen us through so much, and we're forever grateful for everything. I love you.

Big thanks to Paul and my darling nephews, Xavier and Logan, and also thanks to Joni, Courtney, Buddy, Marc, Kip, and Mac. Thanks also to my husband's family, Jake and Stephanie, Amanda and Matt, Pam and Kevin, and especially Martha and Larry Lutringer.

Thanks to my extended family: Delena and Rex; Slade and Keegan; Jessica, Noah, and Trevor; and T-Pa and Feeney. (Huge thanks, T-Pa, for the skeet shooting tips!)

A giant thanks to my East Coast family, starting with Dorthaan Kirk, whose enduring friendship means the absolute world to me. Thank you so much for everything throughout the years, Nana! BRIGHT MOMENTS! Special thanks also to April, Yolie,

Iris, and all the Grands. Big thanks to my Houston family, Charlotte, Shan, Kia, and Akyla. And I'm forever indebted to Rahsaan Roland Kirk, my forever muse.

Massive thanks to my wonderful friends Kim and Chris and Elliot, Shannon and Drew Crawford, Sarah King, Lauren, Lori, Jackie, David and Clara Ward, Bo and Laura Elder, David Hess, Mark and Dan, Betty Neals, Lew Aldridge, Sara Zaske, Cody Daigle-Orians, Alex Giannini, Bob and Shirley, Carole Geffen, Dave and Joyce Dormady, Ron Shelton and Lolita Davidovich, Kellie Davis, George and Fran Ramsey, Henry and Patricia Tippie, Terri Whetstone, Adam and Colette Dorn, Stanley Smith, Guy and Jeska Forsyth, and Sumai and Hannibal Lokumbe.

I will never be able to adequately thank my incredible friend Carmen Costello, who showed me, by example, how to live the artist's life and who pushed me with love down this path. We are always together.

Many thanks as well to Tanda Tashjian and the Zhang family: Li, Bob, Don, and Sharon. Also much gratitude to Kayla Hsieh, Lauren Dechiro, Marissa, Erin, Kelsey, Kristen Rakun, and the whole crew.

Writing can be a real kick in the pants, and I have to give a shout-out to my writing friends. First, to Riley Sager, who gave me much-needed encouragement about this novel and the stellar advice to "write the &*$% out of it." A big high five and toast to my writing mates, El Poquito and Cathy Fast Horse — our continued back-porch chats keep me sane and inspired. A huge thanks to my writing friends in Austin: Marit Weisenberg, my work wife, as well as Amanda Eyre Ward, Owen Egerton, my dear friend Suzy Spencer, Stacey Swann, Amy Gentry, Beth Sample, Hillery Hugg, Leigh Paulk, Michelle Cullen, Nick and Jordan Wade, Alyssa Harad, Stacy Musczinski, Michael and Stephanie Noll, the Writers' League of Texas, and the LLL.

Huge gratitude to Katie Gutierrez (for everything!) as well as my longtime friend Tracy Strauss, Stacia Campbell, Roxanne Pilat, Elia Esparza, and the entire Cabin 20. Massive thanks to Luis Alberto Urrea, who saved my writing life years ago by inviting me into the Cabin. Also big thanks to Ellison Cooper, Alexandra Burt, Samantha Bailey, Kassandra Montag, and Clare Empson.

Many have helped me through the publishing business, and I owe a special thanks to Arielle Eckstut and David Henry Sterry (a.k.a. The Book Doctors), Christina

Hogrebe, Terri Bischoff, Dana Kaye, Dan Mallory, and Scott Montgomery at BookPeople.

A hat tip to all the fabulous bookstagrammers, especially Laura @wonderchick40, Chelsea Humphrey @suspensethrill, Celeste Ní Raois @celesteniraois, Amy @novelgossip, Bex @outofthebex, Jamie S @readwithjamie, and so many others.

The biggest thanks of all goes to my incredible, loving husband, Chuck, for your otherworldly faith in me and for making our lives brighter every single day. I love you. You are the best husband and father ever. And, finally, to my magical son, Johnny, who teaches me every day that miracles exist; I am so lucky I get to be your mom.

ABOUT THE AUTHOR

May Cobb earned her MA in literature from San Francisco State University, and her essays and interviews have appeared in the *Washington Post,* the Rumpus, *Edible Austin,* and *Austin Monthly.* Her debut novel, *Big Woods,* won multiple awards. She lives in Austin, Texas, with her family.

The employees of Thorndike Press hope you have enjoyed this Large Print book. All our Thorndike, Wheeler, and Kennebec Large Print titles are designed for easy reading, and all our books are made to last. Other Thorndike Press Large Print books are available at your library, through selected bookstores, or directly from us.

For information about titles, please call:
(800) 223-1244

or visit our website at:
gale.com/thorndike

To share your comments, please write:
Publisher
Thorndike Press
10 Water St., Suite 310
Waterville, ME 04901